We at the Christian Writers Guild are proud of Kariss and wish her the best with this worthy launch of a promising career. Kudos!

—JERRY B. JENKINS
NOVELIST AND BIOGRAPHER
OWNER, CHRISTIAN WRITERS GUILD

Shaken paints a very real picture of how faith and foundation are both touched by war and catastrophe. Kariss captures not only the heart of a warrior but also the bonds of brotherhood in the SEAL Teams and the adversity relationships face in the midst of our most dire moments. Kariss shatters the Hollywood, too-cool, immortal depiction too often misportrayed of our nation's Special Operators. This book shows what it looks like when a life of service collides with personal struggle and seemingly impossible circumstances.

—NAVY SEAL

A thrilling read! Suspense and romance that will shake your world. This writer is on her way up!

—DIANN MILLS
AUTHOR, FIREWALL AND THE SURVIVOR
CHRISTY AWARD WINNER

Drama, love, hope, and a spotlight upon a future generation…Lynch weaves a tale that has it all. It's been awhile since a story has so fully immersed me into a hub of societal ills yet left me brimming at the end all the same. A job well done for Kariss Lynch.

—HEATHER JAMES
AUTHOR, UNHOLY HUNGER AND HANDS OF
DARKNESS, LURE OF THE SERPENT SERIES

HEART OF A WARRIOR SERIES / BOOK ONE

Shaken

WITHDRAWN

KARISS LYNCH

ReAlms

Most CHARISMA HOUSE BOOK GROUP products are available at special quantity discounts for bulk purchase for sales promotions, premiums, fund-raising, and educational needs. For details, write Charisma House Book Group, 600 Rinehart Road, Lake Mary, Florida 32746, or telephone (407) 333-0600.

SHAKEN by Kariss Lynch
Published by Realms
Charisma Media/Charisma House Book Group
600 Rinehart Road
Lake Mary, Florida 32746
www.charismahouse.com

Scripture quotations are from the Holy Bible, New International Version, copyright © 1973, 1978, 1984, International Bible Society, used by permission; the Revised Standard Version of the Bible, copyright © 1946, 1952, 1971 by the Division of Christian Education of the National Council of the Churches of Christ in the USA, used by permission.

Published in association with the literary agency of WordServe Literary Group, Ltd., 10152 S. Knoll Circle, Highlands Ranch, CO 80130.

Cover design by Bill Johnson

Author photo by Shanna Russell @ www.srussellphotography
.com

Back cover photo collage credits:

NOAA/NGDC, Red Cross

NOAA/NGDC, Logan Abassi, United Nations

U.S. Navy photo by Chief Gas Turbine System Technician
Mechanical Charles Thomas/Released

U.S. Navy photo by Culinary Specialist 2nd Class George
Disario/Released

Visit the author's website at www.karisslynch.com.

Library of Congress Cataloging-in-Publication Data:
An application to register this book for cataloging has been
submitted to the Library of Congress.

International Standard Book Number: 978-1-62136-535-8

E-book ISBN: 978-1-62136-537-2

First edition

14 15 16 17 18 — 9 8 7 6 5 4 3 2 1

Printed in the United States of America

To Dad, Mom, Toby, and Chasya for reminding
me that "no" is simply a prelude to God's better
"yes"

And to the friends and family who prayed for me
throughout this journey

NOTE FROM THE AUTHOR

IN JANUARY 2010 I sat as a substitute teacher in a third-grade classroom in Lubbock, Texas, while the scratch of pencils filled the room. News of the Haiti earthquake still rang in my head. So many hurt, so many lost.

My pen hit the page and began to fill the lines with the story of an American nurse standing amidst the debris in Haiti wondering where God could be found in the chaos. I intended to turn it into a short story. But it sat in my notebook until I signed up for a writing class in September.

One thing led to another, and the page turned into a chapter, then ten chapters, then a novel. I began to research, watch videos, read books, and interview people about Haiti, the earthquake, and the people there. Slowly I fell in love with a people I'd never met and a place I'd never been. The story built in my heart until it spilled onto the page. Then I waited for someone else to fall in love with what I had—the story of a resilient people, the heart of an American young adult, the hope found in Christ no matter the circumstance, and the love of two people in the midst of struggle.

While I waited, I had the opportunity to go to Haiti with a team from my church. We partnered with Mission of Hope, a ministry seeking to transform lives in Haiti with the power of the gospel. They are educating children, building homes, helping adults establish business plans, teaching job skills, providing health care, and teaching Christian values. And things are changing! Voodoo priests are coming to Christ or moving higher into the mountains. Teenagers are stepping up to lead and share the gospel in their villages. Children are learning that they can dream big for the first time in Haiti's history. They have a future!

I truly believe there is hope for Haiti. I believe the vicious cycle of poverty, disease, and death can change. I believe young adults can change the world. I believe change happens one life at a time, and I believe Mission of Hope is helping this happen. If you would like to partner with them to help Haiti, please visit www.mohhaiti .org.

I hope you fall in love with Nick and Kaylan's story as much as I have. I hope the people of Haiti grip your heart. But most of all, I hope you discover the goodness of the God who loved us enough to send His Son to die for us.

Journeying with you,

Kariss

"Two roads diverged in a wood, and I—
I took the one less traveled by,
And that has made all the difference."

ROBERT FROST

Prologue

Dust settled over Kaylan like a shroud. The ringing in her ears pulsed with the beat of her heart, and her face stung as though needles pricked her skin. She swiped at the stinging. Blood. She glanced around the small space. Chunks of cement cocooned her underneath the twin bed. She squinted, trying to remember.

A sliver of blue sky, the only thing not cracked or bleeding, peeked through a hole in the wall, discolored in the chalky air. Within seconds, dust enveloped the beacon. Rolling in a space no bigger than a sleeping bag, she winced as her shoulder scraped the bottom of her bed. She sucked in a breath and coughing seized her, cement dust choking the air more with each passing moment.

Where was Sarah Beth? A shriek rent the air outside the broken house, and Kaylan jerked, her head banging on her bed with a crack. Blood pulsed and her head throbbed as she massaged the spot where a knot bloomed.

Through the cracked walls of her makeshift cell, she searched for any sign of life beneath the chaos. A body lay twisted in the street, bloody, tattered green shorts and flip-flops still in place. A woman bent over the tiny frame, clutching it to herself and crying. Kaylan's stomach convulsed, and panic built in her gut.

"Sarah Beth? Oh, God, she needs to answer me."

The floor beneath her began to buckle.

"Sarah Beth!"

It was happening again.

PART ONE

PART ONE

Chapter One

ON THE EVE of her biggest decision Kaylan Richards's biggest regret walked back into her life. She should have been celebrating. She had crossed the stage and graduated from the University of Alabama just two hours earlier, December class of 2009. Her dreams stretched endlessly before her, beckoning her toward an unknown future. And now, *he* was back: the one who had turned his back on her. Pain from that time in her past returned with a dull ache.

Her oldest brother, David, walked into the kitchen, loosening his tie. "Mr. Fight-and-Flight just pulled up. Did you know he was coming?"

The blood drained from her face, and she slumped against the kitchen cabinet as her mom bustled around them. "Nick's here? Now?"

Ever the faithful older brother, David's mouth stretched in a tight line, and his hazel eyes raked her face. Her heart sank. He wasn't joking.

David nodded. "Micah just went out to meet him. I guess he didn't tell you. Sorry, sis." He reached for a chip in the sea of goodies multiplying on the island counter. Their mom slapped his hand away as she added spinach dip to the mix.

Kaylan groaned. "Why today? I have too much on my plate to deal with this. What was Micah thinking?"

"He's Micah's best friend, and he doesn't have any family." David pulled her into a hug, crushing her graduation cap. "Be confident, Kayles. It was his loss, not yours."

His statement fell flat. It had been her loss. Nick's decision and her heartache.

Decisions...Nick's had changed her life. What of the ones she had yet to make? Had yet to tell her family about? What about Haiti?

Her mom dusted her hands off and placed her arm around Kaylan's shoulders, as tall as her daughter in her heels. "You okay, honey? You want me to ask him to leave? We can help him find a hotel."

Kaylan popped a peanut into her mouth to hide her emotion. "I can handle it. I think." Her heart took off at a gallop at the thought of facing Nick. "Excuse me for a minute?"

Kaylan dashed upstairs to her room, pulling off her cap and gown and heaping her graduation regalia on the bed. What had consumed and defined her for three and a half years had taken less than two hours to conclude, and all she had to show for it was a piece of paper and a robe she couldn't wear again. She almost wished she and Sarah Beth had taken their time and graduated in May with the rest of the class. At least it would have given her one more semester to figure out what she really wanted to do with her life.

She ran her hands through the tassel, enjoying the silky, cool feel. Absent the cap and gown, a different weight settled on her shoulders, one of expectation and years of plans. She was being kicked out of the nest and told to fly with no further direction. Her first "adult" decisions loomed on the horizon, and already she was floundering. From now on, her choices would split between the familiar and the unknown.

Nick fit both of those categories.

Rushing to the window, she lifted the edge of the curtain. Nick lounged against a black Ford truck, his breath evident in the chilly December afternoon. What was he doing here? He'd made his choice. He'd chosen the road that took him as far away from her as possible. She lifted the curtain higher just as he looked up and caught her eye. She dropped the silky fabric like a hot plate, backing away a step. Those eyes, smoky blue like the ocean in a fog, pierced her like a bullet.

Physically, he hadn't changed much: tall, muscled, blond, ever the California beach boy. Even in the chilly weather, she wouldn't be surprised to find him in board shorts and flip-flops as if to will the weather to warmer days.

She threw open her closet door and chose her favorite red sweater. If she had to see Nick today, she might as well look her best.

Nick pushed off the truck to meet Micah, his wide grin infectious. Micah met him with a back-breaking hug. Together the two had weathered college at the University of Southern California, Basic Underwater Demolition/SEAL training, the death of Nick's father, and a deployment in Afghanistan. Their bond was thicker than blood, and Nick considered Micah his brother in arms and in life.

"Hey, Bulldog, you sure this is all right? I don't want to intrude."

"Kaylan said it was fine." Micah shrugged.

"Hmm." Nick studied his friend. "In other words, you didn't tell her so she couldn't be upset about it."

"Why do you have to be so perceptive? It gets really old."

"Well, the team didn't give me the name 'Hawk' because I have a beak and feathers."

"And they don't call me 'Bulldog' because I take things lying down or avoid confrontation."

"They haven't seen you with your sister. She has you wrapped around her finger."

"I guess that makes two of us. Speaking of confrontation, you have a lot of humble pie to eat with Kaylan, my friend. But I have an idea…" A sly grin spread across Micah's face.

"Oh, so I take it that I have your blessing with the sister I crushed by my stupidity?"

"Yeah, Hawk, about that. I know you've changed a lot over the last couple years. And you're my best friend, but if you break her heart again, I swear I'll break your neck." He locked eyes with Nick, and Nick recognized Micah's serious, combat mode that surfaced only when the situation deemed it necessary. Apparently this was such a situation, and Nick smothered a smile at the irony.

"Believe me, I have no intention of doing that again."

"Well, she can't do better than you. If you behave, I'll even put in a good word for you."

Nick held up his hands in mock surrender. "Lead the way, matchmaker." Despite his calm demeanor, Nick's heart raced. Would she forgive? Could she? Nick first met Kaylan when her family visited Micah for a couple days before BUD/S training began. She'd been a kid, barely out of high school, and his best friend's baby sister. He hadn't been far from his party days at USC and new in his faith, girls the last thing on his mind as he grew in his relationship with the Lord.

Nick powered through BUD/S, intent on finishing and becoming a warrior for his country. He'd never experienced pain and the desire to persevere as much as he did during Hell Week. His dad lived to see him complete that phase of training and then passed away. With no family left, Nick threw himself into conditioning his body and mind to become a SEAL in every sense of the word. After completing almost three years of SEAL training, he finally took a mini-vacation. With no family and nowhere to go, he went home with Micah to spend a few weeks in Alabama. But he hadn't counted on Kaylan Richards. She'd been on the cusp of twenty-one and about to launch her third year of college at the University of Alabama. Beautiful, intelligent, and sweet, her innocence had been a breath of fresh air, a welcome change from the girls he had dated before coming to Christ.

He fell hard and fast. She was everything he wanted and never thought he could have. They'd spent a few weeks together on the lake, swimming, picnicking, and enjoying family game nights. Mornings with her had never been sweeter, talking about the Lord and their dreams.

Then he'd left to rejoin his SEAL team and experienced the most difficult season of his life as he began a year and a half of work up to his first deployment. The realities of combat preparation broke his body, drained him mentally and emotionally, and left nothing for Kaylan. So he'd made the call. After months of long-distance phone dates, he ended the relationship and pressed on to deployment. He couldn't be a warrior for his country, couldn't give his everything if she was constantly on his mind. He hadn't seen her since. And today, the day of her graduation from college, was probably not the best time. But he was different, and he would not blow this again.

"Hey." Micah slapped Nick's back, taking him away from lingering sweet memories of that distant summer. "You ready for a whole lot of party food seasoned with a bunch of not-so-subtle questions?"

Nick groaned. "I'm slightly more worried about the look I'll get from your sister when she sees me."

Laughter filtered through the door as Micah opened it. "I'll pave the way for you. But you're on your own with the family."

"Gee, thanks. I think I'd rather face the barrel of a gun right now."

"Speaking of which, I better go hide those." Micah's laughter joined his family's as Nick entered the lions' den.

A knock sounded on her bedroom door as Kaylan finished retouching her makeup.

"Who is it?"

"Your favorite middle brother. Can I come in?"

Kaylan pulled the door open and faced Micah, hands on her hips and ready to breathe fire.

"That mad, huh?" Micah slipped past her into the room and closed the door. "Okay, now you can yell at me."

Kaylan glared at her brother, refusing to let him off the hook. "You stabbed me in the back, Micah Matthew Richards. How could you bring Nick here today of all days? He's already made it clear that I'm not worth his time."

"Kaylan, that's not true, and you know it. He just couldn't deal with a relationship and a deployment. Neither one of us knew just how insane this lifestyle would be. And now our first deployment is over. He's changed, Kaylan. A lot. He's my best friend and a good guy. I'd never bring him if I thought he would hurt you again."

"Don't try to charm me with that grin of yours. It may work on other girls, but not on me. You're my brother. You're supposed to protect me."

She put on an elaborate pout, but the betrayal truly stung. Since childhood, every time she had scraped her knee or a boy had broken her heart, Micah had picked her up and carried her away from it, his back between her and the world. This time he had left her wide open to take enemy fire with no protection.

He flipped one of her auburn curls, and she fought a smile. "Believe me, I will always have your back. And I know he hurt you, but I really think you should hear him out. Give him a little credit. You aren't the same person anymore. Maybe he's changed too."

How could she be so frustrated with her brother, so wary of

Nick, yet somehow drawn to him? Just not today. Any other time but today.

"I just wish you had told me first. I need to…I have some…I have a huge decision today, and I wish I didn't have to deal with Nick."

Micah's brown eyes bore into hers, and she was reminded of how stubborn he could be. She didn't need him asking questions she wasn't prepared to answer. "What kind of decisions, Kayles? And why haven't I heard about this?"

"I haven't said anything because I'm not totally sure, and I haven't even talked to Mom and Dad yet."

"Are we talking about a life-altering, anger-management-required decision? Or small, insignificant, won't-be-a-big-deal kind of decision?"

She avoided his eyes. "Definitely life altering. I'm not entirely sure Mom and Dad will be supportive. Or you."

"Kayles, what are you talking about?" He crossed his arms and took a step closer. That look could convince a lion to retreat mid roar.

"There you are." Kaylan whirled away from Micah's gaze as Seth's russet hair and bulky linebacker frame filled the doorway. Kaylan never ceased to marvel that the youngest Richards child looked the most intimidating but owned the biggest heart of them all. "Are you done primping yet? I'm so hungry, and Mom's making us wait for you. You always look great, so what's the holdup?"

Kaylan was thankful for the interruption. Seth was her constant comic relief. "You're always hungry, Seth."

"Hey, I'm a growing boy. You don't want me to get squashed like a bug on the football field next year, do you? These college guys are huge, and I won't be a redshirt freshman anymore. I gotta pack on the pounds so I don't break."

She patted his stomach, knowing her brother worked far too hard to be anything but muscle. "All right, baby brother, let's get you some food."

"You know, people never believe you when you call me your baby brother. I outgrew you a long time ago. How tall are you? Maybe 5'8"? I've got almost nine inches on you."

"You're a giant. Why haven't you been snacking?"

"Mom keeps slapping my hand away, and David and Dad are hovering around the food, guarding it like squirrels. I need to eat."

Kaylan and Micah laughed at their brother's whiny tone.

"I'm serious, Kayles. If you don't come now, I'm going to throw you over my shoulder and carry you in there."

She held her hands up in surrender and backed into the footboard of her bed as he advanced toward her. "Okay, okay. Let's go feed you."

Micah's whispered tone startled her. "We're not done, Kayles. I want to know what's going on."

It was hard to believe only hours before hats had danced through the air and cheers and camera flashes had bounced off the walls of the University of Alabama's Coleman Coliseum like lightning bugs desperate to escape.

Was she really finished with college, ready to conquer the world? Was she ready to settle down and "get an adult job," as Sarah Beth liked to say? Or should she take that famous "road less traveled," one that could take her to who-knows-where?

"Y'all go ahead and tell Mom to let you snack. I'll be there in a minute."

After her brothers left, Kaylan slipped down the stairs and headed down the back hallway to her favorite spot in her parents' lake house, the sunroom overlooking Lake Tuscaloosa. There she stood at the windows, but her mind was miles away from the view. Her options stretched endlessly to the horizon like railroad tracks splitting in two different directions. One was rife with parental expectations and a solid career track. It was a red carpet to her dreams of becoming a dietician—work at home, start her internship in August, get licensed. The other road stretched in a direction only God could ordain. Poverty-stricken Haiti called to her—families without money, food, and proper health care. It was miles away from normal and safe. So why had she even considered it? The idea had seemed like a great one when Sarah Beth first proposed it—volunteer in Haiti for six months, gaining some real-life experience in dealing with poverty and malnutrition. But now that it came time to pose the idea to her parents, the idea seemed crazy. Was Haiti the lesser road that would make the difference in her life?

She needed to call her best friend. Maybe Sarah Beth could help her face her parents and navigate this final decision that could determine her future.

She found Sarah Beth's name in the list of her favorites and dialed. As the phone rang, her mind bounced from Haiti to Nick to graduation like the ball pinging off the rails in a pinball machine. Her head ached. Or was it her heart?

"Now what, Lord? Stay at home and work, or go to Haiti? And what do I do about Nick?"

Chapter Two

SARAH BETH'S VOICE rang in her ear. "What do you mean you haven't told them yet? I thought you took care of this. Kaylan, go and tell your parents. Now."

"Maybe I could wait a day. Or two."

"Kaylan Lee Richards, if you don't tell your folks by the end of today, I'll do it for you. I'll be over there this afternoon as soon as our family party ends. I'm leaving right after Christmas for Haiti, and if you're coming with me, you'd better get your parents on board. Besides, aren't you ready to actually help people instead of just talking about it?"

Kaylan had known she wanted to study nutrition since high school when she did a school project about malnutrition in children. That dream had led her into a college program focusing on dietetics. The final step to becoming a registered dietician was an internship, which in her case began in August. Because of her grades and her senior research project on nutrition alternatives, a dietetics program in California had unofficially promised her a spot—quite a privilege, since internship spots were competitive. She had planned to spend the next few months preparing for the internship. Then Sarah Beth came to her with the Haiti idea, and a new dream was born. One that she had yet to share with her parents.

Kaylan took a deep breath and shifted the phone in her hand. She wanted to go to Haiti, even if it meant possibly jeopardizing her internship. That realization strengthened her resolve. "I'm coming, Sarah Beth. I'll tell my family after dinner." Sarah Beth cheered, forcing Kaylan to hold the phone away from her ear.

Her heart beat wildly against her ribs. She'd just made a decision that could change the course of her life. Who knew what could happen in Haiti? The looming black hole almost made her second-guess her decision. Almost.

"Why haven't you told them yet?"

"I don't know. Things just happened so fast with my big research project this semester, finals, graduation. I've been so busy, and leaving always seemed so far away, so surreal. Now all of a sudden, I'm out of time."

"You still have time, Kayles. It's not too late. But it's time to stop living safe, and start having the tough conversations. Just focus. Pretend I'm your dad and just shoot straight. Ready?" Sarah Beth's voice grew deep and gruff in a poor impersonation of Kaylan's dad. "Honey, why do you want to go to Haiti?"

"Bubbles…." Kaylan used her childhood name for Sarah Beth.

"Kayles." All sense of joking dropped from Sarah Beth's voice. "Remember when we dressed up as superheroes when we were kids? Sheets on our shoulders and paper masks?"

"You mean our glory days of nerd-hood?" Kaylan laughed. "I still have that cape."

"Good times. It was back before we worried about our future or our grades. We dreamed, and we dreamed big. We always wanted to save the world. And this is our chance to do that."

"So we're taking our superpowers to Haiti?"

"Kayles, you need to think about this. Don't go for me. Go because you want to be there, because you want to see the Lord do big things. I don't have the skills to help heal people, but I can be there for them and invest in their lives. Why are you going, Kayles? Pray about it. Before you make a decision. Before you talk to your dad."

Kaylan's dream stemmed from her desire to help people. She could sit in Alabama for months, working at the dance studio and helping her mom with her interior decorating business. The days would pass as she waited for her internship to begin in August. Or she could go to Haiti and help people who were hungry and didn't have the money for medical care. She could make a difference and begin living her dream now instead of waiting years.

She released a long breath. Her parents had always encouraged her dreams and helped her to think long term. Was this just a selfish craving for adventure, an outpouring of restlessness and change? Was it wrong to think short term? She lacked qualifications and professional experience, but she wondered if she valued those things too highly.

"I'll tell Mom and Dad before I go to bed tonight."

"Awesome! I was hoping I hadn't talked you out of it."

Kaylan laughed. "You think I'm going to let you wear that cape all by yourself? We're a team." Her laughter faded as an old wound surfaced again. "Hey, Bubbles, by the way…Nick's here."

"Really? Knight in shining armor returns to woo gorgeous, distressed graduate. Sounds like a Hollywood smash. Knock him dead, Kayles."

"I'm serious! What do I do? What do I say?"

"Well, would you want to explore a relationship with him again? Maybe he isn't the same guy who left last time."

"He still left, Sarah Beth."

"You didn't answer my question."

Trust her to shoot straight. Kaylan felt like a fickle preteen. "I guess it depends on why he's back." Her voice lowered as she gazed through the floor-to-ceiling windows at the lake shimmering in the light. "Between you and me, he still looks too handsome for his own good."

"I bet all that SEAL training didn't hurt. I gotta finish cleanup so I can make it in time for Richards family football. See you soon. And Kayles, give Nick a break. It's been a few years."

"All right, all right." Kaylan ended the call and gazed at the waves lapping against the dock. Was she ready to see Nick? Was she ready to tell her parents her plans? Was she ready for the changes life was about to throw her way?

"Kaylan!" Micah's voice echoed through the house.

"Coming." With a final look at her reflection, she left the sunroom to join her family in the kitchen. Time to face Nick.

Nick had endured a round of family greetings and grilling, and still no Kaylan. Taking a breather, he poured himself a Coke and crossed the room, pretending to take in the lake view from the windows. Whistles and cheers erupted behind him. Then the sound of her musical laughter. He turned to face the room, and there she stood. Tall and graceful, just as he remembered.

Fierce longing engulfed him at the sight of her. How many nights had he lain awake in Afghanistan wishing, praying he'd never walked away? Nick clenched his jaw, rejecting the sudden rush of pain.

"There's my girl." Scott Richards threw his arm around his only daughter.

Nick lingered in the background, content to allow her family this time before talking to Kaylan for the first time in a long while. She looked good. Her youthful glow had faded somewhat, but it had been replaced by the beauty and maturity of a young woman. Her face lit up under the attention of her dad, the doting of her mother, and the affection of her brothers. She was in her element.

"Where's that diploma I paid an arm and a leg for?" Mr. Richards chuckled as the two shared a smile.

"Well, I guess I could ask them to put your name on it too. But then I might never get a job, and you'll be supporting me for life."

"Well, if Dad's name goes on it, mine should too, since I had to listen to you cry or stress out every time you had a project or test," Seth grumbled.

"Put my name on that list too," Mrs. Richards said as she added the last platter of sandwiches to the kitchen island.

"On second thought, that piece of paper is all yours. Congratulations, honey." Mr. Richards kissed her forehead as he reached for a strawberry. "Dig in, gang!"

"Finally." Seth dove for the food as the rest of the family grabbed plates and lined up around the island.

Nick braced as the space between them cleared and Kaylan's eyes found his for the first time. Her wavy, auburn hair fell a couple inches below her shoulders. The faint crease where her graduation cap sat earlier spoke of her accomplishments. Her red sweater draped her slim body in all the right places, conservative and classy. His memory hadn't done her justice.

"Hi." The word scratched his vocal cords, husky and thick. He cleared his throat as he approached, hoping she hadn't noticed.

"Hi back." Her voice held a million questions, hesitant and guarded as if she'd fortified every wall against him. He inwardly winced.

"Congratulations. You deserve every minute of today. I know how hard you worked for it."

"Thanks." Her voice was soothing, like waves lapping a beach in the moonlight. He'd missed its gentle, musical tones.

He studied her face: the excitement in her green eyes causing them to glow like emeralds, the slight upturn of her nose, reminding him of a pixie, and the light dusting of freckles around her nose, evidence of days in the sun.

"I'm glad you're home safe. How long are you back?"

"Micah invited me for Christmas, and then we have to head back to California right after."

She crossed her arms and took a step away from him, clearly

upset but trying to maintain her calm. Her family moved behind them in the kitchen, talking and eating.

"And clearly Micah forgot to tell you."

"If he invited you, then you're welcome here. No one should be alone for the holidays."

"Thanks."

She turned to grab a plate, then paused. "It's good to see you again, Nick."

"Maybe you'll be seeing more of me."

"Don't make promises you can't keep."

Her words cut deep. "Kaylan…"

"Hey, you two." Micah threw his arms around both of them. "This is a party. Why so serious? Come grab some food."

"What is it with you and Seth and food?" Kaylan backhanded her brother's stomach, and he dropped his hand from her shoulder.

"You are starving us. We had to sit through all those names this morning. It was very draining."

"Hey, that's not nice." She fought a smile.

"Just being honest." His grin could melt ice. As Kaylan gave in to his teasing, Nick remembered how close Micah and Kaylan were.

"You better watch it, bro, or I'll…"

"Where's our Sugar?"

"Pap, Gran!" Kaylan hurried to greet her grandparents as they entered the kitchen carrying a tray of brownies. Nick grabbed a plate and began to fill it, praying about how to navigate a celebration he had clearly interrupted, at least in the eyes of the day's star. He circled back around to Kaylan's side getting close enough to whisper in light of the noise, "Could you give me some time this week? You know, talk, catch up?"

She studied him. "Sure." Without another word she ducked in the middle of her family, joining the festivities.

Nick's hopes rose. It wasn't much, but it was a start. Maybe, just maybe he could win her back. As he joked with Seth and Micah, he silently prayed for the conversation to come.

Richards family football remained a comical, competitive tradition. Usually Kaylan's brothers tested her to her limit, teasing her and pushing her to run harder, hold on to the ball, and score. In a family of boys, Kaylan had long ago learned to never give up. It fed her competitive nature.

"You ready, sis?" Seth whispered in their huddle. She and Sarah Beth sucked air into their lungs in shallow bursts. Her days of prepping for finals without hitting the gym were catching up to her.

"Let's beat these guys!" Sarah Beth high-fived Kaylan and wiped sweat from her face.

Kaylan nodded at Seth. "I'm ready, little bro."

"Remember what I taught you. Don't drop the ball. Butterfingers are not cute to macho SEAL snipers."

"Hey! I'll catch it."

"Watch me for the signal."

"The signal is so dumb."

"Dumb or not, it works. Go, team!" They lined up, Kaylan right across from Nick. His smirk made her hope Seth sent the ball her way, just so she could put Nick in his place.

Sarah Beth hiked the ball, and Seth caught the snap. He stuck his tongue out at Kaylan, and she took off like a shot, dodging Nick and using the strength from years of dance to propel her across the yard to the makeshift end zone between two large trees. She could hear Nick on her heels and Sarah Beth's cheers as David and Micah shouted back and forth, blocking Sarah Beth and trying to stop Seth from sending the ball Kaylan's way. Her parents and grandparents cheered from their rocking chairs on the wraparound porch.

The ball whizzed through the air, and she turned to follow its arc. Rough pigskin burned her fingers as she crossed the end zone. Then strong hands grabbed her waist and pulled her to the ground. She landed on her attacker before being flipped on her back to stare at bare tree branches, the ball held close to her chest. She drew in a sharp breath. Nick knelt over her, a victorious grin on his face.

"Real subtle, Hawk." Micah joined them and popped the back of Nick's head.

"I got it. That counts." Kaylan scrambled to her feet, daring them to challenge her. Nick and Micah burst into laughter as the others joined them.

"Wasn't this *touch* football?" Seth scanned Nick up and down, looking every bit the protective younger brother.

Nick shrugged. "I just couldn't resist. She looked too cute running across the field. And who can resist a girl who makes touchdowns that gracefully?"

Kaylan glared. He had no right to come along and make her heart race or say those kinds of things, especially in front of an audience.

"Told you he would like it if you caught the ball," Seth snickered.

Kaylan turned on her little brother. "Hush your mouth, Seth Richards. I can still whip you." She hoped Nick missed her glowing, red face.

"I'm not sure I'd put money on you, but I'd definitely like to see that." Nick slapped Seth on the back, his chuckle causing her temperature to rise.

She stared Nick down, ready to shoot a few bullets of her own. He seemed to sober as he received the full impact of her gaze and smothered his smile. "I take that back. Right now I would definitely put money on you."

He winked and turned to Micah. "How about a break for some of that sweet tea I've been missing in Cali? They just can't make it quite right."

Nick and Micah headed for the house with David and Seth trailing behind. Kaylan studied him as he greeted her parents and grandparents on the wide porch. What had gotten into him since his deployment? If he was this obvious already, she wasn't sure she was ready to face the full intensity of a talk with him.

She turned to Sarah Beth. "What do I do about Nick?"

"Kiss and make up, of course. What kind of question is that?" Sarah Beth's eyes sparkled.

"I'm serious! He wants to talk. Just the two of us." She bit her lip. "This is really awful timing. First Haiti, now him."

The smile that rarely left Sarah Beth's face dimmed, and she pulled Kaylan close in a hug. "You aren't that hurt girl anymore, and you have no obligation to him if you don't want to explore a relationship. Okay? Sorry, girl, but I need some of your Gran's sweet tea too. Meet ya inside." After a quick squeeze, Sarah Beth ran to the house.

Kaylan walked back to the house, feeling abandoned. Everyone else seemed willing to give Nick the benefit of the doubt, but she wasn't ready. Not until he explained a few things.

She trudged onto the porch, stretching her muscles. Everyone had disappeared inside except Pap.

"Hey, there, Sugar. Come sit with your Pap for a minute."

Pap's Southern drawl comforted Kaylan. She remembered many sweet moments with him on this porch. His green eyes so much like her own twinkled as she faced him.

"He's a good-looking guy, isn't he, Sugar? And a military man at that."

A blush blossomed again, and she cursed the genetic trait. "Pap…" She groaned, settling into the rocker next to him and setting it in motion.

"Can't lie to your Pap now, Sugar. From what I hear, that young man is the kind of man we always prayed you would marry. Maybe he deserves a second chance. He was a catch several years ago, but neither of you were ready. I think the Lord has probably knocked rough edges off both of you over the last few years."

Once upon a time she would have said the same. Had everyone forgotten Nick's phone call with some excuse about no time for anything except God and country? He'd basically told her she wasn't worth the time or effort.

Pap handed her a glass of iced tea, his solution for everything. Gran had brewed this batch to perfection with the precise mixture of sugar and lemon. More sugar than tea, she suspected. It was the Southern way.

"Talk to your Pap. How're you feeling about today?"

Kaylan struggled to sift through all the emotions. Nick crowded her thoughts, filling her senses with his dominating, quiet presence. She wanted him out of her head. Away from her heart. She ignored Pap's references to Nick and focused on her graduation instead. "I can't believe I graduated, Pap. I'm so excited to be done, but I'll miss college. Whose bright idea was it to release us into the wild without any more direction as soon as we finish school?" She laughed. "I'm a mess, Pap."

"Well, now, I think that's pretty natural." He studied the afternoon sky. It was a brisk December day though the sun shone. Kaylan closed her eyes and enjoyed the rays kissing her face.

"Something else bothering you, Sugar?"

She opened her eyes and met his steady gaze. Those eyes had once intimidated criminals in his courtroom, but he didn't fool her. They held a sparkle and wisdom Kaylan coveted. He was the picture of the South: strong, sure, warm, inviting. Pap was safe. He was home. And she was leaving him for Haiti.

What was she thinking?

"It's been quite a day." Should she tell him now? It wasn't like her to keep something this big from her family, especially Pap or Micah. "Pap, did you ever think about living in another country?"

"Alabama's always been home. But there was a time your grandmother and I considered moving to Africa."

"Why didn't you?"

"I was moving up in my career. The kids were settled and excelling. So, we sent money, we prayed, we supported those who could go, and we served in our own community here. Both places are mission fields. The Lord assigned us to our own family and friends here in Tuscaloosa. My place on the bench afforded me the chance to influence our community." His sharp eyes met hers. "Where's this coming from?"

"Well..."

"Hey, you two, it's about time to eat," Seth shouted from inside the house, gaining her more time to process.

Pap rose and squeezed her knee. "We'll talk again after dinner, Sugar."

Kaylan sighed. It was hard to believe she had walked across the stage that morning. The day had taken one twist after another. Two things were certain: Nick was back and determined to prove himself, and she wanted to go to Haiti, which unfortunately meant it was time to have some heart-to-hearts. Kaylan prayed everyone would understand.

Decisions, and now confrontation. How she hated those words.

Chapter Three

THEIR VOICES SWIRLED around her head like a tornado in the spring, wreaking havoc on her already confused thoughts. Her graduation dinner clearly wasn't the best time to discuss her decision to go to Haiti. The storm broke in all its fury with her confession, made just after the graduation cake was cut and served. Her piece, covered in white frosting with a few red flowers, sat untouched in front of her. Everyone had an opinion, and everyone was talking at once.

"Kayles, isn't this kind of sudden? I mean, you would need to leave a few days after Christmas. That's less than two weeks away." Always practical, David immediately resorted to number crunching.

"Aren't the conditions pretty rough?" her mom chimed in.

"How are you planning to pay for this?" Her dad frowned.

"Is this a good idea? You've never lived outside of Tuscaloosa," Gran interjected.

"Have you really thought this through?" By the look on Micah's face, Kaylan knew she should have told him earlier.

"That sounds like an adventure. Where can I sign up?" Seth's enthusiasm drew a small smile.

"When were you planning on telling us?" Her dad's voice rose above the fray, but before Kaylan could respond, Sarah Beth rose to her rescue.

"Mr. Richards, Kaylan and I have prayed about this for a while. We really feel like the Lord is calling us to Haiti now. I know we can make a difference."

Only Nick remained quiet, his eyes taking in the action. A quick glance at his face reminded Kaylan why she'd been drawn to him in the first place. He assessed a situation before he responded. As his eyes swerved to hers, she saw a glint of admiration and curiosity before she looked away. She didn't want to deal with that now.

Her head buzzed. Could she really do this? If God had called her to it, He would see her through it. Wasn't that what she had always been taught? Yes, this was a commitment the Lord had placed on her heart. He would walk with her through every step. The sweet reassurance sank and took root in her soul.

Silence descended as Pap stood, knuckles rapping on the table, every bit the retired state judge who could still command a room. "Now, let's stop asking all these questions, because the last time I checked, the Lord seldom calls us to do what is realistic. He calls us to be obedient, and that sounds like what my Sugar is trying to do here. Now I, for one, am going to support her." He nodded at his wife and wrapped her hand in his, taking his seat.

Tears filled Kaylan's eyes.

"Before you say anything else, can I at least answer why Haiti? Haiti is the most impoverished nation in the Western Hemisphere. I want to help train parents how to take care of their kids' nutritional needs, and I want to teach them about Jesus." A current welled in her heart and spilled out of her mouth. "Haiti is right in our own backyard. The people are stuck in an awful pattern. I want to help fix it, not just stick a Band-Aid on it. Sarah Beth and I believe we can help change things." Passion burned within her and would not be quenched. She had finally put a name and a task to a calling she had feared to voice.

She held her breath, looking to her parents. She didn't need their approval, but she craved their blessing and the support of her brothers.

"Mom, Dad?"

Micah winked at his sister and then looked at their parents. "If this is something Kaylan feels she needs to do, then I think we should support her. I won't lie; I'm a little worried. Haiti isn't stable politically or economically, and from what I've heard, that often causes unrest among the people. But whatever happens, she's tough, and God's in control."

Her mom turned to her. "Kaylan, could you tell us more about what you would be doing?"

Kaylan nodded. "Sarah Beth heard about this organization called Hands and Feet for Haiti, which is dedicated to helping the people of Haiti. Rhonda Ames, one of their staff, runs a clinic close to the slums. I've talked to her over Skype, and she would train me in some basic medical care so I can help out in the clinic. She says I would be able to use some of the things I learned as part of my nutrition degree too, since Haiti ranks among the bottom three countries in the world for daily caloric intake. They need major help."

Her mom gestured toward Sarah Beth. "What about you, Sarah Beth? Your degree is in teaching, not anything medically related."

Sarah Beth jumped in. "This mission also engages kids in the slums who can't afford school. I'll work with some of the kids during the day to teach them basic reading or writing with the help of local translators."

"And where would you stay?" Mrs. Richards kept her tone light, but hesitation marked her words.

"We worked that out too. Rhonda, the woman who runs the clinic, has a room available at her house with two beds that Kaylan and I can stay in."

"And how long would you be there?" Her dad's question was the one Kaylan had been dreading.

"Six months, but they'd really like us to stay a year," Kaylan responded.

Her dad frowned. "Wait a minute, Kaylan. Do you mean that you might forgo your internship to stay in Haiti? You may not get another shot. Those internships are hard to come by."

"I know, Dad. But I don't have to make that decision right now."

From the corner of her eye she saw a glimmer of a smile light Nick's features. She fought the urge to look at him.

"Honey, you know how competitive this internship is, and you know how hard you've worked. I will have a difficult time blessing this trip to Haiti if it will put your future career in jeopardy."

"I thought about that. And believe me, I will weigh my options very seriously when it comes time to make that decision." She swallowed hard, refusing to second-guess herself. "I have to trust and believe that the Lord will show me the next step. And Haiti is my next step, Dad. This is so much bigger, so much more important than just Sarah Beth or me. These people are the poorest in the Western Hemisphere. I don't have to be completely qualified or equipped to help; I just need to be faithful. I've really prayed about this, and I'm so sorry I didn't talk with you sooner. I just got so busy that it snuck up on me. But I want to do this now, more than I want to sit home waiting for my internship to start. I need your support on this."

"So you two have made up your minds? You both want to go to Haiti? Y'all worked hard and decided to graduate a semester early. Are you sure this is what you want to do with that time?" Kaylan's dad looked from her to Sarah Beth and back.

"Yes, sir," they answered together.

"What's communication like? Would we be able to talk with you?" Mom asked.

"Internet is really sporadic, so we might be able to Skype at night. Phone reception might not be clear all the time, but I'll get an international plan set up so that I can call home."

Her dad sighed and ran a hand over his five o'clock shadow. "Well, sweetheart, this is ultimately your decision, and it sounds like you have all the details worked out. I hope you know what you're doing."

"Let me know how I can help you get ready, hon." Her mom offered a small smile before she began to gather plates.

The family rose to wash dishes and clean up after a long day of celebration. As Kaylan left the dining room to see Sarah Beth off, she caught Nick studying her, a hint of admiration in his eyes. He'd definitely added a twist to her graduation day. As much as she was drawn to Nick, she wasn't quite ready to deal with what he had to say. Maybe it was nothing. After all, their romance had been brief, close to two years before. But after the way he'd looked at her today… Her heart raced, and the response scared her. She still cared, more than she wanted to, more than she'd realized.

She would at least give him a chance to talk, and she would pray. As Micah had reminded her, the Lord was in control and had good plans for her, but on a day of so much change, it was hard to see the direction this train was taking her.

"If this is a taste of life after college, I should never have graduated," she groaned as she walked her best friend out to her car.

Sarah Beth wrapped her arm around Kaylan's waist. "It's not that bad, Kayles. One tough conversation down, only about a million more to go." Kaylan shot her a look that drew a laugh from Sarah Beth. "You're an adult now, Kayles. You are fully capable of making your own decisions. Your parents understand that and will adjust. This is a new life stage that everyone will get used to. The question is, are you going to allow their hesitations to dictate how you respond to what the Lord is calling you to?"

Kaylan nodded as she hugged Sarah Beth good-bye. She had an odd feeling that as difficult as it had been to face her parents, and as hard as it had been to see Nick again, Haiti would be a whole different kind of difficult, one she looked forward to with terrified anticipation.

Chapter Four

EXHAUSTED FROM THE day's events, everyone turned in early, but Kaylan was too energized to sleep. The excitement and discussions of the day sent her pacing. Change emerged as her new companion, and she wrestled with the implications. She needed to go outside, clear her head.

Grabbing her coat and a flashlight, she tiptoed down the stairs and into the dark night. Her shoes pounded the familiar path traveled many times with her brothers. Smoke from a campfire drifted in the stillness, adding to the wood's aura. Out here she felt free, weightless.

Minutes later Kaylan arrived at their childhood tree house, a testament to a family weekend of hard work and bruised thumbs. Two trees bent close together, thick branches gnarled and overlapping. It created the perfect place for a tree house, capable of holding all four Richards kids.

Moonlight peeping through the trees illuminated the area above her as she climbed the rickety steps. She ducked through the doorway, sat down on the dusty, old rug, and turned on the battery-powered lamp. The urge to return to her childhood beckoned. Maybe it would somehow clarify her present.

Toys from years past littered the corners of the rough-hewn room. She smiled at the footballs in Seth's corner, action figures in Micah's, cars and trucks in David's, and the dolls and books in hers, all worn with weather and age. Even as kids their interests provided glimpses of who they would one day be. The realization warmed her. Pulling a cord, she opened the hatch in the roof to reveal the branches and a smattering of stars. The night was still, and the moon hovered above her. The rustle of leaves and whistle of chilly wind greeted her in the winter air. She lay down on the rug and gazed at the sky. For the first time all day she relaxed.

"Permission to come up?" Micah's voice broke through the stillness.

Kaylan bolted upright and scrambled onto the small platform. Her brothers stood below, and she chuckled, remembering them covered with mud in their younger years.

"Move over, sis. We're coming up anyway." Seth began climbing without waiting for her response. His large frame sent the ladder wobbling.

"Don't fall, Seth. You're not pint-sized anymore."

"Is that a fat joke?"

Kaylan burst out laughing as he pulled his body up on the landing. "Absolutely. Look at you."

"I work hard to be big."

"Oh, I know. Your mouth works overtime on more than talking."

"Hey!" He dropped her in a headlock and dragged her into the tree house as David and Micah hauled themselves into the space.

"We sure don't fit like we used to." Micah squeezed into his corner, knocking over his Superman action figure.

"That's because you and Seth decided to grow out and up." David punched Micah's shoulder, and Kaylan feared the tree house would topple to the ground as a result of their roughhousing.

"Another fat joke. Just because you can't gain weight, don't knock those of us who can," Seth said, sending David a haughty grin.

"Touché, little bro. But not all of us need the extra padding."

"So much for peace and quiet." Kaylan rolled her eyes, knowing she wouldn't trade the interruption for the world. She needed this more than silence.

Micah grew serious. "Kayles, why didn't you tell us about Haiti before?"

"I wasn't sure I was going."

"When did you decide?" Seth pulled a cheese stick from his pocket and bit into it.

"Today."

"Kaylan, that really isn't like you."

"I know, Dave, but it's something I've been thinking about for a while."

"Why didn't you tell us you were thinking about it? Didn't you think we would support you?" Micah lounged against the wall.

"Of course I did. I'm just…" She sighed and wished she could pace. "I'm just overwhelmed and tired of all the decisions. I mean, don't you wish we could just go back to being kids?"

"I'm nineteen, so technically I'm still a teenager. I consider myself a kid."

Kaylan laughed, reaching over to tousle his russet hair. "I don't think you'll ever grow up, Seth, but that's not what I meant."

Silence descended. Micah studied the art work on the walls and the toys in each corner. "Time seems to stand still in here. We're shadows of who we were back then, but that doesn't mean that those kids aren't still part of us."

"I guess I'm just tired of the decisions. How do you know which path to take? Dave, how did you know you wanted to be an accountant? Micah, when did you decide to be a SEAL? Why was it so easy for you guys and not for me?"

David leaned toward her. "What makes you think those decisions were easy? Kayles, I love cars. I wanted nothing more than to be a NASCAR driver or a car salesman." She chuckled as he picked up one of the cars in his corner. "But I'm good at what I do. Both of those things were dreams without substance to me. When it came down to it, I pursued what I was good at. I want to help people make wise financial decisions, be good stewards of their money. And I'm good with numbers. Accounting fit, and I'm happy there."

Micah chimed in, "Don't you remember that horrible fight Dad and I had when I decided to become a SEAL? Let's face it, sis, I've always had an uncontrollable hero complex. I love the brotherhood and patriotism of the military. It wasn't easy, Kayles. Decisions that change the course of your life are rarely easy."

Kaylan admired her brothers. They pursued life with their heads and their hearts, but she was still conflicted.

"Have you prayed about it, sis? Prayed more than you worry?" Seth grabbed a book from her corner of the tree house. It was a small pocket Bible she'd received in church as a child. The pages were weathered and worn. He flipped it open and began reading from Jeremiah, "'For I know the plans I have for you,' declares the LORD, 'plans to prosper you and not to harm you, plans to give you hope and a future.' He knows where you're going, sis."

Micah massaged a kink out of her shoulders, and she leaned into his strength. "I think what I'm really wrestling with is choosing my dream over a calling."

"That's tough," David said. "The question is, which one trumps the other?"

Kaylan thought about it for a moment. "I think I'm struggling because both carry equal weight. Dave, my internship is similar to your decision to be an accountant. I'm good at putting together meals and helping people understand living a healthy lifestyle that is within their budget. And Micah, Haiti is a lot like your decision. My heart is to help people in a tangible way. One is a means to an end, and the other requires immediate action and blind faith."

"Kayles, are you worried about going to Haiti because it's unfamiliar?" Micah knew her so well.

"Yeah. How do I know that's right? I could sacrifice everything for the temporary chance to help people. If I just waited a year, until after my internship, I could have both."

Seth chuckled. "God's clock runs faster than ours. I think He may be shoving you out of the nest early."

They all laughed. When silence descended, David spoke up, "You think you're supposed to go, don't you?"

She nodded. Deep down she knew the Lord was opening the door for Haiti. But the reality of her choice had just begun to hit home.

"Then go, Kayles. There isn't one mission that I go into worried that the Lord isn't right there with me. He'll be with you in Haiti, and He'll help you decide the next step when the time comes," Micah encouraged.

Peace descended again in the cold night air, and the stars seemed to shine brighter. She laughed, "Do y'all ever let me off easy?"

"Absolutely not. We gotta toughen you up somehow. Besides, my coaches push me because they know it makes me better. I push you because I love you…and I love to see you squirm." Seth dropped his arm over her head, putting her in a headlock.

Kaylan chuckled and shoved his chest, struggling to pull loose. "And what are you going to be when you grow up?"

"We already established that he'll always be a kid," David said.

"Big kid in a giant's body," Micah said, tossing one of Seth's balls in the air and catching it with a snap.

Seth joked, "I'll just be Kaylan's personal shrink. God knows she's going to need it if she can't make up her mind about her first decision as an official, graduated adult."

"Very funny."

Micah nudged Kaylan with his bulky shoulder. "You know we love you and are in full support of this. We'll look forward to pictures and stories of you saving the world one calorie at a time."

Their laughter joined similar echoes of the past in the cool Alabama night, leaving Kaylan's heart full. The perfect end to the day.

Chapter Five

THE WOODS GLOWED as if on fire behind the dusky lake, the early morning sky like pink lemonade and mango tea. Kaylan sat in the family sunroom with a mug of coffee watching golden rays burst past the rosy hues and spike above the tree line. The glassy lake mirrored the colors.

Morning had always been her time. A biological clock woke her just in time to view God's first visible act of glory for the day. Waves lapped against the dock, wind whistled through the old oaks, and birds dipped down and grazed their wings on the water. The sights calmed her, helping her feel closer to the One who had created her.

She burrowed under the blanket, avoiding the chill from the floor-length windows lining the room. On the coffee table her Bible lay open to Lamentations. "The steadfast love of the Lord never ceases, his mercies never come to an end; they are new every morning, great is thy faithfulness." Her whisper reverberated in the stillness. She set down the coffee cup and wrapped her arms around herself, imagining the Lord's arms around her. New day, clean slate, fresh possibilities. God was so good.

"I love that verse."

Kaylan jumped, whirling toward the open doorway. Nick lounged against the doorpost, one hand in his pocket and the other gripping a steaming mug of coffee.

"Sorry, I didn't mean to startle you."

"No one is usually up at this time."

He chuckled. "Micah sleeps like the dead until noon when he's on leave. It's a wonder he can be on time for zero four hundred bus rides to the drop zone."

Silence settled in the room. Dark circles pooled under his eyes, and Kaylan wondered if something had roused him earlier than usual.

"You know, you shouldn't sneak up on people like that. It's a really bad habit."

Nick offered an apologetic grin. "They don't give me the sniper rifle because I'm loud and clumsy."

"Well, they should give you some kind of over-sized cat tag, like Panther or Mountain Lion instead of Hawk. Where did that nickname come from, anyway?"

Nick pushed off the doorway, set his mug on the coffee table, and sat down on the edge of the couch. "Well, that was Micah's suggestion. Maybe you should ask him."

"Come on. We both know Micah is the king of exaggeration. Let's hear it."

Nick smiled and leaned back, crossing his arms and peering out at the now-risen sun. "We were training for our first deployment, one of those ten-day isolated mock missions with our team at a remote location. We were tasked with locating and eliminating a terrorist camp. Since I'm a sniper, I was camped out on a hill a little ways from the rest of the team in what we call an overwatch position. The air asset, or remote-controlled plane, had called 'no enemy activity' in the area, but that wasn't good enough for me. As much as they are there to help, I don't trust the lives of my team to mechanics, electronics, and an unknown person's judgment coming from a different zip code. I scanned the area, focusing on the shadows and recess movements beyond the cover of vegetation blocking my view.

"Then I saw them. A team of Army Rangers all posing as terrorists for the exercise were creeping into a perfect ambush position against my team. I could barely detect them in their camouflage netting covering their hide site, but I recognized the heat signature, a reducing cloak that had probably fooled the unmanned drone overhead." Nick smirked, but Kaylan noticed the challenge and severity the memory aroused in him.

"In real life, my team would endure heavy casualties in an ambush like that. So I treated the exercise like it was real. No one touches my team. And no one beats a SEAL. In combat, my job would be to take out the enemy threatening my team, but in simulation, practice shots aren't made for long distance, so I radioed my team to give them a heads-up about the Rangers. Just as my team rounded the ridge, one of the Rangers made a move and tried to shoot, but Micah shot first with a paint round. The Rangers lost the element of surprise, and we completed the mission. The exchange of paint rounds meant a few bruises and a few drills for my team, but it was more than worth it."

Kaylan studied him, new respect dawning for his job. He shot first, or his teammates died. He had their backs, a huge responsibility. His team obviously trusted him completely. It was written all over his face, in the casual way he told the story, confident, sure, protective. He was good because he had to be, and he trained to stay that way.

"So where does the 'Hawk' part come in?"

"A hawk's eyesight is about eight times as powerful as a human's. They see what we can't in greater detail. That's my job. I'm the eyes of the team, the point man. I see what they can't, and I protect them. A hawk soared overhead on our way back to camp that evening. Micah slapped me on the back, pinned me with the name, and I've been Hawk ever since." He smiled, and his eyes carried confidence and knowledge of his responsibility. "My role really helps me understand how dependent we are on Jesus, how important it is that we trust Him to see what we can't and to have it under control. That's what I have to do for my team on a much smaller scale."

"So, where did Micah get his name?"

Nick hung his head and chuckled. "I bet you can figure it out."

"Well, he's a bulldog in the morning. I hate waking him up."

"He's more like a grizzly."

She laughed. "Very true." She thought for a moment. "You don't mess with someone or something he cares about."

"Bingo. Micah would jump in front of any of us if we're staring down the barrel of a gun. Even if he doesn't agree with us, he defends us and then tells us how stupid we are later. He's our resident bulldog. Kind of the team's mascot." The affection and appreciation for her brother was unmistakable, and Kaylan was glad Nick watched her brother's back.

"So, you look out for the team, protect their backs. And Micah defends them. Not a bad combination. You sound like a pretty good team."

"We are." The corners of his mouth twitched, and his blue eyes seemed to shimmer like the water outside the window. "He thinks you and I would make a pretty good team too."

Her jaw twitched. It was too early for this conversation. She thought they would spend some time together, maybe find a more steady footing before addressing this topic—if it even came up. He reached for her hands and she kept them limp in his, not encouraging, simply listening.

"Kayles, give me a chance today to take us back. Before I left."

She shook her head. "We can't go back, Nick."

He leaned forward, and his grip on her hands tightened. She fought the urge to lean back. The intensity in his eyes startled her. She'd never seen this side of him before. Playful, affectionate, gentle, sure. But vulnerable? Not mighty Nick Carmichael. He was a modern-day knight with armor a mile thick, and he was stripping it off for her. She worried what she would find if she put her own shield down. He was a flight risk. Hadn't he shown her as much?

Kaylan jumped as Nick's fingers brushed her cheek, tucking a wayward strand of hair behind her ear.

"You're right. We can't go back to yesterday, but we can take the best of yesterday and build today and a thousand tomorrows on it. Will you give me a chance?"

Her heart responded to his touch, his words, the burning sincerity in his gorgeous eyes, but her brain cautioned her to wait. He'd crushed her last time, but a part of her longed to return to the beauty and joy of that time.

"That's a big promise, Nick. Can you follow through? Will you even stick around to try?" She wasn't handing over her heart that easily. Beautiful words were just that, beautiful, unless action followed. His actions had told her she wasn't worth investing in. She didn't have a place in his life.

"A lot's changed, Kayles. I'm going to prove that to you."

Her heart teetered on the edge of a cliff, debating a dive. She couldn't do that yet.

Closing her Bible, she slipped from beneath the blanket and stood, looking down at him. Confusion, fear, and frustration swirled like a whirlwind in her head. She willed his words to be true but was afraid of what she would find if they were.

She squeezed his shoulder. "I'm going to hold you to that, Mr. SEAL."

His eyes lit up, but she pulled away and hurried from the room, not ready to handle any more talk just now. Why were there always two paths? She wanted to run into Nick's arms yet flee as far away as possible. Who knew what the future would bring with a man like Nick Carmichael pursuing her?

Chapter Six

NICK HEADED TO the kitchen to pour his third mug of coffee, shaking off the effects of a rough night. His dreams hovered in the light of day, forcing him to relive the nightmares of his deployment. How long would it take before they ceased to haunt him? He squeezed his eyes shut, forcing the faint pop of gunfire and screams from his mind.

"Tired, son?"

Nick nearly spit out the hot liquid. Keith Matthews sat at the breakfast nook, a coffee cup and book in front of him.

"Mr. Matthews. Sorry, sir, I didn't see you there."

"Call me Pap." He chuckled, and the deep rumble set Nick's nerves at ease. He was the white-haired, slow-talking, Southern grandpa of many a classic movie. "America's elite don't usually spook that easily." His quiet perusal caused Nick to grip his mug. "Rough night?"

"New bed, different room. I'll be fine. I'm used to broken sleep."

"Understandable. Why don't you come join me?"

Nick crossed the room and took a seat. Silence settled over the table, and Nick locked gazes with the man next to him. He wasn't used to examination. That was a role held only by his father, and he'd been gone over two years now. Sorrow washed over Nick, and he shifted his gaze to the water outside the bay windows, always his escape.

"Nightmares are nothing to be ashamed of, son. You just got back from combat. They're understandable. If you need to talk, I'm here."

"I appreciate it, sir."

"All right, then. Now I wasn't around much the summer you spent here in Alabama. Tell me about yourself. Micah said you grew up in California?"

"Yes, sir. Right on the beach."

"And your parents?"

"Passed away. Mom my senior year of high school, and Dad a few years ago."

"I'm sorry for your loss. Micah said you were adopted. What about your biological parents?" Nick shook his head. "I've never met them. My parents adopted me as a baby. I've been piecing together bits about my biological parents since college. There's not much. Maybe I'll never know."

Pap stood and squeezed Nick's shoulders, leaning down to look in his face. "Sometimes answers are closer than you think. Keep looking. Keep asking." He turned to fill up his mug. "Take care of my granddaughter today. I like you, but if you have no intentions to pursue her after you leave, then don't lead her on today."

Nick's heart pounded against his chest. "Yes, sir. I have no intention of hurting her again." He grew weary of repeating that line but knew he deserved the skepticism.

The man's smile caused his eyes to crinkle. Nick stared into eyes just a little lighter than Kaylan's.

"Then have a good day, Nick. Ah, to be young and in love." He chuckled and left the room.

In love? Nick wasn't sure his feelings stretched that far. Yet. Love was a strong word. He rubbed the back of his neck and ran through his checklist for the day. Kaylan waited, and he would only get one second chance.

"Of all the things we could do today, you chose horses. Didn't you fall off Micah's horse the last time you were here?" Standing in the barn, holding her horse by the bridle, Kaylan laughed at Nick's glare. After time with the Lord and a breakfast complete with Seth's and Micah's hilarious antics, Kaylan felt at ease and willing when Nick proposed a ride through the woods for the morning.

"Your brother has a big mouth."

"Only with me." She nuzzled her horse, Black-Eyed Pea, stroking her silky mane. "So, why horses?"

"Because I know you love them, though I'm starting to regret this particular act of groveling. Where did that horse get its name again?" He examined the buckskin mare as though studying a deadly disease.

"She won't bite. Well, unless you smell like apples or carrots." She caught his hand and tugged. "Come here, you wimp." She directed his hand to the mare's nose. "How are you going to ride a horse if you won't even touch one?" Kaylan had been riding since she could walk. The Richardses boarded two horses a few miles away on a friend's land.

"I'm taking my time. Give me a break. I grew up on the ocean." Nick smirked. "About that name?"

Kaylan began saddling Black-Eyed Pea as she explained. "The first time I saw her, I thought she looked like a black-eyed pea with her tan skin and the black mane and tail. Mom fixes them for New Year's. Says they're lucky. The name just stuck."

She finished saddling Black-Eyed Pea and then led Nick over to another stall containing a black stallion with a white star on his forehead. King's Knight stood tall as she led him from the stable and handed the reins to Nick, who looked at her skeptically.

"He won't buck you this time. He promises." Kaylan laughed and climbed onto her mare's back with ease, then watched Nick gingerly mount his horse.

"Hold the reins loosely, and grip with your legs."

"Right." His knuckles turned white on the reins.

She led him into the woods. "Pretend the reins are your sniper rifle. You don't have a death grip on it, do you?"

"Depends on the situation."

She frowned and opened her mouth to ask more but stopped at his steely look. She noted the dark circles again.

"Are you sure everything's okay this morning? You look tired. Maybe we shouldn't do this."

"Oh, no, you got me on this horse. I'm not getting off until we get to the spot I picked out."

They rode in silence, the nippy air blowing softly. Kaylan whispered to her horse throughout the ride, brushing her fingers through her mane and patting her neck. She loved riding. Pap had always told her it was a way to wash away the stress. "The horse knows where she's going, Sugar. Let her lead you for a while."

This time she allowed Nick to take the lead. The thought made her hands slip on the reins. He would protect her physically, but she wasn't sure he would protect her heart. The horses broke into a clearing in the trees, the bare limbs forming a canopy over the sleeping grove. She'd come here often with Pap. In the spring, wildflowers blanketed the pasture; yet even in the dead of winter it held a solace and beauty. Kaylan slipped off Black-Eyed Pea and hurried to Nick's side in case he needed help. He swung off with a slight stumble.

"Well, you definitely aren't a Southern boy."

"Surfing's a lot more my style. I don't have as much time for it as I would like, though."

"What do you like about it?"

"I love being in the water and mastering the waves. They're so strong. If you can stay on top, ride them to the end, you somehow prove yourself worthy." He grinned. "It's a rush. I'll take you sometime. Payback for the horseback riding."

"We didn't have to ride."

"Yeah, well, I remember you talked about it the last time I was here."

A pang pierced her heart at the thought of last time. Nick pulled the pack off his back. A blanket, sandwiches, thermos, and cookies spilled out—perfect for a winter picnic. He spread the blanket, and they sat.

The pang eased. She'd told him that her ideal date was a picnic and was touched that he'd remembered. His memory of their past conversations contradicted his decision to leave. They needed to talk, but it was if she had lost the ability to speak or even think clearly.

"Thank you for this. It means a lot."

"My pleasure."

He stopped shifting food and met her eyes, his grin inviting. Her breath caught at the intensity in his gaze, and she snatched a sandwich from the spread.

"Peanut butter and jelly. My favorite." A smile warmed her face, and she chuckled. Nothing ruffled his Hawk feathers, but she felt as though she were floundering in the middle of the ocean.

Nick shrugged. "I'm no cook. And be careful. Micah helped."

Laughter slipped from her lips. The weight of Haiti was distant. The yesterdays they'd once shared appeared closer than she believed possible.

"David's the cook in the family. He won't need to be much longer, though, if he ever asks Melody to marry him."

"I like your family, Kayles."

"They like you too."

"And what about their only girl? Do I still have a shot with her?"

As quickly as the laughter came, clouds crowded in, ushering in uncertainty. She had never struggled with honesty, but she did struggle with saying what was necessary. She prayed for the right words.

"Is that what you're looking for, Nick? A shot?"

"If you'll let me. I've missed you."

She struggled to keep her voice even. This wasn't fair.

"I missed you too. But you ended things."

"I messed up, Kaylan. I'm so sorry." The look in his eyes mirrored her stormy thoughts.

In Afghanistan Nick had lain awake countless hours, thinking of Kaylan's gentleness, her laughter, and the way she looked at her brothers as if they could do no wrong. He had missed talking about the Lord with her and the way her forehead crinkled when she was thinking of how to respond to a problem in a loving but bold way. He'd missed the way she bit her lip when she studied and the blush that colored her face when he complimented her.

They'd kissed once. Nick remembered cradling her face and playing with her hair, waiting for her to trust him. Her hands rested lightly on his chest, unsure. He'd almost cheered when she'd wrapped her arms around his neck and forgotten the world with him for just a moment. She'd smelled and tasted of oatmeal cookies, fresh from the oven. Her lips and body molded to him, and he knew he'd found his perfect fit. Their relationship had been so unlike the others in his past, controlled by physical chemistry and infatuation. With Kaylan, the relationship had revolved around laughter and common interests, deep conversations, and quiet, shared moments—what he had always longed for.

And then he'd blown it.

The truth was, he'd never stopped caring, but after only weeks together, the depth of his feelings had alarmed him. She loved the Lord. It resonated in everything she touched, the way she responded to the people around her, and it shone in the innocence and peace in her eyes. Peace that wasn't present in her eyes when she looked at him now.

He'd hidden behind God and country. In reality, he wasn't a man the caliber of those in her family. They trusted God completely. Nick was still finding his way. Surrendering control of what he cared about was difficult for him, but she was too precious not to entrust to the hands of the One who directed both of their steps. Even if it meant losing her.

He finally broke the silence. "Kaylan, can you give me a second chance?"

"Nick, I like you…"

"I feel a 'but' coming."

A small smile lit her features.

"I don't know that I can trust you. You made big promises last time, promises I bought into. And you broke my heart with one phone call."

He reached for her hand, and she let him take it. The progress gave him hope. At least she wasn't pulling away from his touch.

"Kaylan, I promise I won't do that again."

Frustration colored her tone for the first time, and he realized she was struggling to hold her anger and hurt at bay. "Do you really think it's that simple? Those are just words unless you back them with actions, Nick. Keeping your word, loyalty, those are big things to me. Things I don't take lightly or for granted. When you say you'll do something, I count on your follow-through. I pin my hope on it. You exist to protect others. You never leave a man behind. But you didn't live out that code with me. It got hard, and you backed out, even when I wasn't demanding anything. I fully supported your position in the SEALs, but it wasn't enough."

He cleared his throat. *Lord, I need her to understand.* He made sure she was looking at him and then took a deep breath.

"Kaylan, when I left, I wasn't a man worthy of you. I looked at the men in your family, and I fell short. When I stayed with your family the first time, I never factored you in. I was a party boy in college. Girls existed for me to lead on and dump. I never had strong feelings for a woman until I met you." He moistened his lips. "What I felt for you scared me. And what I saw in you and your family intimidated and shamed me. I wanted you more than anything, but when I left to deploy, I couldn't do it. I couldn't be a man like your brothers or dad. I couldn't handle it all. So I called it off and didn't come back. Kaylan, I was so immature. I thought combat would make me forget, but it only intensified. I saw…"

His jaw clenched, and he pushed the thought away. Now was not the right time. "I saw things that changed me. I understood trusting God in a new way. I studied my Bible and prayed. Micah really helped. And I changed. I started to become a man I could be proud of."

Her eyes softened minutely and a smile flirted at the corner of her lips, giving him an energy boost as if he'd downed an espresso shot.

"I'm not perfect, Kayles. I never will be. But I'm not that guy anymore. I know who I am, and I know who my God is. I know trust is earned, and I will be a guy you can trust again." He brushed a wayward curl behind her ear. She didn't pull away. "Let me try. We can be the couple we dreamed of being last time I was here, only a better version of those two."

He leaned forward and kissed her forehead. Her green eyes held a small measure of the peace he had missed. It was time to be the man he'd just claimed to be. Hopefully, somewhere down the line, he would be worthy of her.

Kaylan's face heated as he brushed the hair out of her eyes. Sweet words, but she still wasn't sure. Trust remained elusive. Still, it took courage for him to share his heart, and she appreciated his effort.

He released her hands and took a bite of his sandwich. "Man, I'm glad that's over. I'm so hungry." He clutched his stomach.

She shoved him, thankful to have a break from his intensity. For the next few minutes they ate in companionable silence. As Nick grabbed the last of Gran's homemade brownies, her phone blared in the silence of the clearing.

"Hey, Micah."

"Kayles, come...Pap...hospital." The connection broke, and Kaylan stood, heart racing as she rushed around the clearing, searching for a better signal.

"Micah? What's wrong? What happened to Pap?" She heard sirens in the background before she lost the connection. The blood drained from her face, and she turned to Nick, who stood alert next to the blanket.

Her knees felt like noodles as she walked toward him. "We need to go. I think something happened to Pap. Micah said something about the hospital, and I heard sirens." She felt lost. This was the first time she'd experienced an emergency like this. How to handle it? She bent to gather the remains of the picnic and jumped when Nick's hands gently grabbed her arm, pulling her up and into his arms. She sniffed back tears.

"It'll be okay. Go get the horses ready, and I'll pack up. I'll get you back as fast as I can." She nodded and stumbled to where the horses grazed, checking the saddles and bridles. Moments later Nick's hands grabbed her waist and lifted her on the horse before he climbed onto King's Knight. He urged his horse to a gallop, and Kaylan did the same, this time thankful to follow his lead.

"Lord, don't let anything happen to my Pap. I don't know what I would do without him."

The only response was the whispering wind.

Chapter Seven

THE EMERGENCY ROOM buzzed with practiced urgency. As the doors slid open, Kaylan searched for a familiar face. Spotting Micah, she wound around chairs, anxious to hear the news.

"What happened? Is he okay? Where is he?"

"He's fine, Kayles. He had a ministroke while he and Mom were eating lunch. Doctor says he just needs to rest. They want to watch him for the next twenty-four hours, in case of another stroke."

Kaylan sighed in relief. "Ministroke. I can handle that. I'm glad he's okay."

"Good, because he's asking for you." Micah's eyes darted between her and Nick, who stood like a bodyguard behind her. "He wants to know how your date went and apologize for interrupting."

She laughed, tension leaving her body. "Of course he does. Although there's not much to tell." She glanced back at Nick to see a look of challenge on his face. A thrill coursed through her, sending shivers down her spine. The warmth in his eyes made her thankful they weren't alone.

"Looks like you're falling down on the job, partner. Is your charm wearing off, or is my sister just able to put you in your place?" Micah slapped Nick's shoulder and led them back to Pap's room.

"Very funny, Bulldog." Nick slipped his arm around Kaylan's shoulders, startling her just as they came in view of the rest of her family. David and Seth eyed him suspiciously. If her brothers ever acted on their protective instincts with Nick, it would be an interesting duel. She wasn't sure who would win.

"Is he okay?" Kaylan needed to hear it from her mom.

"We need to watch him for the next few hours, but I think so."

Kaylan feared what this stroke meant for the future. If he had one now, would they increase over time until he had one he couldn't recover from?

Her grandmother stepped forward and smoothed the wrinkles on Kaylan's forehead. "Pap wants to see his Sugar. No use fretting about what we can't change. God's in control, honey." She smiled and tapped Kaylan's nose. "Now, get your beautiful self in there and tell Pap about your date. Nick can stay out here with us." Gran looped her arm with Nick's.

Micah pushed her toward the door. "We won't be that hard on him. Besides, if he can't handle the pressure, he can't stick around."

"We won't hurt him too bad, sis." Seth cracked his knuckles and shot her a wicked grin.

"Good luck." She envied him. Pap was a talented interrogator, and she was not quite sure what she would say about her time with Nick.

An old John Wayne movie played in the dark room. Kaylan's heart jumped to her throat again. Minor stroke or not, she was worried what she would find.

"There's my Sugar."

Kaylan sank onto the bed and squeezed his hand, her eyes flitting over his body to check for herself. She hated the hospital gown on her strong grandpa. His silver-white hair stood up in a couple places on his head, and despite the dark circles under his eyes, they still sparkled as they met hers.

"Stop fretting. I'm fine. I've survived worse than this."

"Like what?"

"Strep throat. You can't get over that dadgum sore throat for a week. Your gran makes me drink her awful-tasting hot lemonade. Much worse than this." Pap shook his head and grimaced.

Kaylan couldn't help but laugh. "Pap, that's not funny. This is serious. Now that you've had one stroke, you're at risk for another one."

He shook his head and patted the back of her hand. "We don't fear what we can't control. I can only do my best to stay healthy and let God take care of the rest. If it's my time to go, it's my time to go."

Don't fear what you can't control. The thought reverberated in Kaylan's mind like a gong. Much easier said than done. She feared her relationship with Nick, her decision to go to Haiti, what the future would bring.

"Hey." Pap tapped her knee, drawing her away from her frantic thoughts. "It's okay to fear the unknown. We're only human. But when we let that fear inhibit our faith in the Lord, that's when we walk into trouble."

"Things are so crazy and uncertain right now, Pap. Blind faith is hard."

"Sure it is, Sugar. But faith by definition isn't easy. It requires action and sacrifice on our part. When the Lord told Abraham to leave his home and family behind, he had to just start walking until the Lord told him to stop. How's that for lack of direction? But the Lord never left him. He had good plans for that man, and he became the father of a lot of people. That's a little overwhelming to think about, though, isn't it?"

She nodded. "If the Lord was faithful to Abraham, He'll be faithful with me."

"Always, Sugar."

She leaned down and hugged him, breathing in the smell of peppermint and coffee. "You can't leave me yet, Pap. What would I do without you?"

"Ah, I don't think it's my time to go. But one of these days I will. Life isn't forever, and you'll be just fine."

Kaylan wasn't so sure. Where would she be without his quiet

reassurance and wisdom? He always calmed her and pointed her to Jesus. Just as Nick had at one point in time.

Nick. How long ago the morning seemed. Pap squeezed her hand, and she met his steady gaze and knowing smile.

"Now, why don't you tell me about that young man out in the hallway? Can't keep secrets from me."

She was glad the room hid her blush. "One conversation doesn't fix everything, Pap, but it sure was enlightening. I don't want to let him back in too quickly, but I don't want to avoid the risk, either. What if I miss out this time because I'm the one to say no? But then, where does Haiti fit into all this? This time *I'll* be leaving."

"Whoa. Slow down there. Do you love him?"

"Pap." She felt as though she were back in grade school, telling him about her first crush. "That is a really strong word."

"That's what I've heard. Well, all right. Do you like him, then?"

She shrugged. "Sure I do."

"Why?"

Her cheeks heated, and she was thankful for the dim lighting. "He's confident. And he quietly leads. I felt frazzled when Micah called to tell me you were in the hospital. Nick took control. He calmed me down. He hates horses, yet he never looked more comfortable on one as he led us back to his truck. He loves the Lord. He fights for what's right and defends those who can't fight for themselves."

Something slowly dawned on her: if she had a list of the perfect guy for her, Nick was quickly meeting every requirement.

"Well, I'm sold. Did he kiss you yet?"

Kaylan smiled and leaned in close to her grandfather's ear. "None of your business."

"Now, Sugar, you're only young once, and I need to live vicariously through you. Details. Don't you hold anything back from your Pap now."

"No, Pap, he didn't. I'm not ready for that."

"Good. I would have needed one of you to bring my shotgun up here." His rich baritone chuckle filled the room, though weaker than normal. "I want to talk to you about Haiti. You still set on going?"

"Yes, sir, but…"

"But what, Sugar?"

"What if I leave for Haiti and you have another stroke?"

"And what if I don't make it through that one, and you don't get to tell me good-bye? Is that it?" As always, he read the fears splashed across her heart. "Remember what I told you earlier? No fear. God's in control."

"Yeah, but what if I stayed here and took care of you? I could work at the dance studio and help Mom with her interior design business while I wait for my internship to start in August. And I could take care of you." She met Pap's eyes as he allowed the silence to linger.

"Well, now, that sounds like a much safer option than going to Haiti. Practical, even. But when was the last time the Lord called us to what was practical? Sometimes, in our most difficult decisions and transitions, the Lord works the most."

"Then this is going to be big, because this has been the hardest decision of my life."

"Go, Sugar. Pray, trust the Lord. Your gran and I want to sponsor your trip. So don't worry about the money. Just go do your thing."

A nurse bustled in to take Pap's blood pressure, followed by Gran. With a wink and nod, Pap released Kaylan, and she headed out to rejoin her family in the waiting room.

Nick was quickly learning the Richardses' family dynamics. David and Seth, reassured that Pap would be okay, had headed home. Kaylan had arrived back in the waiting room and announced that, in light of Pap's stroke, she was reconsidering her trip to Haiti. Her parents had accepted her decision, but not Micah. As soon as they left to check on Pap, Micah turned on his sister.

"Kaylan, Pap would want you to go to Haiti, not stay here for him." Micah paced back and forth—rarely a good sign. Nick silently applauded Micah. Kaylan needed to take this trip, needed to spread her wings. Nick loved her sacrificial spirit, but this time she needed to direct it to helping the Haitians.

"But I could help Pap. Mom and Dad need to work, and Gran still has her responsibilities with the school board. Your leave is up right after Christmas, and no one else can make sure he's taking care of himself."

"He's a grown man, Kayles. And he wants to get better." Micah squeezed her shoulder.

"What if he has another stroke while I'm gone, Micah? I couldn't handle being so far away if that happened."

"That's not in your control, Kaylan." Micah hugged her. Nick knew Micah viewed himself as Kaylan's protector. Nick wondered if he and the rest of the family protected her too much. Out of all the Richards kids, she'd lived the most sheltered life. He thanked the Lord she hadn't experienced the pain of life in the way he had. However, he had learned firsthand that brokenness shaped a person, and growth didn't occur without it. It wasn't his or Micah's job to protect Kaylan from life. Only Jesus could do that.

"I feel so bad leaving right now while he's unhealthy." She grew quiet and looked at Micah. "Pap told me he and Gran would pay for the cost of my trip."

"That's awesome! Huge answer to prayer. Smile a little. It's what you've been praying for, isn't it?"

"Sure. I just feel guilty letting him do that now."

"I think you won't have much choice one way or the other. When Pap sets his mind to something, he usually makes it happen."

"I know."

"No one is making you feel guilty but you. Snap out of it."

She nodded, her lips thinning. Nick knew that face. She would listen, but she would struggle to release the guilt.

Micah threw his arm around her, tugging her close. "I love that you want to take care of everyone, little sis, but let us do that here. It's time for you to go. It's not your concern."

"The ones I love are always my concern," Kaylan said, shoving Micah playfully. In her statement Nick saw the quiet strength and determination that so often came to the forefront. She might wrestle with making decisions, but there were some areas of her life where she never wavered in her commitment and devotion. People she cared about topped that list. Nick wanted the top spot.

"Then pray for him. And trust God and us for the rest."

"Okay, okay. Just let me see him one more time." Kaylan rose to check on Pap again, leaving Micah and Nick alone in the waiting room.

"Lord, take care of her." Micah lifted his voice in the quiet room. He turned to Nick. "She carries the weight of the world too much. She needs to learn to give that to God."

"Give her some credit, Bulldog. It took you a tour in Afghanistan and a near-death experience to learn to trust God in a new way. Maybe Haiti will be exactly what she needs."

Micah nodded, and a grin spread across his face. He pulled out his phone and scrolled through his contacts. "There's only one person besides Seth who can put a smile on her face."

It didn't take a genius to know who that person was.

Their voices blended in the sterile hall, "Sarah Beth." Micah stepped away to make the call as Kaylan joined Nick again in the waiting room. Without hesitating, she settled beside him on the couch, leaning in to his embrace.

"Feel better?"

"I talked to the nurse. The stroke was minor. He'll be fine."

Nick thought she was trying to reassure herself. He rubbed his fingers along her arm. "He's a tough guy. He'll make it." Just like his granddaughter.

"I know. It's just hard to see him like this."

Nick leaned over and kissed her forehead. They'd moved leaps and bounds since their morning picnic. She was allowing him to comfort her, something she rarely allowed others to do when family was present.

"Why don't you get out of here for a little while? He's fine and resting."

She nodded and leaned her head against his chest. "Thank you," she murmured.

"For what?"

"For being here. For being nice when I panicked on our date." She chuckled. "That was embarrassing."

He leaned back so he could see her face and brushed his knuckles along her cheek. "You're stronger than you think, Kaylan Lee Richards. And never apologize for crying or freaking out in front of me."

"Growing up in a houseful of brothers, you have to get tough, or you get run over."

Nick tipped his head back and laughed. "Knowing Micah, I bet that's right."

Micah popped back into the waiting room and thrust his phone at Kaylan. "Someone wants to talk to you."

Kaylan's look of surprise quickly gave way to relief as she heard the voice on the other end. Nick recognized the bond. It was blood-thick. Kaylan and Sarah Beth were the kind of friends who had long ago breached the line of friendship and moved to sister-hood. Similar to the bond of Navy SEALs.

After a few minutes of serious talk, Kaylan's voice changed. "Sounds perfect. You can pick me up out front at the hospital entrance." Kaylan handed the phone back to Micah, and a smile lit her face.

Nick's interest rose. "Wait, where are you going?"

Kaylan smiled at him over her shoulder as she left the room. "Dance studio."

Chapter Eight

DANCING WAS KAYLAN'S favorite pastime. The polished wood floor was as familiar as the sound of waves lapping her dock at home. She and Sarah Beth stretched in one of Madame Sally's dance studios where they had danced since they were five.

"What are we going for today?" Sarah Beth held up her iPod and skipped to plug it into the speakers at the back of the room. "Jazz, pop, ballet? What are you in the mood for?" The smack of her bubble gum bounced off the mirrored walls.

"Let's burn some stress. Pop or jazz." Kaylan stretched, slipped on her shoes, and stood as an old 'N Sync song blared over the speakers. Sarah Beth danced to her side.

"Old school, huh?"

"I thought we could test our memories on the routine from our senior dance recital. You still got the moves?" Sarah Beth nudged Kaylan and then rushed to restart the song.

"Bring it."

The music began again, and Kaylan closed her eyes and moved with the beat, the old routine flowing naturally. Instinct took over. She was no longer in the studio. She was in Nick's arms, the relationship restored. He was strong and safe. She kicked and leaped in rhythm with Sarah Beth, imagining herself in Haiti, surrounded by orphans, teaching them about Jesus and helping them live healthy lives. She could feel their little hands, hear their voices singing.

They continued to dance, the steps growing more intricate. She was with her brothers playing football and with Pap horseback riding. Sarah Beth held up cards of nutrition facts with funny acronyms. She was with her dad in his study, telling him the exact proportions of a mast as he crafted a model ship. And she was with her mom and Gran, picking out paint colors and wall decorations to create a homey atmosphere at the lake house. Sarah Beth bumped into her, and they both giggled, bringing her back to the moment.

Songs continued to play, and with each, Kaylan moved with more intensity, the stress and anxiety flowing with her sweat. She focused on her favorite memories and wishes. Strands of her hair clung to her neck as she kicked and twirled, while Sarah Beth followed or created her own movements.

Without fail, time with Sarah Beth refreshed her. No words were necessary. They danced as two who shared one heart, letting years of friendship heal and do the talking. The polished wood under Kaylan's feet was a welcoming sensation. The room smelled of sweat and accomplishment.

A slower song filled the room, and Kaylan slowed her movements to match. She closed her eyes again and willed herself to feel the movement of the music and act on it. Her art teacher had once told her that creative expression was often a product of music. Dance was Kaylan's version of creative expression. When she danced, she was truly herself. No hiding. Emotions released with the flow of her body, refreshing her spirit.

The final strains filled the room, and Kaylan dropped to the floor, adrenaline leaving in a rush. Drained and soaked, nevertheless she felt alive, just as she did in the mornings when she watched the sun rise. She was back in control, and life felt less overwhelming.

A deep cough bounced off the walls, and Kaylan bolted upright. Sarah Beth was gone, but Nick leaned against the wall, watching her.

"I think I need to teach you to be more aware of your surroundings."

"I think you need to learn not to sneak up on me," Kaylan shot back, her heart dancing to a new cadence. "Where's Sarah Beth?"

He shrugged. "Went home, I guess." He pushed away from the wall and joined her where she sat in the middle of the dance floor. Her heart rate doubled. His nearness and the intensity rippling in his eyes told her that she could no longer deny their chemistry. They were treading into unfamiliar territory, approaching a point of no return.

"Do you think we could finish our conversation? We were interrupted earlier."

She nodded and bit her lip, bracing for what could come next.

"I need to understand something." His relaxed manner eased her fluttering pulse. "Why Haiti, Kaylan? Why now?"

"Because I want to change the world, or at least a part of it. I want to do something that matters, Nick."

"You have a red carpet to your dreams. Why not wait?"

She shook her head. "I don't want to second-guess myself again, Nick. I see that child, his ribs sticking out from hunger, or that mother thinking of giving up her baby because she can't feed him, and I want to change the cycle."

"You want to be the catalyst." He nodded, but his eyes held caution. "You can't do it on your own."

"No, but I can change one life. One piece of the world in my own backyard. I can make a difference."

"And us, Kayles? Where do you see that going?"

She swiped her hand across her forehead and shivered, the sweat on her body cooling in the chill of the studio. Her body shook from more than the air.

"You asked me to trust you again. To give you a chance. I can give you that, but it's my turn to leave, Nick. And I don't know what's waiting for me or when I'll be back."

"That's usually my line."

She wished she could read minds. His poker face denied access. It was his turn to study her, not the other way around. "I was counting on you. I can't stay here just to give you another chance. It's my turn. I want to see the world, people I've never met, make a difference. It's what you wanted when you left."

"I wouldn't ask you to put your life on hold for me, to just stay at home and wait. Not if Haiti is something you really feel you need to do."

Relief filled her, and his support bolstered her trust. "I've sat on the sidelines my whole life. Always waiting for a better time, always following the plan in my head. But I feel like the Lord is calling me to step from my comfort zone and take this unexpected adventure. Yes, this is something I want to do."

He grabbed the backpack he'd been carrying that morning and withdrew a box, the red wood stained and rustic. He handed it to her. She traced the wood grains and then lifted the latch. Inside lay a stack of letters, all addressed to her and bound by a rubber band. Wondering, she met his eyes. They churned like the sea about to break over the rocks.

"There's a letter for every week I was deployed last year. Well, once I realized I was missing you, which didn't take long. Twenty-six total."

She swallowed hard, her eyes darting from him to the box and back again. What was he saying? And what would she find within these letters?

"I don't understand."

"I meant what I told you today, Kayles. I missed you and thought of you while I was gone. Ending our relationship was the biggest mistake I have ever made. Right now you don't trust me completely. I made a lot of promises to you before I left, and while I meant them, they were premature and hurt you. I am so sorry, Kaylan. I'm not that guy anymore. I know it will take a while to let me back into your heart. But for now, can you please let me be part of your life?"

He moved closer to her and reached for her hands. He'd never been this vulnerable with her before, but her thoughts were wrapped as tightly as a ball of twine. She couldn't find the end to release them into a coherent strand.

"My heart is in those words. How much I missed you, how much I wished I could take it all back. My dreams of someday. Read them in Haiti, and I'll be waiting when you get back."

"You would do that?" She tipped her head, needing to know. "You would let me leave, let me figure this out for months, and still promise to wait for me? Why?"

"Because I care about you as more than a friend and more than my best friend's sister. I love who you are." He returned the gentle pressure on her hands and leaned toward her. "Kaylan, if this relationship progressed and we looked at forever, I would be asking you to support me as a Navy SEAL, a soldier for my country. That would mean long deployments, little contact, secrecy, and blind faith. How could I do any less for you in what you feel the Lord calling you to?"

Her heart raced and roared in her ears. "If you promise to wait for me, then I'm going to hold you to it."

"I won't let you down." His voice sounded low and husky. He brushed his knuckles across her face and slowly pulled her to her feet. "I want to follow the Lord, Kaylan. I want to do this right. And to do that, I have to trust Him with you. I've let you down, but He never will."

She smiled. "Trust is a big word."

"Very true." He leaned forward until their foreheads touched, his grin making her weak.

"I've got another chance, don't I." It wasn't a question.

"Well, I guess so. Who am I to resist a pining frogman who wrote me letters in the heat of combat?"

"You wouldn't be a lady if you tried."

"Hey!" She pushed him away, but his cheeky grin mended the scars on her heart, reminding her of moments when her mom had applied Neosporin to her cuts and scrapes as a child. The cut would heat and sting, but a few days later it would be gone. Kaylan wondered if this was the start of a new normal. Her heart and her mind could barely keep up with all the changes. *Is this really happening, Lord?*

He held up his finger, motioning her to wait, and moved to the stereo system in back. "One more surprise."

She smirked. "You're just full of surprises. By the way, what did you do with my best friend?"

"I bought her off. It was easy. She knows what's good for you."

"And what's that?"

"Me."

"Can You Feel the Love Tonight?" drifted through the speakers. Nick jogged back to her, slipping his arm around her waist and bringing her hand to rest on his chest.

"*Lion King*, really? Who would have thought?" She laughed as they rotated in place, this time unable to clear her head as they danced. His nearness was like a drug, one she didn't want to quit.

Whispering in her ear, he pulled her closer, "What can I say? I'm a man of many secrets." He softly sang the words she'd known since childhood. "You know, love's a pretty big word too," he commented.

Kaylan met his eyes. "It's also demonstrated best over time." She kept her tone light, but her message was clear. He better tread lightly.

His smile grew as he acknowledged her gentle warning. "How about this: I promise I won't say it until I know for sure."

"I can handle that."

His eyes grew intense again, and she fought the urge to pull back. "But when I finally say it, Kaylan, I'll be playing for keeps. And you'll need to make a final decision on whether you can trust me or not."

She nodded, speechless. He pulled her near again as the song wound to a close, and they stood breathless in the middle of the studio.

His lips lowered to hers, his fingers weaving through her hair, challenging her resolve. Her racing heart galloped like Black-Eyed Pea in an open field. Heat poured into her face. She wasn't ready for the feel of his lips on hers again. Not when everything was still unsure. Before she could change her mind, she gently pushed against his chest and away from his embrace.

"Make good on your promise," she whispered. "Let's see what happens."

He nodded, pulling her close again and resting his forehead on hers. He chuckled. "You won't let me say good-bye like I want, will you?"

She shook her head, tempted to change her mind. Her arms slipped around his neck, and they swayed in the silence. In the moments that passed, she stored the memory in her heart to recall when she was miles away and this seemed only a dream. His arms, warm and firm, made it seem as though all was right in the world. He chased away the shadows. But it was time to face her future. Only God knew if Nick would play a part.

Weaving her fingers into his hair, she brushed his cheek with a kiss before pulling away, her eyes looking to his heart, to the hole in his armor he'd opened for her alone. Her whisper echoed in the gilded room: "It's how I want to say hello."

"You can bet on it, beautiful." He slipped his rough hand in hers, linking their fingers, and brushed her fingers with his lips. Her breath caught and a future with him materialized in her mind again piece by piece.

As they left the studio to rejoin her family at home, Kaylan felt as if she could conquer the world with him at her side.

With his promise to sustain her, the trip to Haiti shone all the brighter.

PART TWO

Chapter Nine

THE STREETS OF Port-au-Prince, Haiti, buzzed with goats and children. A chicken ran across the road in front of Rhonda's small car, flapping and clucking, and Kaylan leaned out the window to watch its frenzied trek. She had just arrived, and already the vibrant colors in this tiny country astounded her—bright reds, deep turquoise, kelly greens, and sunny yellows and oranges marked people's lives and art in the tropical environment.

Mothers poured buckets of water over naked children less than a foot from where cars zoomed past. Cars played chicken in the streets, traffic lines completely ignored, speed limits disregarded. If a car moved too slowly, others simply zoomed around it, dodging oncoming traffic. Women walked with baskets or buckets of water balanced on their heads, their daughters trailing behind with smaller balanced bundles.

Homes stood pieced together with sheets of rusted metal and worn wooden boards. Clothes hung loosely and mismatched on adults and children wandering the streets, but smiles adorned many faces, and children played in the street with rocks and flattened balls. Though many were destitute, the people made up for the squalor by accessorizing their lives with color. Her first glimpses of Haiti filled Kaylan with a strange mixture of horror and hope. She was ready to roll up her sleeves and dive in.

"What's that terrible smell?" Sarah Beth wrinkled her nose in protest at the scent of burning plastic. Since debarking the plane, Kaylan had fought the urge to hold her breath.

"It's garbage and waste. People don't have a way to dispose of trash properly, so they burn it. You'll get used to it after a while. It's worse in the city than farther out in the country."

Rhonda gripped the steering wheel, winding her way among cars and trucks zooming past, some with men perched precariously on the car roof. Kaylan sent up a silent prayer for safe arrival at their destination.

A tap-tap, similar to a small bus, navigated the street in front of them. Kaylan stared in awe at the array of colors coating its sides. It was as if a rainbow had broken apart into odd shapes and pieces and melded together to form a unique piece of artwork on the vehicle—a hippie experiment gone terribly wrong. The sides of the bus were covered with voodoo and Christian symbols, and men peered at the white women from the small door in the back of the bus. A motorcycle skirted past their car, carrying four people and a small pig.

Their car bumped and swerved over potholes. Kaylan pressed her hand to the roof of the car, anchoring herself in the seat. The sides of the road overflowed with clothes, flip-flops, food, and artwork. Packed bodies scurried from one side of the street to the other, resembling ants on a mission to carry supplies back to the queen. Cars honked, people ran to and fro, and vendors yelled from the side of every street. A thin, bald man stood on a corner, handing out pills to locals who bartered with him.

"He's the local pharmacy," Rhonda pointed out. Kaylan sat up straighter and took a closer look. That couldn't be healthy. A basket rested on his head, and he periodically reached up to grab a package of unmarked pills.

Rhonda jerked the car then slowed as a mass of humanity came in view. Sarah Beth squealed from where she sat in the back. "What is all this?"

"It's one of the biggest marketplaces in Port-au-Prince." Rhonda gestured to the women and children outside. The mothers spoke with their hands, their voices rising over the clamor of people arguing for the necessities. "Despite what they barter for here, people still have very little. Hardly enough to survive."

"They must be pretty tough." Kaylan watched a mother corral her children through the mass of bodies.

"They're resilient. Life is hard, and the people here roll with it. In a sad way they've accepted that it will probably never get better. It's a sick cycle."

"Then how do we stop it, Rhonda?"

"One person at a time. Sometimes it's like trying to swim upstream. You fight the current the whole way, and only those determined to tough out the heat, animals, natural disasters, and blasé attitude make it. This country isn't for the fainthearted or idealistic."

Kaylan's heart broke for the Haitians, and her affection swelled for the lady driving. From the moment Rhonda Ames collected them from the airport, Kaylan sensed a humble strength from this tiny woman.

"Rhonda, how did you end up here in Haiti?"

The corners of her eyes crinkled with her smile, a mark of years in the Haitian sun. "I was young and idealistic like you. I got married right out of college, and we both wanted to save the world. Haiti was the forgotten country, the underbelly of the United States, with little resources and big problems." She shrugged. "At first we were determined to change it. But my husband left me three years after we married. He hated the heat and the lifestyle. I said we could go back to America and serve there, but he said it was too late for us. I couldn't bring myself to leave. Haiti was home. My family is here now. Haiti can drain your motivation or make you more determined." She looked at both of them in the rearview mirror. "Be careful not to let life here discourage you."

Kaylan studied the scene outside her window. Poverty, pure and simple. She never imagined it could be this bad. How did people live like this? Before she boarded the plane, she questioned her sanity. Haiti had more nonprofits trying to help than almost any other country. Maybe she should pick somewhere else to help. But those thoughts were immediately dispelled as she drove through human squalor. This country needed more help than it was getting. And she and Sarah Beth were ready and willing.

"We're excited to help. Just put us to work, Rhonda." But Kaylan wondered who she would be if she spent years in Haiti as Rhonda had. Would she lose her passion, or would she grow even more motivated? Only time would tell.

Evening had descended on the California coast. As much as Nick missed Kaylan, it was nice to be back in the home he shared with Micah close to the beach in Coronado. It was definitely a Navy community, and Nick had missed the sound of the waves and the smell of salt in the air. As much as Micah was a Southern man with the accent to prove it, Nick had been born and bred for the ocean.

He and Micah had returned to California a day before Kaylan left for Haiti. After spending his first deployment with the SEALs in Afghanistan, it was comforting to be back with these men, his family.

Music drifted from Micah's room as Nick took advantage of the down time to compose a letter to Kaylan. Words spilled onto the page.

A football whizzed through the air and landed next to Nick on his bed. Nick looked up to see Micah cross the room with an envelope in his hand, a grin the size of Canada lighting his features.

"Well, Hawk, looks like you made more headway with my sister than I thought. Maybe your charm worked after all." He tossed the envelope on the bed, and Nick wrestled to keep his expression mild. If Micah knew just how much this meant, he would never hear the end of it.

"Looks like it got lost in our pile of mail on the kitchen table." He smirked. "You gonna open it?"

"Not with you watching, Nosy."

"C'mon, Hawk. I need something on my mind besides all these drills they've run us through since we got back." He massaged his shoulder and neck. "They must be prepping us for something big."

Nick nodded. His muscles ached from drills and the weight room. He may have overdone it a bit, but anything was better than losing his mind worrying about Kaylan. He wanted to kick Micah out of the room and read her letter, but years of discipline kept his emotions firmly under control.

Micah shifted back against the wall, this time massaging his calf muscle. "What do you think it is?"

"What are you yapping about?"

Micah snatched the envelope and twirled it between his fingers. "If you can't get your mind off my sister and into combat mode, we may be in serious trouble on our next deployment. Is that why you've been hitting the weights during every free moment? You're making me look bad, man."

Nick punched him in the arm. "I'll be good when it counts. Kaylan won't be an issue." Yet, Nick silently wondered. She invaded his thoughts, made him second-guess his moves in combat. He didn't need her on his mind to stay alive. The natural drive was strong enough. Micah was right, though. If he couldn't start focusing here, he'd be in big trouble on the next op.

The letter landed on his chest lightly, and Micah rose to leave the room. "Maybe I should find a girl so I'm motivated to hit the gym more often." A sarcastic smile lit his face. "Tell my baby sis I said hi."

Nick tore through the envelope and found her familiar script, as elegant and graceful as she was.

Nick,

We watched our last sunrise together this morning, and tomorrow afternoon I will board a plane for a country that has a name but no face to me right now. It comforts me that no matter how far apart we are, we are both under the same sunrise. I will watch them in the mornings and pray for you.

The art of writing letters has been all but forgotten, but thank you for braving my brother's endless teasing and your own embarrassment to make the effort. It means more than you know. You asked me to trust you, and you have made that easier every day of this holiday. You've lived up to your word and your mantra.

As I leave for Haiti, I leave with hope. I will spend time with my best friend and serve with her because I love her; I will help people physically because the Lord has gifted me; and I pray their hearts will change spiritually, because He came to heal body, soul, and mind.

Your calling and mine are not all that different. You fight for your country because you love it. You would lay your life down, because you believe some things are worth it. You would pay the ultimate sacrifice for people you have never met, because Jesus did the same for you. I find myself praying for that courage and servant's heart. I will help people, because the Lord cared about the broken, abused, poor, and needy. I will be the hands and feet of Jesus. In the process, I pray I can learn the sacrificial heart of a warrior. That's what I admire about you, Nick: your strength.

Praying for you from an ocean away,
Kayles

Nick skimmed the page again, seeing her quiet strength. He stood and paced the room. She trusted him. How precious was that gift, one he didn't deserve after his past with her. He prayed for courage and for strength. She weighed heavier on his mind than she had in days, and he felt an urgency to pray.

She would receive the gift he'd sent in a few days, and he hoped she saw the heart behind it. He folded the letter and slipped it into his Bible, two precious treasures united. If she spent the early morning hours praying for him, then he would do the same.

He grabbed his running shoes to stamp out the urgency and longing knotting his gut. He was just beginning to appreciate the strength and perseverance it would take to ask her to wait for him at home while he served his country.

Micah stood in the center of the living room, stretching. A grin spread across his face again. "Ready for that run?"

"You know me too well." Nick laughed. "See if you can keep up."

"No problem. Now you gonna tell me what that letter said that has you in need of clearing your head?"

Nick grabbed Micah in a headlock. "If I talked about it, it wouldn't clear my head, now, would it? Besides, I would hate to ruin my mysterious reputation."

Micah fell into step with him, his laughter echoing off the houses in their neighborhood.

Chapter Ten

THE FIRST THREE days in Haiti passed in a blur. While Sarah Beth roamed the neighborhood getting to know the children, Rhonda worked Kaylan mercilessly at the medical clinic, training her in skills she lacked, like suturing and giving shots. Kaylan had knowledge of nutrition practices, health needs, the body, and basic chemistry, but the practical, hands-on skills escaped her. As Rhonda trained her, she realized how little she actually knew. Book knowledge only went so far. In a country like Haiti, though, whoever was present to help handled any and every emergency. Doctors and volunteers alike became masters in the art of "winging it" for the sake of saving a life.

Patients came and went. Kaylan brought them water as they waited and spoke to children who shyly smiled back, curiosity shining from big, dark eyes. To build relationships, she and Sarah Beth had even joined in a soccer game the night before. A rolled-up lump of trash had served as a ball until Sarah Beth presented the checkered ball she had slipped in her suitcase in place of a pair of shoes. The excitement of the children shattered the language barrier. Laughter became the means of communication. Kaylan had fallen in love—not with a man, but with a people.

Today was her day. Rhonda had declared her ready to start seeing patients on her own. This day might test everything she held dear about her new romance.

Her interpreter, Abraham, entered the clinic with a big grin, his white teeth gleaming against his dark skin. Sunglasses rested on his head, and his designer jeans spoke of American attempts to provide for this country. The Haitian flag on his T-shirt spoke of his pride. Kaylan warmed at his presence, thanking God for this lanky teen.

"I feel called of God to lead my people, Kaylan. I will teach them the truth about Jesus Christ," he had told her on her first day at the clinic. He was in his first year at the local seminary and volunteered as an interpreter with Rhonda in his free time.

"I'm ready." Her eyes flitted around the room, finding her first patient, a young girl of about fifteen with a child in her arms.

"You be God's hands today, and I will be His mouthpiece, and together we will make a great team. *Wi?*" Abe held up his hand for a high-five, something Sarah Beth had taught him. His grin was infectious.

"*Wi.*" The crack of their hands drew several curious looks from those waiting.

Kaylan knelt down in front of the young girl and brushed her fingertips across the head of the sleeping baby.

"Are you Tasha?" The girl nodded as Abraham translated, Kaylan understanding bits and pieces from her study of French. "Tasha, I'm Kaylan. Let's go back and check you and your little man out, okay?" Tasha rose and followed Kaylan to a small room in the back of the clinic where Rhonda inventoried supplies. She had promised to listen and observe, stepping in only if necessary.

"May I hold him?"

Tasha handed her baby to Kaylan reluctantly. Kaylan placed her hand on his tiny back, feeling the rattle through his thin shirt as he breathed. "What's his name?"

"Kenny."

"He's beautiful."

Tasha grinned, her hesitancy dropping away. "*Wi.* A gift."

Kaylan placed Kenny on his back in a small basinet then displayed a pamphlet she'd brought with her, outlining in Creole good foods to eat so Tasha and Kenny would receive the nutrition they desperately needed. "Do your best to eat chicken or pork daily to satisfy your protein requirement. Fruits and vegetables are necessary too, as well as grain or bread of some kind." She stopped and waited for Abe to translate. He looked at her, his eyes wide and confused.

"Sorry, Abe. Do I need to slow down?"

Tasha's eyes swiveled back and forth between them, her forehead wrinkling.

"Kaylan, I cannot tell her that."

"But that's what she needs while she breast-feeds, so she and Kenny will be healthy. I've researched this. I have a plan. It'll be okay."

"I do not think you understand the ways of Haiti." He shook his head sadly and spread his hands, imploring. "Do you not know what she is?"

"She's a teen mom who needs help."

Rhonda's brisk voice sounded behind them in the small room. "Kaylan, may I speak with you for a moment?"

Kaylan followed Rhonda from the room as she replayed the scene again in her mind. Had she done something wrong? She knew what she was saying. How many times had she designed a plan like this in class or for a project in a local school with students who rarely received proper nutrition? Rhonda shut the door of the small office behind her.

"Did I do something wrong?"

"Kaylan, Tasha is a teen mom because she is a prostitute. Her dad doesn't work, and her mom has several small children. Tasha is the oldest, and to help her family, she did the only thing she knew how—she sold herself."

No girl should ever need to resort to that. Kaylan's anger built like a storm cloud toward Tasha's father and the men who took advantage of the beautiful teen. Tasha had seen far more than Kaylan could even imagine. Alabama grew more distant by the hour, and the safe bubble Kaylan had always known seemed like a cruel joke.

"I'm sorry. I didn't know. But I still don't understand. Why wouldn't Abe translate what I said?"

"Because her family can't afford to buy chicken or pork. They barely afford one meal a day for the whole family. Why do you think she and Kenny are so malnourished?"

"But, Rhonda, she can't get healthy if she doesn't eat protein and more than one meal. What am I supposed to tell her? She can't afford it, but she needs it." Kaylan paced the small room. She could fix this. She needed to fix this.

"Kaylan, this is the reality for many who live in the shanty towns. Think of alternative ways she could have protein and grain, maybe with less expensive food."

Kaylan raked fingers through her hair, yanking when they caught in her curls. "What if I help pay for some of her food? What if we had her over to the house and cooked a meal for her? Rhonda, there's got to be something."

Rhonda shook her head. "Are you going to do that for every teenage mother, every hungry family, every malnourished child?"

"If I have to." Kaylan's voice rose and cracked. How could she help so many? How could she not? There had to be a break in this terrible cycle, a way to teach and train these women.

Rhonda hugged Kaylan. A tear slipped down Kaylan's cheek, and she swiped it away. She felt helpless to change the life of one. How could she change the lives of so many?

She pulled back from Rhonda and paced the room again, her mind whirling with possibilities.

All right, Lord. You wanted me here, and I'm here, so now what? How do I help Tasha and those like her? How do I fix this?

She remembered something from a study one of her classmates had done of nutrition alternatives in Africa. If they couldn't eat meat, then they needed to understand the nutritional need to make a whole protein with beans and rice or peanuts and a grain. She knew some of them couldn't even afford that. Maybe she could help them combine these cheaper alternatives to get the proper nutrients for themselves and their malnourished children. Her mind spun.

A soft laugh came from Rhonda, who stood watching her from across the room. Kaylan stopped pacing. "What's so funny?"

"Did you come to change the world, kiddo? 'Cause that's not your job."

"Maybe I forgot." She shrugged. "But I'm not sure how to help Tasha. Everything I've learned seems useless here."

"It's real life. This isn't a classroom. These people live in poverty daily, and they accept it. This is their normal." Wrapping her arm around Kaylan, she led them back to Tasha. "The question is, kiddo, what are you going to do about it?"

Kaylan's fists clenched at her sides. She wasn't sure what to do yet, but she wasn't done trying.

"Miss Kaylan, pass, pass!" Reuben jumped up and down, his green shorts catching the dust from the street. Kaylan shot the soccer ball in his direction through the tangled legs of kids from the nearest shanty village. His bare foot stopped the ball mid-roll, and he propelled it toward the makeshift goal between two dilapidated homes. Some of the kids had never played with a real ball.

Kaylan cheered him on, admiring the grace in his small body. She and Sarah Beth had stayed up late the night before to welcome the new year, and after a long Saturday at the clinic, they pulled out the soccer ball again. Local kids flocked en masse to meet the girls, their beautiful, dark eyes focused on the ball in Sarah Beth's hands.

More hands had touched Kaylan's hair in the past hour than in her entire life. Her auburn hair and green eyes were an anomaly, a beacon amid the dark bodies and dust. A woman in the market had already asked to paint her.

Reuben ran to her, jabbering in Creole about his victory shot. "Goal, Kaylan, goal."

She rubbed his short hair, his joy infectious. *"Bon travay,* Reuben."

He ran to Abraham, grabbed his hand, and pulled him over to Kaylan. Abraham translated. "He wants to know how to say it in English. He says he will be a great soccer player someday, and he must learn English before he can play in America."

She knelt down in front of the boy. "Good job, Reuben."

His eyes squinted, and his mouth worked to form the words.

She laughed and motioned back to the game as he butchered the phrase for the fifth time. "We'll work on it."

A hand grabbed the back of her thigh, and Kaylan jumped at the light contact. A little girl with round eyes and stickers covering her face gazed up at Kaylan. Sarah Beth skipped toward her.

"Just added the beads to Sophia's hair. What do ya think?"

"Trèe bèl, Sophia." Kaylan's heart went out to the small child, remembering Tasha. Would it be this little girl's fate to sell herself for a loaf of bread or a bag of beans? Kaylan grew up hearing how beautiful she was, how treasured, knowing her worth was in Christ. Did this little girl understand that there was something more than the struggle for food? When survival was paramount, the black-and-white rules became a murky gray.

"She wants to know if you will kick her the ball," Sarah Beth said, breaking into Kaylan's thoughts.

"Wi, Sophia." The smile she received could have melted a glacier. Kaylan pointed and Sophia took off running, her little arms pumping and her bottom lip puckered in focus. Reuben grabbed her hand and showed her where to go. Kaylan was proud of him. His talent hadn't gone to his head yet.

Kaylan blew a whistle, and the kids shifted from foot to foot in anticipation, their eyes on the black and white checkered ball. Kaylan kicked it to Sophia. The other team tried to intercept, but Reuben wouldn't have it. He ran in front of Sophia, blocking any other child who came close. She stumbled on her dress as she ran, her five-year-old legs pumping as fast as they could. Children across the field shouted encouragement, and teens emerged from the homes to cheer.

As the ball bounced off a tree and feebly rolled through the goal, Kaylan shouted. She called for Sarah Beth as some of the seminary students took their place on the field. "I have an idea."

"It's about time." Sarah Beth smirked. "I could hear you thinking from across the field."

"Very funny." She shoved her friend. "Listen, I'd like to host a class for young mothers to teach them how to feed their families. Maybe we could even make them a meal to take home at the end of the meeting. We could ask for sponsorship from someone at church back home."

Her mind jumped from one possibility to the next. She could do this. She could help Tasha and little Reuben and Sophia. Only Jesus could fix Haiti, but she could give hope by pointing them to Him. The idea grew in her head and took root. She officially had a purpose.

"Done and done." Sarah Beth clapped. "I'm proud of you, Kayles. Let's do it." Sarah Beth held her hand out. "Go team, on three?"

Kaylan laughed. "You are such a kid sometimes."

"Guilty. Twenty-two going on ten." As Sarah Beth placed her hands over Kaylan's, dark hands of all sizes slowly covered their pale skin. Children giggled, fascinated with the new game, and the lanky teens matched their enthusiasm.

Sarah Beth counted in Creole, "One, two, three, go team!" The girls threw their hands in the air, eliciting cheers and clapping from their loyal crowd.

The sun began to set, and Kaylan knew it was time to leave the streets. She had plans to make, and the soccer game had been a success with the children.

As they walked to Rhonda's, Reuben ran to them, dragging a boy of fifteen or sixteen bearing similar features. Abraham joined them to translate.

"This is Reuben's brother, Stevenson. He trains with Eliezer, the local houngan, voodoo priest." Abraham's eyes darkened. "Reuben is proud because Stevenson is training with Eliezer to read palms so he can make money from the tourists. Most of those in this slum who practice voodoo follow Eliezer. The temple is close by." Abraham shook his head.

Kaylan's heart went out to the youth. "It's nice to meet you, Stevenson."

"I speak English." His accent was thick as he carefully formed each word.

"Very good. Where did you learn English?"

"Only little. Eliezer teach me for tourists."

Kaylan nodded. She used her hands as she spoke. "Reuben said you read palms."

He held his palms up and nodded. "I tell you future?"

She shook her head and smiled, hoping he wouldn't be offended. "Only Jesus knows my future." She grasped his hands and used one finger to press down in the middle of his palm. "His palms bled to give me a future because He loved me." Stevenson cocked his head in confusion.

His eyes grew big as Abe translated. "Jesus love palms? Tell future?"

"Yes, Stevenson. Only Jesus knows future."

"Tell me." He put his palms on his chest and leaned toward her, then froze and backed away quickly. Sarah Beth appeared at her side, and Kaylan turned to face a skinny man towering over her. His head was shaved, and above distinguished cheekbones his eyes were those of a dead man. Despite its dingy hue, his button-down shirt set him above the rest of the men, speaking of his concern with his appearance. His khakis had dark stains on both knees, and he wore sandals.

His face remained emotionless, but his mouth spewed venom. "Do not talk to him about this Jesus. He is in training. The spirits show us the future. Our ancestors call to us."

Abraham stood calmly beside her. "Eliezer, this is Kaylan and Sarah Beth. They are from America and want to help our country."

He nodded slowly, and a glimmer of a smile touched his mouth. "Then we will both help Haiti. But do not speak of Jesus to my student." Motioning to the young man, Eliezer faded back among the homes.

Abraham shook his head again. "He will cause trouble."

"Why? Maybe we can help improve things just a little bit." Sarah Beth's enthusiasm triggered a small smile from Abraham.

"You do not understand. Eliezer is one of the extreme voodoo priests in Haiti. He believes that all of Haiti's problems can be traced back in our history to the white man."

The idea sounded antiquated to Kaylan. "How's that, Abe?"

"Many years ago, Haitians were slaves on our own island until an uprising overturned the white man's rule. Eliezer is under the impression that Haiti would thrive if all white men would leave Haiti, particularly Americans, and especially Christians. He thinks the Christian faith ruins our ancestral, African tribal roots."

"Well, that's a little extreme and outdated, isn't it? I mean, all that happened a long time ago." Kaylan waved at the woman on the corner painting in the market as they walked the few blocks to Rhonda's house.

"Eliezer thinks his way is best. You need to understand how he thinks in order to share Jesus with him or those he influences. I'll see you tomorrow." Abraham left them at the corner with high-fives.

Sarah Beth and Kaylan walked in silence the last block to Rhonda's house, Kaylan praying for wisdom. She never dreamed she would face a real voodoo priest in Haiti, and his warnings against talking about Jesus had both chilled and angered her. She was glad that his fate was not her ultimate responsibility. For only the Lord could change the heart of a man like Eliezer.

Chapter Eleven

ER FIRST WEEK in Haiti had drained Kaylan emotionally, but on this muggy Sunday morning, she had never been more spiritually filled. Sweaty bodies in their own versions of Sunday finest packed the small church just outside the slum. Torn and dirty dresses, hats, and suit coats adorned each Haitian. Kaylan had donned one of her sundresses for the occasion.

She had never experienced worship on this level. Several men and women stood in front of the congregation leading the songs. No screen with lyrics, no microphone, no instruments—just the beautiful voices of Haitian believers singing about the goodness of God.

Kaylan's eyes welled with tears. She struggled with missing Nick or wondering how her future would work out. These people didn't even know where their next meal would come from. Their children looked several years younger than their actual age because of malnutrition. Yet, they praised the Lord with lifted hands. They had seen hurricanes devastate the island, Westerners promise help and fail to deliver, their crops fail to grow, their coasts devoid of fish. But even then, they sang and they trusted and showed up in the best they had to worship.

After an hour of standing and singing, Abe stood to lead the church in prayer. He led first in Creole and then translated his prayer into English. "Lord, we thank You for the chance to worship You. We pray that we would follow You and know You better. Amen."

The congregation sat, squeezing together to fit everyone in the room smaller than Kaylan's living room back home. A lazy breeze drifted through the open windows, and gnats buzzed around Kaylan's head. She wiped sweat from her forehead. She had never been more thrilled to be in church.

Sarah Beth caught her eye, and a smile lit her face. As the pastor passionately shared his message with loud responses from the congregation, Sarah Beth leaned close to Kaylan's ear. "I think this is what heaven will be like someday. How are we so subdued in worship back home? It's like we've missed it."

Kaylan couldn't help but agree. After experiencing church Haitian-style, she couldn't imagine returning home and worshipping the same way ever again. These people with nothing truly showed Kaylan that God was their everything.

Kaylan arrived back at the clinic for the afternoon after a Sunday lunch at Rhonda's house a few blocks away. While Sarah Beth played with local kids and Rhonda worked with a patient in the main room, Kaylan took advantage of the lull in activity to familiarize herself with the supplies.

A shout filled the street outside the clinic, and Kaylan dropped the needles in her hands back into the drawer and ran into the main room of the clinic. Stevenson ran through the door, Reuben in his arms. Blood dripped from a jagged, deep cut on Reuben's leg onto his brother's arm, then trickled to the floor.

"Lay him here, Stevenson." She rushed to clear the space. Rhonda appeared at her side to help.

"He needs stitches. You want to watch or try it?" Rhonda remained detached, professional. Her hands moved nimbly and gently around the cut. Kaylan wished she could gain that emotional distance. This was a child, a child she had just gotten to know but already loved.

Kaylan gulped. She needed to learn how to do this to help Rhonda, but the thought of making a mistake terrified her. She clenched her hands to still the shaking and took a deep breath.

"Kaylan?"

"I got it. Just stay here in case, please?"

"Of course." Rhonda squeezed her arm as she applied pressure to the bleeding.

Low, lilting Creole sounded in the small room as Rhonda reassured Reuben. The boy whimpered, his jaw clenched, but he fought his tears. Kaylan admired his strength. He was a young leader in the making for his people, and he didn't even know it.

Stevenson's eyes resembled saucers as Kaylan gave Reuben medicine to calm him while she cleaned the wound. She concentrated on keeping her voice steady. Her confidence grew as she moved her hands quickly, preparing the needle and thread. "What happened, Stevenson?"

"He cut on metal." He motioned wide. "Sharp, big. He climb on roof of house."

Kaylan looked at Rhonda. "Will it get infected?"

"We'll just have to wait and see." She spoke more to Reuben in Creole. A small smile lit his face. "I told him he shouldn't be crawling on rusty roofs. Even tough little boys get hurt."

Reuben pointed to Kaylan. "*Eske ou se yon gerisè?*"

"What does that mean?" Kaylan prepared Reuben's leg for stitches. She silently prayed for steady hands and a strong stomach.

"He ask if you 'healer.'" Stevenson's eyes darted uneasily from Kaylan to his brother, looking like a caged animal. "Eliezer say he heal us with help of *loa*. Spirits. My brother should not say these things about you."

She turned her focus back to Reuben and began to stitch. Reuben's breath caught, and then his body relaxed. He watched her work as the medicine numbed his pain and made his eyes droop.

"I'm not a healer, Stevenson. Only Jesus can heal. I can only help you feel better." She smiled to herself. "Sometimes I can't even do that." She continued to work while Stevenson translated for Reuben. The boy fought grogginess and sleep as if his life depended on it.

"He want to know who Jesus is. He say you make him better, so where is Jesus?"

Rhonda chuckled and ran her hand over Reuben's head. "From the mouths of children, you get the most difficult questions. Good luck."

Kaylan gently tugged the thread, praying for the right words. "When your mom tells you to do something while she is away, you remember her words even when she is gone and you complete the task." Rhonda translated, and Reuben responded in Creole.

"He said that sometimes he likes to play instead." Rhonda rubbed his head again, laughing with Kaylan.

"I like to play too." She was glad he was distracted. The cut was long and deep. "Jesus came a long time ago from heaven, because His Father wanted Him to save people."

"Like you come to help Haiti?" Stevenson's eyes locked with hers.

Kaylan had never thought about it that way. Jesus had come to a broken and hurting earth to give people hope, like what she wanted to do. She'd come to heal bodies. He'd come to heal souls.

"Yes, Stevenson, like I have come to help you. Only Jesus came because He loves you."

Rhonda translated, and Reuben pointed to himself.

"You too, Reuben. People didn't like Him, so they killed Him. But He didn't stay dead."

Reuben's eyes widened, and his mouth dropped open.

"He came back to life again three days later. But His Father wanted Him to come home to heaven. So Jesus went back to be with His Father because He'd finished his job. And He is alive and making a home for us someday, if we choose to believe He died on the cross and rose again."

"So how do we meet this Jesus? Is He in Haiti?"

"He is in every country. He lives in the hearts of people who love Him."

"So he is like *loa*? A spirit?"

"We have His Spirit with us. But He is the only God, Stevenson. He is not a *loa*. He speaks to people personally."

"So, how He be healer?"

"Jesus helped a crippled man walk again. The blind could see. The deaf could hear. The dead were raised and the sick made better. But He didn't come to heal our bodies alone. He came to heal our hearts."

"People not like Him, like Eliezer do not like you."

"That's right, Stevenson."

"If He healer, why they do not like Him?"

"Because they didn't understand that He loved them and came to give them hope and healing."

"Haiti need hope and healer."

"Yes, it does."

"Reuben want to know how he can see Jesus someday."

Kaylan continued to tug the thread, closing the wound. "You have to tell Jesus you love Him, that you know He died to heal you and that you believe He rose again. Then you promise to follow Him and obey." She smiled into his eager face. "Even when you want to play instead."

Kaylan bandaged his leg and watched the brothers' exchange. "He say he will talk to this Jesus and want to know if He like soccer as much as Reuben."

"He made every bone in your body, and He made you good at soccer. I bet He loves to watch you play."

Reuben looked down at his leg and brushed the bandage with his fingers before pointing at the ceiling. *"Se jezu sel ki kon geri."*

"*Wi*, Reuben. Jesus is Healer." As the boy finally succumbed to the medicine, she put away the supplies and moved to other patients. Deep in her heart she knew Reuben would come to know the Lord. Maybe her mission in Haiti was simpler than she thought.

Later that evening Kaylan lay in bed reading one of Nick's letters from his deployment.

> Dear Kaylan,
>
> You're on my mind daily. Micah calls you a distraction. I call you a regret, a dream I walked away from. I'm surrounded by heat, dust, hurting people, and enraged militants, but when I think of you, the world fades away. It makes me groan to think how sappy I sound, but one of my pivotal mistakes was not sharing my heart with you the last time we were together.
>
> I can't tell you what we're doing here, though I wish I could. My body is primed for combat at every second. When we aren't in the field, I'm in the gym or writing to you. Fear hangs like a canopy in this place. I feel less than a hero.

Kaylan paused. Nick had always been a hero, even when he'd walked away. The description of his assignment in the Middle East made her skin crawl. She'd feared coming to Haiti. Nick had chosen and committed his life to serving other people. He didn't walk away from a dream. He embraced the calling of a bigger one. Her eyes found his words again.

> I'm afraid, Kaylan. As I lie on my bedroll, I know men plot to take my life. I know they use their sons and

daughters to lay the IEDs that take American lives. I know death is a part of their culture, less of a tragedy and more of a daily event. How do you fight a mentality? How do you war against a religion? In my fear, I remember God is in control. Yet He seems so distant here. Micah reminded me today that bravery and courage are not the absence of fear, but rather the acknowledgement that we serve the One who has promised a peace despite the circumstances. Our story is already written.

Kaylan remembered Eliezer's confrontation. His eyes had bored to the core of her being, daring her to speak the name of Jesus. She knew voodoo was a cultural practice in Haiti. She knew many Haitians often mixed Christianity and voodoo practices. But never had she faced such animosity toward herself or her faith. Nick did daily. He was hated because he was an American and Christian.

Shame colored her vision. Fear had quickly turned to anger in light of Eliezer's veiled warning. Nick seemed to rest in who Christ was. Kaylan kept discovering just how weak her faith was when challenged.

My mom used to call me her "mighty man of God." I'm just now coming to accept that. I don't fight against flesh and blood. These men and women are products of a warped culture. I fight my fear, my desire to run to alcohol, my anger, my desire to control. I fight what I can't see and am equipped by a God who is invisible yet ever present. Does that calm you, Kaylan? The Lord is training me to be His mighty man. I fight for my country because I love it. I fight for my faith because I want the freedom to share it. And I will fight for you because you are more than worth it.

With all my heart from the deserts of the Middle East,

Nick

"Kayles?" Sarah Beth entered the room, dabbing her wet hair with a towel. The curls multiplied in the heat and humidity. She sat on Kaylan's bed and nodded at the letter in her hand. "Missing him?"

"Yeah. It amazes me that words he wrote months ago help me today."

"God sure knows how to time things, doesn't He?" Sarah Beth shuddered and shifted closer. "Did Eliezer make you nervous yesterday?"

"A little bit. It was more his manner than what he said, you know? Like he could see through me, like he was in total control."

Sarah Beth nodded. "You ever wonder how people can be so confused? I was talking to Rhonda about voodoo, and she said that many people mix it with Catholicism here. Like the saints are equivalent to spirits in voodoo. Apparently, it's a pretty relaxed religion. People are one with nature and the earth."

"Sometimes the most accepting religions are the most dangerous."

"Rhonda said we should be careful. We won't accomplish anything by offending his culture."

"True. But how do you love someone who has such a hold over a young kid like Stevenson? I mean, if it was just Eliezer, it might be a little easier to be sympathetic. He's bought into a lie. But to take Stevenson with him? It makes me angry."

"I understand." Sarah Beth squeezed her hand. "This is when the gospel gets tough."

"I never expected to come down here and deal with religious clashes. I thought they would just want to hear about Jesus. This battle of religions was not in the game plan."

"And was Haiti in your game plan?" Sarah Beth laughed. "Looks like God had even bigger plans for you than just coming to Haiti. He wants you to use your gifts to make an impact."

"I can't do it by myself."

"Girl, you're not alone. Rhonda's been here for years. I'm here. Don't be discouraged in doing good. The Lord's bigger than the problems in this country or the dysfunction in America." Her eyes shone, and in response an invisible force seemed to well up in Kaylan, increasing her determination. She longed to be as strong as Sarah Beth and as rooted as her family.

As night descended on Haiti, Kaylan fell asleep planning her first meeting with the young mothers.

Chapter Twelve

RHONDA'S HOME HUMMED with feminine laughter and the cry of babies. Sarah Beth and Rhonda moved throughout Rhonda's living room, talking to women and playing with kids. Kaylan packed food for the women to take back to their homes. The first Tuesday night meeting about nutrition and diet couldn't have gone better. Kaylan had taught the women about the importance of proteins, such as beans or peanuts, and how combining them with a grain, like rice, forms a complete protein. Both of them knew that even with this knowledge, most of these women wouldn't be able to afford a substantial amount of food, but it was a start.

Tasha approached, a pregnant girl of about the same age beside her. Kaylan immediately reached for Kenny, enjoying the feel of his smooth skin and fuzzy, dark hair. Her heart skipped a beat, and her determination doubled. For babies like Kenny and women like Tasha, things needed to change.

"Thank you." Tasha's smile carried hope, and with it Kaylan's excitement grew for the next meeting. "This Yanick. She married."

The woman smiled shyly at Kaylan, keeping her hands wrapped around her swollen abdomen.

"Yanick, it's nice to meet you. I'm glad you came."

The door banged open, and Eliezer barged into the entranceway. Kaylan froze in confusion. Silence settled among the women, and several swept their toddlers from the floor, holding them close. Eliezer's eyes traveled the room and settled on Tasha and Yanick. He began to yell in Creole as he stormed over, grabbed their arms, and shoved them toward the door.

"Kenny!" Tasha cried, reaching around Eliezer but unable to break from his grip. Kaylan hurried after them, bringing Kenny and the two sacks of food for the girls' families.

Eliezer ushered the girls to a man waiting in the dark street. The man roughly grabbed Yanick, yelling at her in Creole. Tasha remained calm. Meeting Eliezer's eyes, Kaylan handed Kenny to Tasha while Eliezer watched her solemnly. Once again, his clothes, though still shabby, spoke of his desire to dress more affluently than those who inhabited the slums. Kaylan wondered if it gave him more credibility with the people. They feared him and heeded him too much. She refused to show fear in his presence, and by the fire in his eyes, she could tell that bothered him.

"We leave, now." Eliezer hissed through his teeth. His eyes blazed.

"No worry. Jesus here tonight." Tasha pointed to her heart, and with the shadow of a smile, she turned and followed Yanick down the street, soothing a squalling Kenny as she walked.

Despite the spectacle, laughter escaped from Kaylan's lips, and she tipped her head to the night sky, thanking the Lord. Whether anyone had learned from the meeting or not was irrelevant in light of Tasha coming to the Lord. Turning to reenter the house, she bounced off Eliezer.

"Oh, I'm sorry, Eliezer. I didn't see you." She attempted to walk around him, but he blocked her path.

"You interfere where you do not have rights."

"I'm here to help. Don't you want a better Haiti for your people?" She wished she could read his face. He stood in the shadow, and the light from Rhonda's house splashed her face.

"Then you stay with the ones who claim your God. I am responsible for those who follow me."

"Sir, your people respect you. Don't make them choose between doing what they feel is right for themselves and their families and their respect for you."

"Do not meddle, and it will not be a problem. I respect you came to Haiti to help. I respect Rhonda has come to help. But I will care for my own. You worry about the rest of Port-au-Prince." Dirt billowed in a cloud as his feet pounded the street, and he blended into the dark night.

"You okay, Kayles?" Sarah Beth moved from the doorway and glanced up and down the street.

Kaylan stared at the place Eliezer had disappeared, almost expecting him to materialize from the shadows. "He creeps me out." She shuddered, pulling Sarah Beth toward the sound of laughing women. It was not time to dwell on her fear.

Her friends celebrated the life of one in light of the threats of another. The light and laughter surrounding Kaylan repelled the darkness of the streets outside the small house. Haiti was a whole new kind of difficult, but she wouldn't trade a night like this for a hundred nights back in Alabama. She'd made the right decision. Yet, despite the success of the evening, she couldn't shake the twinge of uncertainty. Eliezer loomed larger than life, lurking in the shadows of Kaylan's dreams.

Nick concentrated on extending the bar completely above his chest. His arms shook, and sweat poured off him, dripping into his eyes as if he were in a sauna instead of the Naval Amphibious Base in Coronado, California. Micah stood above him, hands ready if Nick needed help. They had already run a couple miles along the coastline with several guys on their Naval Special Warfare Support Activities team, and now they were hitting the weights. While they were part of a larger SEAL team stationed on the West Coast, Nick and Micah were also part of NSWSA-1, a Support Activities team and smaller group that deployed for very selective and secretive assignments for however long necessary in addition to normal

SEAL deployments. They had to keep in shape, ever ready to be called on a mission.

When they weren't working out, they were training for professional development on their individual jobs for the team. After a few months of this, they would travel to different sites and conduct real-world training in environments they would see overseas. Then they would work on months of Squadron Integration Training, where they focused on mission-specific aspects. In the midst of all the training, Micah, Nick, and their fellow SEALs knew how to kick back. Surfing was Nick's and Micah's vice, but the other guys also enjoyed anything from hiking and fishing and time with their families to hanging out at local bars. Work hard, play hard—SEALs knew how to do both.

"Hey, Hawk?"

Nick gritted his teeth and forced words out as he exhaled, "Yeah?"

"On the phone the other night Pap asked about your birth parents, wondered if you'd found out anything. He said y'all talked about it when we were home. Why didn't you tell me you were on this quest to find your birth parents? When did this start?"

Nick nearly dropped the weights on his chest. Micah came to the rescue and helped lift the bar back in place.

"Sorry, I didn't mean to throw you off."

Nick wiped the sweat from his forehead and grabbed his water bottle. "It started a little bit after my dad died. When we were in Afghanistan, and I was pining over Kaylan, I decided some things needed to change, that I needed to change. It's something I'm curious about."

"And why's Pap curious?"

Nick shrugged. "Maybe he wants to make sure my blood is good enough to pass on to his grandchildren."

Micah groaned and rolled his eyes. "Watch it, bud. That's my sister you're talking about." He smirked. "Pap's not that way.

Maybe he just wanted to make sure you didn't have any identity issues. You know..."

His voice trailed off, embarrassed, but Nick understood the implication. Several adopted kids he'd known had a rough time in their teens, seemed to go off the deep end. His struggle manifested itself in college, after his mom died. Parties, girls, alcohol, and a couple close brushes with the law had left him feeling empty and alone. He'd had great adoptive parents. Then his dad got sick. Cancer ate away over a few years, all while he cheered Nick through BUD/S. Alone now, with both adoptive parents gone, a deep longing had sprung up in him to find his family. His birth family.

Micah spoke up again. "Not to pry or anything, but it just surprised me that you hadn't mentioned this."

"I wasn't hiding anything. It's just sort of...embarrassing."

Micah laughed and threw him a towel. "Why would it be embarrassing?"

"I had great parents. It just seems weird to look for ones who didn't care enough to keep me."

"There's no shame in wanting to know where you come from."

Nick appreciated the support. He'd found his family in the SEALs. He'd found a brother closer than blood in Micah. "Thanks, man. That means a lot."

"My family will help you find your parents if it means that much to you."

Nick wondered why it mattered so much, why it burned in his heart and mind to find these unknown, biological parents. He just knew it did, and until he knew the truth, he would keep looking.

"So, what are you going to do when you actually find them?"

"I honestly have no idea, Bulldog. Maybe nothing. Maybe knowing will be enough. Maybe I'll reach out to them. But I don't want to disrupt their lives, and nothing will be accomplished by rehashing the past. I have no regrets. Just an overwhelming curiosity."

Micah rubbed the back of his neck and avoided Nick's eyes. "Man, I gotta ask. Are you hoping that you'll find your parents, introduce yourself as the son they lost, and magically become part of the Brady bunch?"

"I'm under no illusions. I have brothers through the SEALs. I had parents. I've found a great girl."

"Are you trying to tell me something, Hawk?" Micah grinned.

"Believe me, if Kaylan and I get to the place of making this permanent, you'll be one of the first to know."

"*One* of the first? That's all I get?"

"Don't push your luck." He took a swing at Micah and missed. "Seriously though, have you ever had an idea or dream that just ate at you until you fulfilled it? That's what it's like with my birth parents. If I never know, I won't have lost anything. My life is full. But if I can find them, I could gain something I'm not even aware of yet."

Nick stood and moved to another machine, beginning his reps.

Micah sauntered to his side. "So where do we look now?"

Nick smiled and shrugged. The pieces would fall together in their own time. They had a good break before they were deployed again to who-knows-where, unless the Support Activities team called on them first. For now, they would train and be ready to leave at a moment's notice, but he would definitely take advantage of the time to track down more information, even if he wasn't quite sure where to look yet.

Kaylan's excitement since her young mothers group the night before quickly dissolved as she stared at the mother on the bed in front of her. They had tried, but there was nothing she or Rhonda could do. The baby was gone. Kaylan's fingers dug into her face, choking back a sob. The young woman lay passed out in exhaustion. Rhonda wrapped the tiny bundle in clothes and walked out of the room.

"Why?"

The word slipped through her whitened fingers. Every day she fought a battle of two steps forward and one step back. She shared the gospel with Stevenson, but he went back to Eliezer. She tried to help mothers understand the importance of nutrition, but Eliezer dragged two of the mothers away. She tried to help mothers deliver healthy babies, but Eliezer interfered there too. Was there no way to counter his influence? No way to stop his evil? How many would run to Eliezer's medicine because they lacked knowledge and education? How many more mothers would lose children? A dark cloud hovered over Haiti in the form of voodoo and years of extreme poverty. Would the shadows ever fade?

She wrung water from a cloth, soothing the sweaty brow of the mother who would never hold the child she had borne for eight months. It was the way of Haiti. With so many uneducated, with the heat, and the need to constantly make a living, there were those who grew tired of pregnancy and sought help from local voodoo priests to induce labor. She still wasn't sure what Eliezer gave them. Some natural remedy, or so she'd been told. But many times it ended with loss of life and an aching mother. A flash of anger startled Kaylan. How could this mother risk hurting her own child to shave off one month of pregnancy?

Some days she hated Haiti as much as she loved it. She longed to see change. Like the unfulfilled mother before her, Haiti should be beautiful and vibrant, but her need to provide for the day without thought to a hundred tomorrows left her barren and childless. The people couldn't provide for themselves. Land was deforested, reefs devoid of fish, people without schooling, children sold as slaves, women employed as prostitutes, and men left wandering the streets without knowledge and skill to provide for and lead their families. Lack of education and resources left them destitute, and an apathetic attitude gripped many. Could anything worse happen to Haiti? Had God forgotten these beautiful people? Some days the battle felt hopeless.

"You can't save them all, Kaylan."

Silence reverberated in the room, and Kaylan's eyes drifted over the woman's sleeping frame.

"How do you live like this, Rhonda? Don't you want to save them all?" She turned on her mentor, her eyes flashing. "You've grown callous. That was a baby. A baby who never had the chance to live because of this woman's naiveté and impatience to be back on the streets selling herself."

"You've been here less than two weeks. I've invested ten years. You think I don't care? You can't fight the culture, Kaylan. You can't change years of oppression and voodoo and grinding poverty. She needs to feed her other kids, so she acted. Wrongly, naively, but she did."

Kaylan stepped back at the cold emanating from Rhonda, but the current building within her would not be quenched.

"So, you accept it? You don't fight to change it?"

"Before you change a culture, you must understand the basic drive behind every poor decision. Families need food, so they sell their daughters. Men can't afford to provide for their families, so they leave. Welcome to extreme poverty, Kaylan. Don't you dare tell me that I don't care. I've been fighting this battle for years. You don't know anything. You're acting like a spoiled, selfish, rich girl who has never been out of her comfort zone. Tell me, Kaylan, are you really here for the people or to be a hero? This isn't a game or a movie. This is real life."

Kaylan drew back as if slapped. The fight left her. Was that why she was here? To be a superhero, as she and Sarah Beth had joked about back home? Tears pooled in her eyes. She felt helpless and hopeless. How could she ever have thought she could help here, that she alone could turn things around?

"I'm sorry, Rhonda." She brushed tears away with the sweat. Tears wouldn't save the baby or cure Haiti's need. "I had no right to question you. I'm not superwoman, and I've tried to be."

Rhonda crossed the small room and rested her hands on Kaylan's shoulders, tilting her chin up. "Kiddo, I've seen more than you can imagine, cried more than you will ever know, buried more children and treated more people than you could hope to see in your time here. It never gets easier. It is what it is."

"But it doesn't have to be."

"No, it doesn't." She wiped a tear winding down Kaylan's cheek. "Kaylan, do you remember how you felt when you first arrived?"

Kaylan nodded. "I fell in love with these people so quickly, Rhonda. I want to protect them from the world. Give them everything I have and more. I live so sheltered, and these people have so little. Some days I wonder if God cares. And then every day I see some small miracle in the midst of hardship, and I remember that He does. I just still don't understand why it won't change more quickly."

"I love your heart for these people, Kaylan. But your mind-set is still very American. This is not an instant gratification society. We can't bring America to Haiti. We have to meet these people where they are at, and help in any way we can."

"I understand that. But how do we change a country and a mind-set after years of hardship?"

Rhonda crossed her arms and studied Kaylan. "Kaylan, how do you finish a test?"

"What?"

"I thought you were a brainiac."

Kaylan chuckled and lowered her head.

"Think about it, Kaylan. How do you finish a test?"

"One question at a time?" Kaylan felt stupid. Surely it wasn't that easy.

Rhonda's voice lowered to a whisper, burning with passion. "Kaylan, how do you change a country?"

Recognition dawned in Kaylan. She lifted her chin and squared her shoulders. "One life at a time."

"One life at a time, we will see Haiti changed. One mother understanding the intricacies of the life within her, one child knowing the love of two parents and a full belly, one father knowing how to provide for his family. One by one."

Compassion welled for the woman on the bed who would open her eyes to empty arms and a barren womb. Kaylan would teach her, so she never forfeited another child again.

"One life can save Haiti."

Chapter Thirteen

RHONDA, RHONDA!" THE shouting and banging woke Kaylan, and she sat up with a start, glancing around the dark room for the offensive sound and then at the clock by her bed. Two a.m. It had been almost a week since they lost the baby, and more tragedies had followed in its wake. Kaylan could barely keep up with the never-ending stream of patients who entered the clinic each day, needing help with malnutrition, child abuse, dehydration, malaria. Exhaustion made her eyelids heavy as she struggled to identify what had roused her from her nightmares.

"Kayles, what's going on?" Sarah Beth's Southern drawl lengthened in the dead of night, and Kaylan rubbed her eyes. The house was hot and sticky. The pounding continued. The door. Someone was at the front door. Kaylan stumbled from her bed and hurried to the door.

"Kay-lin, Kay-lin!"

Kaylan jerked open the front door as Rhonda entered the hallway, pulling a robe tightly around her. Tasha fell into Kaylan's arms, her words a jumble of Creole and English. "Yanick's baby need help. Must come, now."

Rhonda darted into her room without a word, and Kaylan stood in the hallway, stunned.

"What happened, Tasha? What's wrong with her?"

She shook her head and opened her mouth to speak, then immediately covered it with her hand, her eyes growing wide again.

Kaylan tugged her hand down. "I need to know, Tasha, so we can help her."

"Eliezer. Pain. Big pain. He hurt me for telling you."

Eliezer. Kaylan's heart dropped to her toes. The last woman he'd helped in pregnancy lost her child. Her anger broke like the surf, spreading and out of control.

"Not this time." She ran from the room and grabbed clothes, throwing them on.

Sarah Beth bolted from the bed. Her blonde curls stuck out at odd angles on her head.

"What happened? Where are we going?"

"Eliezer gave Yanick herbs to make her baby come faster, and now she may lose her child too. That can't happen again. It just can't." Her hands and voice shook slightly, and she grabbed her head, turning in a circle, struggling to concentrate.

Sarah Beth came and shook Kaylan. "Don't panic, Kayles. We'll do our best to get there in time. I'm coming with you. Another set of hands always helps."

Kaylan stood staring at her best friend as Sarah Beth grabbed towels and several water bottles and bolted through the door. She glanced back at Kaylan.

"You coming?"

Kaylan rushed to the car where Tasha and Rhonda waited. *Lord, keep Yanick safe, and please, help us save her and the baby in time.* The pint-sized car bounced over the uneven dirt roads. Kaylan clenched her jaw to keep her teeth from rattling and counted the minutes to Cité Soleil. Her sweaty palms gripped the medical supplies, and she struggled to keep her breathing even. Cité Soleil was not a friendly place to travel in the dead of night, and Eliezer was not a character she wanted to mess with on so little sleep. She prayed for steady hands and patient words.

Cité Soleil was known as the worst slum in the Western Hemisphere and one of the largest in the Northern Hemisphere. What began as a shanty town soon grew to contain hundreds of thousands of Haiti's poorest and most dangerous. Homes were pieced together with cement blocks and steel. Gangs had once terrorized and ruled the territory, until the government took extensive measures a couple years before. Now, only remnants of the gangs remained, but the slums were still a place of extreme poverty, illiteracy, raw sewage, and massive crime.

Sarah Beth hummed "Amazing Grace," and Tasha's voice joined in the soothing tune from the front seat. Kaylan smiled. The peace and steady voice of one who had experienced the worst and lived to tell the best made her feel two inches tall. How unworthy she was to help these people. They taught her more each day than she could possibly teach them in a multitude of lifetimes. They knew what it meant to survive—and not only survive, but also thrive. They defined *resilient*.

Gritting her teeth, she thought through Scripture to give her courage. Fear wouldn't paralyze her tonight. The life of a woman and her child rested on their shoulders. She would be strong and fight...like Nick.

They rounded another bend, and water and trash pooled in front of them in the moonlight. Kaylan jolted as the car stopped, and she scrambled to grab her things. The walls across from the dilapidated house bore the scars of bullets and gang wars. She was about to deliver a baby into the fray.

Kaylan squared her shoulders and followed Rhonda into the house. She would fight, but could she win against a country so entrenched in poverty and despair that the rest of the world seemed to have given up on it?

"Push, Yanick, push!" Rhonda's firm, almost frantic tone betrayed the urgency. Daylight crept over the houses in the slums. The pop of gunfire had evaporated in the heat of a new morning, and the offenders had slunk into the shadows to await a new night. Sarah

Beth pushed her frizzy curls out of her face, before dipping another towel in water to cool Yanick's feverish head.

Yanick screamed, and Kaylan braced her back as she arched it in pain. Kaylan used her body to take Yanick's weight as she perched on the edge of the bed, using it as a makeshift delivery table, while Rhonda coached the delivery.

"I see the head. You must push." Rhonda remained in control, but the early morning hours had been long. An ambulance could not be called during the night, and there were few who would brave the streets of the worst slum in Haiti for the sake of one woman who had grown impatient with her pregnancy and sought other options.

Kaylan glanced at the door, a mere sheet blowing in the morning breeze. Eliezer stood just outside, refusing to leave. His words had awoken the neighborhood and sent more gunfire popping skyward upon their arrival.

"She is my charge. Be gone. I will handle her."

"You gave her something to make the baby come early, Eliezer, and it isn't healthy. What did you give her? I need to know, now." Rhonda left no room for argument. She and Eliezer seemed to have a grudging understanding, one that drew both Kaylan's respect and frustration. It felt as if Rhonda had compromised sharing her faith for peace with the locals. Kaylan couldn't help but wonder where her own faith would be at the end of the year, browbeaten by the hopeless cycles of poverty and human insignificance.

Yanick's baby spelled hope for Kaylan, and she watched in rapt attention as Rhonda kneaded the womb and coached Yanick.

"Kaylan, I need you now," Rhonda called.

Kaylan moved from her place on the bed, transferring Yanick's weight to Sarah Beth. Yanick gladly collapsed back against Sarah Beth's chest in exhaustion. Sarah Beth cradled Yanick's back, smoothing her hair, and talking softly in her ear to calm her as

Kaylan moved to the foot of the twin bed and leaned in close to hear Rhonda.

Rhonda kept her voice steady and low. "The baby's neck is caught in the cord. You must slip it over the head. She can't stop pushing, and the cord is pulling tighter."

Kaylan hesitated, her eyes widening at the tiny bloody head protruding from Yanick's body.

"Now, Kaylan."

With a deep breath, Kaylan tugged the cord over the baby's head, feeling the tautness. The baby slid free, and Rhonda handed him to Kaylan to clean as she walked Yanick through the final stages of labor.

A boy. His bloody body soaked Kaylan's T-shirt, and she quickly cleared his mouth and wrapped him in a blanket, patting his back to make him cry. She stared in wonder at the bundle before her. Life, new life, pulsated in the middle of a slum of death. The blood coating her arms and shirt marked something new, beautiful, and tiny. What would his life be like? Would he grow up to be one of the many who fired guns in the night hours in Cité Soleil? Kaylan's heart ripped at the thought, and she cuddled him closer, sheltering him from the world outside his metal walls.

"Bring him to Yanick when you're finished, Kaylan." Rhonda delivered the placenta, and her low Creole tones danced through the shoebox house, joining the cries of a new Haitian child.

Kaylan walked to Yanick and laid the baby in her outstretched arms, a new fear developing. "Rhonda, he's underweight and premature. He needs to go to the hospital. I'm worried he'll get sick if he stays here without proper care."

"No one goes to the hospital in Haiti, except by accident. We'll take him to the clinic. I'll monitor him from there." Rhonda began to pack the bloody cloths and the medical supplies, her dirty blonde hair frizzy after a night of exertion and heat.

Sarah Beth knelt next to Yanick and smoothed the new

mother's hair away from her face. Her eyes filled with wonder at her tiny son. She touched the baby's hands and smiled when they opened and grasped her finger.

Kaylan knew victory. This baby had survived. His future was uncertain, his health worrisome, but his chest rose and fell, his voice sounded through the neighborhood, and his mouth groped his mother's chest for something to eat. He lived.

The sheet flew open as Eliezer and Rolin, Yanick's husband, rushed in. Relieved at the sight of his wife and son, Rolin broke into a wide smile. But Eliezer's chocolate-brown eyes glowed like black coals. Kaylan stood slowly, approaching him, hoping to make peace.

"He lives, Eliezer. But he is too small. We will take him back to the clinic to watch over him." At the fury in his eyes, Kaylan immediately knew she had said too much.

Eliezer snapped. "He will not go to the clinic. I will care for him. The spirits of his ancestors will make him strong. If he dies, he will join them."

Kaylan exchanged glances with Rhonda, who remained silent, pushing Kaylan to take the lead. "He needs the care of trained professionals. And Yanick needs to be checked for any lingering effects of the drugs she took."

"I said no." His finger almost poked her eye out, and she backed up a step. "These are my people. I will care for them."

Kaylan struggled to keep her voice even, anger burning in her chest as if she'd been branded. "You caused this. He is early because of you. A baby died because of you. Yanick is sick because of herbs you gave her. We are here because of you. You do not help your people. You hurt them."

Kaylan silenced her anger as his eyes shot bullets. *Love him, Kayles. He is stuck in the ways of his people.* Remembering Sarah Beth's admonishment, Kaylan fought to control her temper, searching for something to smooth over her harsh words. "Eliezer, did you know your name means 'God has helped'? You can help your people more by following the God above all gods rather than spirits who have no real power." She reached to touch his arm. "I'm still praying that you will find the one true God."

His hand struck like a cobra, and her head snapped to the side, her cheek stinging. Sarah Beth tugged her shirt, jerking her backward and to the floor with a thud. A string of angry Creole filled the house. Rolin leaped up and confronted Eliezer, his temper apparent in the tone of his voice and his steady stream of dialogue as he maneuvered Eliezer out the door.

"Curse your God! He has no power here. Curse you!" Eliezer's shouts echoed long after his departure.

Kaylan shivered despite the humidity, wondering how far Eliezer's temper would carry him. Had she brought trouble to this fragile family because she hadn't kept silent? She eyed the small bundle in his mother's arms, and her resolve strengthened. A new Haitian. A new hope for his people. Kaylan only hoped they could coax his little body to health quickly.

Chapter Fourteen

Shots whizzed past Nick's head, and the ground rumbled. He ducked into a shop and scanned the darkened interior for hidden insurgents. This op was not going as planned.

"We moved too early."

Nick blew a bubble with his chewing gum. His eyes roamed the streets and rooftops. Micah was right. They had moved too early. Their intel had been wrong. When he got back to camp, that little weasel of an informant would pay.

"Stop the smacking, Hawk. I can't hear over your chewing."

Hawk ignored Micah and radioed in for their other team members' positions. A primary al Qaeda leader was meeting two blocks away, and they couldn't reach him. The insurgents guarding the alleys and streets were thicker than flies on the cows that wandered free in the dusty country. Afghanistan was fly-infested and war-torn, and still the people protected the men who terrorized them.

"On my go, Bulldog, we run to that building." He pointed across the street. "Josh and Daniel are waiting in the trees to the right. We'll skirt around those buildings on the corner of the street and find a new position to take this dude out. Got to get some use out of these long guns today." He blew another bubble. The flavor had faded hours ago, but it kept him focused. He popped another piece into his mouth, adding to the wad.

The road quieted. They were in the eye of the storm. Nick had no choice. It was now or never. "Go." He flew across the street, Micah to his right. Crouching low, he scanned the perimeter, his steps short and quick. Gunfire began again in earnest, kicking up dust near his feet. He bit back a curse.

A yell sounded from the meager tree line, and he turned. His heart stopped and dropped to the dust. A boy no older than twelve held a rocket-propelled grenade launcher, loaded and aimed. The high whiz signified release, and Nick's eyes widened.

They were in the direct line of fire, and it was too late. He couldn't shoot a kid. He swore, grabbed Micah, and threw him on the ground seconds before the grenade whizzed over their heads. He was up and running again, tugging Micah with him as they stumbled over loose rocks. The explosion threw them into the building. Heat seared his face. His ears rang like a gong.

No. God, no. The tree line was in flames, and two bodies lay scorched on the desert floor. Smoke stung his nose, and his eyes watered, intermixed with tears of grief and rage.

"Oh, God. Josh! Dan!" Micah yelled, and Nick held him back. Running into the fire would only cost two more lives. They were gone.

If only he'd killed the kid. His fists clenched, and sweat poured down his face. He couldn't breathe. He couldn't think. An angry cry spilled from his lips, overflowing like the ocean in a hurricane.

"Kaylan!"

He bolted out of bed, his hand searching frantically for his gun before he realized he was at home. He shivered as the sweat on his bare chest began to cool in the chilly night air.

The light flickered on, and Micah stood, rubbing his eyes and squinting. His chocolate- brown hair lay upturned from his pillow.

"You yelled. Nightmare?"

Nick nodded. He grasped at his hair and then threw his hands in frustration, pacing the small room in the house he and Micah shared. Throwing open the window, he braced himself against the frame. He could still smell the acrid smoke, hear the cries of celebration from the lips of a boy ecstatic over his first kill.

"I should have killed him."

"The boy?"

Micah knew him well. It was the mark of a best friend and brother in arms. They'd had this discussion many times. Always it was the same.

"Maybe if I'd shot, then Josh and Dan would still be alive."

"If you had, we might be dead. The whiz of that grenade sounded before we hit the dirt. It was already in the pocket." He clapped Nick hard on the shoulder. "Let it go."

Micah walked to Nick's closet and slid the door open. Nick's University of Southern California sweatshirt and sweatpants flew through the air and landed with a soft thud against his chest. His running shoes landed in front of his feet, and Micah slipped from the room to change.

Running away never solved anything, but running to forget was Nick's specialty. He slipped the clothes on and tied his shoes. The flash of the explosion blinded his vision again. Something wasn't right. Something else had pushed him out of that bed, digging into his instincts to protect.

It wasn't until the crunch of sand and the chilly breeze whispered in his ears that he remembered the name he'd yelled in his darkest moment, the name that weighed heavily on his mind. Kaylan.

He couldn't shake the feeling that something was wrong. He wished he could call her, wished it wasn't almost dawn. Micah's breathing was steady and even beside him, his feet beating in perfect rhythm.

Their neighborhood was quiet, full of SEALs who would wake in a couple hours once again for training evolutions to serve their country and protect its citizens. He had scheduled a Skype date with Kaylan for that evening. Could he wait that long?

Sunrise hovered on the eastern horizon, and Nick remembered the green-eyed beauty an ocean away. He couldn't shake her from his mind or heart.

As the first hints of sunrise cracked the navy sky, Nick lifted Kaylan up to the only One who could protect her in the coming hours and days. Then he prayed for peace, the peace to forget and forgive, and the courage to keep going when quitting seemed an easier option, especially on nights like these.

The letter arrived at the clinic shortly after lunch, and Kaylan slipped to the back room to open it. Yanick's baby was being monitored and was receiving the proper nutrients. Kaylan prayed the Lord would raise him to be a mighty defender of his people, an instigator of change.

Her fingers tugged at the envelope, and her eyes soaked in the sight of Nick's familiar scrawl. Something spilled from the envelope and fell with a metallic clink on the floor. A lily dangled from a silver chain, its center on display and petals peeled open. She slipped it around her neck and clung to it as she read Nick's words.

> Hey, Beautiful,
>
> I know I'm cheating because you already have a box of letters, but consider this a very delayed Christmas present. It would honor me if you would wear it. The lily symbolizes everything beautiful and pure. It embodies you.
>
> We're training hard for another op, though where and when it will take place, I don't know. I focus my body and pray my mind follows suit, but all too often I

think of you. I received your latest letter, and it was the highlight of my week. I think it highlighted Micah's week too. I'm still hearing about it. I'll have to be first to check the mail from now on.

Your words humbled me. Why I never allowed you to share in my career before is a mystery, my mistake. But, you have shown me you understand my calling and will not ask me to change course. I couldn't have hoped for more. I hope you are finding all you dreamed of in Haiti. Saving the world yet?

Every sunrise now, I think of you. As much as I hate the separation, I'm thankful we have this time to grow individually while growing together.

How are the kids there? How many soccer games have you played? Kissing babies and saving lives yet? Know I am praying and that I couldn't be more proud.

Thinking of you at sunrise,

Nick

P.S. Don't forget, you owe me a kiss.

Kaylan traced the chiseled lines of the petals and ached to be with Nick. She checked the calendar on the wall. January 12: Skype date tonight at nine. With renewed energy after a mostly sleepless night, she skipped back to work, counting the hours until her overseas date. She hoped the Internet cooperated.

Kaylan plunked down on her bed. No rest for the bone-tired. The bed, like much in Haiti, was more practical than comfortable, but tonight it would feel like a feather pillow. She kicked her shoes off and snuggled her pillow, her eyes drifting closed. Maybe just thirty minutes of sleep before dinner...

Dinner! Kaylan bolted upright as Sarah Beth took a flying leap and landed on her twin bed on the other side of the room.

"This thing feels like a wonderful, cozy rock."

"The moms are coming over tonight. Sarah Beth, get up. We have to cook. I totally forgot."

"Can't think straight. Thirty minutes."

Kaylan glanced at her watch. It was 4:30. The women would be there at six. Maybe they could fry some of the plantains Rhonda picked up earlier. Her mind drifted, and her fingers played with Nick's necklace.

"Did lover boy send that?"

"It came in the mail today."

"Just in time. Don't you have a hot date tonight?" She giggled when Kaylan threw one of her pillows. "Well, what are you going to wear?"

"That lacy green shirt and my pajama bottoms."

"Cheater." Sarah Beth lobbed the pillow back and Kaylan snatched it, feeling more energized. "I forgot to tell you, but I got an email today from Northington Elementary. Mrs. Thurgood is leaving, and I unofficially have her spot to teach second grade next fall." Sarah Beth squealed. "I am beyond excited."

"Congrats, Bubbles. That's awesome. Know how you're going to decorate your classroom yet?"

"Of course. I was thinking of doing a *Finding Nemo* theme. Talk about the ocean and friendship lessons from the movie. Decorate the walls with waves made from blue crepe paper and tape fish nametags on the desks. I can talk about the seven seas and beaches and different countries like Australia. I can have a buried treasure box for goodies."

Kaylan laughed. "Those second graders are going to have the best teacher in Tuscaloosa."

"Thanks, Kayles." Sarah Beth sounded wistful. "I hope so. The kids here are definitely breaking me in." The room grew still, and

Kaylan loved the ability to say as much in the stillness as in conversation. Only the closest of friends shared this trait.

Sarah Beth broke the silence. "I guess I'll have to leave Haiti in July in order to get ready for the school year. Do you think you'll go back then for your internship?"

"I think so. The internship seems unimportant here, but I have so much left to learn. I desperately need more training." Kaylan pushed off the bed and stretched. She checked the time again. 4:51. "I need to start supper. You coming?" She sat down on the floor and slipped on her shoes.

"Ugh. Give me five more minutes."

"Deal." Kaylan gazed up at her bed, wishing she could crawl beneath the covers. She would be less than awake for her Skype date later, but at least she would get to see Nick, even if she wasn't completely coherent.

Suddenly Kaylan's bed pitched as the floor and walls buckled and rolled. Kaylan screamed and dove under the bed, her head clipping the stiff wood. "Sarah Beth, duck!"

Crashes shook the room. Her head struck the wall beneath her bed as she was tossed like a rag doll. Something warm dripped into her eyes before everything went black.

Chapter Fifteen

NICK SLIPPED THE whole chicken into the oven and set the timer for an hour. He was trying his hand at cooking something more than a sandwich or noodles so he could tell Kaylan on their date. She would be proud. He grinned to himself as he imagined her shocked face. Maybe he would cook her something the next time he saw her. By then he would be a pro. Work had seemed to drag, but it was almost time to see her face, even if only on the screen.

"What time's dinner ready, man?" Micah slapped him on the back and hopped up on the counter.

"About five o'clock."

"I should have set you up with my sister when we first met if it meant you would start cooking. It better taste good."

"Well, you could try your hand at it. You are related to her. You must have some artsy or domestic ability in your blood somewhere."

"Naw. It skipped me and went to her. She stopped trying when she found out she was fighting a losing battle. Better to let me mooch off your success."

Nick grinned and snapped Micah with a towel, starting a war that turned the house into a battlefield of tipped furniture and a couple broken lamp bulbs.

The door banged open, and Nick and Micah immediately stilled, battle senses taking over at the sudden action.

Caveman stumbled in, breathing hard, his keys rattling in his hand. He pointed to the flat screen. "Turn it on. The news. It's all over. Bad." He held a hand on his chest and bent over, inhaling hard.

Micah jumped over the couch and flipped to CNN, where a white-bearded announcer declared, "We are following an earthquake in Haiti originating about ten miles from the capital of Port-au-Prince. Early reports estimate the earthquake as a 7.0 magnitude. It occurred about 4:53 local time, and we estimate significant casualties. High magnitude aftershocks continue. Buildings are collapsed, and cries appear to come from the rubble. Landslides and tsunamis are possible because of the shallowness of the shakes. We are monitoring the situation closely."

Nick whirled to find Micah diving for his cell. Nick grabbed his phone too and dialed Kaylan's number. A busy signal buzzed in his ear like an annoying fly. He threw the phone on the couch and ran to his laptop in the bedroom, pulling up Skype and attempting to call Kaylan. Nothing.

He dashed back into the room. Micah's conversation and the news reports blended in a hurricane of noise around his head.

Oh, God, not Kaylan. Please, anything but that.

"Mom, turn on the news. Something happened in Haiti."

Nick could hear Marian Richards's confused voice coming through the phone as he muted the television. He didn't want to listen. He needed a plan. Caveman stood in the door. At Nick's nod, he turned to leave.

"Thanks for telling us."

"I'm sorry. I hope she's okay."

Nick could only hope.

"We can't get a hold of her, Mom. Nick already tried." Micah looked to Nick for confirmation.

Nick nodded.

"The phone lines are down. We'll try to do something. Maybe we can get down there?"

The question in Micah's voice was aimed at Nick, and his mind traveled through his list of contacts. Who could he call?

"Tell Seth and David and the rest of the family. I'll call when we have a plan. I'm praying, Mom. She has to be okay." Micah hung up the phone and swung his arm with the phone in the direction of the wall. Nick wanted to throw something too, but that phone would become a precious lifeline in the coming hours.

"Can we do something?"

Nick scrolled through his contacts. "I can't sit here. If there's a way to get out of Florida with a team of Marines in the morning, are you in?"

"Absolutely."

"Then let me make a few calls. We can hop a flight."

"I have to find my sister, Hawk."

"We both do." In the back of Nick's mind he relived a very different disaster in the desert, one filled with fire, guns, and the death of good men.

His eyes wandered to a plaque hanging over the front door. "The Lord is good, a stronghold in the day of trouble; and He knows those who trust in Him," he muttered under his breath, knowing he would cling to that promise in the days to come.

Chapter Sixteen

D<small>UST SETTLED OVER</small> Kaylan like a shroud. The ringing in her ears pulsed with the beat of her heart, and her face stung like a hundred needles pricking her skin. She swiped at the stinging. Blood. She glanced around the small space. Chunks of cement cocooned her underneath the twin bed. She squinted, trying to remember.

A sliver of blue sky, the only thing not cracked or bleeding, peeked through a hole in the wall, discolored in the chalky air. Within seconds, dust enveloped the beacon. Rolling in a space no bigger than a sleeping bag, she winced as her shoulder scraped the bottom of her bed. She sucked in a breath and coughing seized her, cement dust choking the air more with each passing moment.

Where was Sarah Beth? A shriek rent the air outside the broken house, and Kaylan jerked, her head banging on her bed with a crack. Blood pulsed and her head throbbed as she massaged the spot where a knot bloomed.

Through the cracked walls of her makeshift cell, she searched for any sign of life beneath the chaos and dusty cloud. A body lay twisted in the street, bloody, tattered green shorts and flip-flops still in place. A woman bent over the tiny frame, clutching it to herself and crying. Kaylan's stomach convulsed, and panic built in her gut.

She remembered the earthquake. She wished she didn't.

"Sarah Beth? Oh, God, she needs to answer me."

Digging trembling fingers into her tangled curls, she drew a rattled breath. She winced. Something warm and sticky coated her skin. Blood. Her blood. Yet even the sight of it couldn't unleash the tears. She felt numb. Buildings, people, lives—now dust and shambles. Gone. Kaylan wanted to scream, to rewind the clock, but nothing could change it.

How long had she been unconscious? Wailing tore through the air outside—uncontrollable, chaotic, eerie. No Reuben playing soccer. No Sophia dancing and skipping with her rag doll, singing *"Wi, Bondye Bon"* in her sweet, off-key voice. No mothers scolding or Rhonda handing out food. Screams controlled the people. In the violence of the quake, hearts and minds had been shaken as well. For that there was no cure. Only Jesus. And even He seemed to have forsaken Haiti.

"Sarah Beth, please, answer me." She inhaled dust and coughing consumed her, choking her precious clean air. She had to get out of the tiny space and into the room, or what was left of it.

The floor buckled beneath her back.

"Sarah Beth!"

It was happening again. The crack of rock falling and the rumble of more collapsing buildings drowned out the frantic cries of helpless people.

Not another one, not so soon… Kaylan braced her hands on the bottom of the bed and tried to hold her body on the floor, but she was powerless. Her body jerked and tumbled as if on some kind of demonic roller coaster. The tremor smashed her into the bed and then back down to the ground, adding to the bruises. A scream ripped from her chest before she realized the sound came from her. Tears poured.

"God, please, God, please." Concrete blocks shifted, screeching and rumbling as they tumbled into the streets. As fast as it hit, the ground stilled. Her body buckled in pain, every nerve alert and angry.

"This can't be happening." Kaylan glanced around her, trying to move beneath the structure of Rhonda's home. She was pinned.

Through the cracks in the structure she could see dust smothering the air and survey pieces of the street.

This was her own personal horror film. She wished she could hit rewind, anything to change the events of the past fifteen minutes. She reached for her phone, her hands brushing denim. The screen lit up but was cracked beyond use. The already sporadic cell towers were probably down all over the city, anyway.

"Sarah Beth?" Kaylan shouted, the sound shattering the stillness in Rhonda's house. She tried to move again while straining to hear a reply. Taking a deep breath, she fought off the numbness to deal with the rising panic building in her gut. Her bed had shielded her from the structural cave-in, cocooning her in a deceptive bubble of safety. Had Sarah Beth made it under her bed before the ceiling collapsed? Panic threatened to overwhelm her, and she took several deep breaths that immediately induced a coughing fit in the dusty air. Usually a safe place, would Rhonda's home become her tomb?

"Okay, Kaylan, one thing at a time." She wiggled her toes and then worked the motions up the rest of her body, testing her legs, stretching them as long and wide as the space would allow. She took deep breaths, gently pushing on her chest, checking for any blood or busted ribs. The body did funny things when in shock, and she needed to know if she had any broken bones. Nothing would keep her from clawing out of her cave to find her friend.

"Lots of bruises, a few cuts and abrasions, and a nasty bump on the head. Not bad, considering." Kaylan let her medical training take over as she finished her self-check. Her body was banged up, but she would live. She focused on her surroundings, and her panic slowly built. Time to get out. Claustrophobia and fear overwhelmed her.

"Help! Is anybody out there? Help me, please. I'm stuck." Kaylan shouted toward the street as she began to wiggle, now testing the strength of her prison. The cement chunks around her head shifted ever so slightly, and Kaylan prayed the weight resting on the bed wouldn't cause it to collapse.

"Sarah Beth? Please answer me. Sarah Beth!" She braced her feet against the wall and used the angle to throw the rest of her weight against the cement pieces near her head. The seconds slid by, and the crack and grind of boulders rolling past one another rang through the house. After minutes, she pulled her willowy frame through the tiny hole created by shifting two large chunks. As she pulled herself to a sitting position, blood roared in her head, and the room spun.

The room shook again, and more cement fell nearby. She dove for cover but couldn't slither back under the bunk. Curling into a ball as close to the bed frame as possible, Kaylan braced herself for a rogue rock to land on her, ending her life.

After what seemed like hours, the earth stilled. Kaylan could hardly believe only seconds had passed, each one excruciating, every aftershock determined to break even more bodies. Kaylan couldn't consider how many lay dead in the street. What would she find if she escaped these walls? Panic tore through her and ran rampant, threatening to rip from her sore throat.

Outside, screaming began again in earnest as more structures caved in and people were crushed underneath. Kaylan could only imagine the horror. Her own nightmare confined her to this room, no larger than a hotel room in the States. A pebble skittered past her head, and she uncovered her face. Dust overwhelmed her, and the taste of blood permeated her mouth. She slipped the neck of her T-shirt over her nose and breathed deeply, welcoming the salty odor of sweat and tears. It smelled of life and struggle.

The faintest whisper of sound emerged from the shambles.

"Sarah Beth?"

"Kayles." This time she heard it.

"I'm coming. Hang on." Kaylan shimmied under the roof, held up by the cement from the walls that had settled before it. Wire and metal protruded from the blocks, and Kaylan did her best to maneuver around them.

She froze at a cough nearby. Dust obscured her view.

"Kayles, hurry." The raspy voice turned Kaylan cold despite the humidity. Dust caked her arms, turning them whiter than normal. She shifted rock frantically and pulled herself onto a particularly large slab, the ceiling scraping her back as she slid through. Pain ripped through her leg, and Kaylan bit back a cry. She turned her neck to find a scarlet pool soaking the rock, a jagged metal rod protruding inches above the surface. Heat rushed to the area, and Kaylan stifled a gasp, tears unwittingly coursing down her cheeks.

She lifted her leg as best she could and slid off the rock, landing in a heap on the glass and rock on the floor. Her face stung from the impact. Pulling herself to a sitting position, she squinted, studying her leg in the dusty fog. A six-inch gap on her thigh exposed muscle. Blood poured from the wound. Praise God it had missed her artery.

Pain built, ripping through Kaylan's body, threatening to paralyze her and send her into hysterics. She attempted to stop the flow with shaking hands.

"Hang on, Bubbles, I'm coming. I promise," Kaylan's use of Sarah Beth's childhood nickname elicited a weak laugh, pouring new adrenaline and hope into Kaylan's system. Her palm now stained with a flow that could not be squelched, she glanced around for anything to use as a tourniquet. Clothes littered the room from the upended dresser, buried beneath the rubble.

"Sarah Beth, for once, being messy is paying off." Her favorite shirt lay wedged under a slab nearby. Tugging it loose with a rip, she fastened it above the gash and pulled it tight. The blood flow slowly tapered off.

Her friend chuckled weakly in the dusky corner, and a hacking cough sounded like a gong in the room. Kaylan was at her friend's side in seconds, pulling her leg behind her like a troublesome sack of potatoes.

She froze. Full-blown panic seized her for the first time as she surveyed her friend.

"Oh, God, oh, God, oh, God."

Curly bleach-blonde hair caked with drying blood and cement dust protruded beneath a section of roof that rested on Sarah Beth's ribs. Her left leg lay lifeless next to her other leg, twisted at an odd angle and pinned beneath more concrete and rubble.

Kaylan turned away, gagging. Her hand swiped angrily at her tears. She had to be strong. Sarah Beth had to be okay.

"That was my first earthquake." Sarah Beth's lips were cracked and bleeding. Blood rolled down from one of the corners.

"Me too."

"Rough day." Sarah Beth wheezed, trying to smile. Kaylan brushed the pebbles and dust from her lashes and cheeks. She blinked slowly, squinting to discern Kaylan's face hovering above her own.

"Can't breathe."

"I'll see what I can do about that." Kaylan examined the slab resting on her friend. It was wedged underneath debris from the wall piled onto the other twin bed. Sarah Beth had managed to roll onto the floor before getting pinned.

Kaylan shoved against the cement, unable to gain much leverage in her hunched state on the floor. Smaller rock rested on the slab, and Kaylan swiped at the debris, desperate to remove any of the weight from her friend. As the rock shifted, the slab groaned, and the remainder of the ceiling shifted, filling the room with a loud crack.

"Kayles, leave it alone. Please leave it alone." Sarah Beth sobbed.

"Just let me try, Sarah Beth."

"You can't move it by yourself."

"Do you think you could push?" Tears filled Sarah Beth's eyes.

"I can't feel anything. Everything is numb. Just...be here with me, Kayles. Tell me a story. Anything."

Kaylan swallowed hard, still examining the concrete pinning her friend. She would need help to move it, and even then, she wasn't sure if she would be able to move Sarah Beth without hurting her further.

"What would you like to hear?"

"How we met."

Kaylan turned back to her friend and found her hand under the slab, entwining their fingers. She lay down next to her, cradling Sarah Beth's head under her arm and stroking her tangled curls.

"I like that one. Let's see, we were in kindergarten, and it was our first day in Mrs. Zuckerman's class. You were carrying your hot-pink Barbie lunch box and wearing a tie-dye shirt with your curly hair all over the place. Your blue eyes were so big, I thought you looked like a cartoon character. You wouldn't stop talking, and I remember you had to pull your card the first day because you kept talking over Mrs. Zuckerman."

Sarah Beth's laugh was weak, and she wrestled to talk. "You were in that little denim skirt with your boots and your hair pulled back in a ribbon, looking all cute and shy. You wouldn't say one word. You were my goal for the day."

Kaylan laughed softly. The commotion seemed so distant now. She knew she should cry for help, but time with Sarah Beth was slipping away, and she wouldn't leave her.

"We were at recess, and I was sitting on the steps playing with bubbles. You came up and sat down with another bottle. You even popped some of mine."

"I just wanted to make you talk. And they were so pretty."

"We blew bubbles the whole hour, and you never stopped talking. You told me about your dog, Toto, and the names of all your Barbies. You told me about your brother, Tom, and how you had to share your room and be quiet while he took naps. But you were so excited to have a baby brother." A smile tipped Sarah Beth's lips upward, causing more blood to trickle.

Kaylan swiped a tear from her cheek, dust caking its trail. "At the end of the hour you threw your arms around my neck and said, 'You may not like me yet, but you're gonna be my new best friend.'" Kaylan chuckled at the memory. "You never got rid of me after that. You've been my best friend ever since."

Sarah Beth's head drooped to the side, and Kaylan rolled it back. "Bubbles, you have to stay awake. You have to. Stay with me."

"Bubbles. How did I get...Bubbles?" She wheezed.

"When we were blowing bubbles and you wouldn't stop talking, I thought you were like the bubbles, colorful, all over the place, happy, fun. I called you Bubbles that day for the first time, and you just said, 'I like Bubbles. That name works for me.'" It stuck ever since."

"You were so serious when you said it. I made you laugh. We played the whole day. Then dance started."

Kaylan wiped away the blood, her own leg pounding. She tugged the T-shirt tighter. "Yes, we started dancing at the studio a couple months later and were Sugar Plum fairies in the December recital. You were so excited to wear pink."

"You never looked prettier."

"Are you trying to tell me I peaked in appearance at the age of five?"

Sarah Beth's laugh sounded like a bark, and she winced. "Well, you got all tall and gangly after that."

"Don't be jealous just because your genes didn't allow you to grow past five-three."

"We're like David and Goliath." She coughed. "But I still love ya, Kayles. Height and all."

"Love you too, Bubbles. I need to call for help. Hang on."

"Kayles, stay. I'm not going to..."

"I don't want to hear it." Kaylan cut off her own fears. "Someone will come. Rhonda knew we were here. If the clinic is still standing, she'll come or send help."

Dust hovered in the small room, and darkness draped the broken capital. The night hours would make locating people in the rubble even more hazardous. Based on her experience in Haiti, she doubted anything had been organized yet to begin relief efforts, just desperate people searching for the living among the dead.

Kaylan lit her phone and scanned the nearby walls for a gap to the outside. A crack large enough to stick her arm through winked back at her through a pile of cement blocks. She pulled her weight forward, wincing as her leg dragged across glass and sharp rock. She maneuvered her arm through the rock and began to yell, hoping someone from the street outside would hear over the screaming. She lit the phone, using it as a beacon.

"Help! Two of us are alive in here. We need help. Can anyone hear me?" She waited, yelling every few minutes, but the chaos in the street prohibited any notice of the plight of two Americans in the midst of thousands of Haitians.

"Help, someone's hurt!" She turned the phone on again. If she couldn't call anyone, at least it was useful as a flashlight. A small, sticky hand grabbed hers, causing her to yank back in fright.

"Kay-lin hurt?" Creole followed, but the small fingers continued to grasp hers, tugging her arm and then pushing feebly on rock. "Kay-lin. Sophia."

"Sophia? Oh, thank You, God. Sophia, find Stevenson, Abraham, or Reuben. Tell Rhonda. We need help. Me and Sarah Beth."

"Yellow hair?"

"Yes, Sarah Beth. Help, Sophia. Get help." She used her limited Creole, and Sophia's fingers slipped away. Kaylan moved her arm and peered out to the darkened street, hoping the little girl would bring the older boys. Her little legs kicked up more dust as she rounded the bend and vanished, taking Kaylan's prayers and hope with her.

She yelled for help a few more times, her voice growing hoarse. Water. They needed water. Where were the water bottles Sarah Beth had used that morning for Yanick? They had brought several back to the house.

Her new mission poured adrenaline into her aching limbs. Loss of blood made her light-headed, but with no ability to stand, Kaylan hoped she wouldn't pass out.

Using the phone once more, she pointed it around the room. "Bubbles, do you remember where we put the water bottles?"

"Under my bed. At foot."

Kaylan's heart sank. Rock and pieces of the ceiling ensconced Sarah Beth's bed. Nevertheless, she scooted past her friend and shoved with all her might, shifting a few rocks, careful not to dislodge any large pieces holding the remainder of the ceiling from crushing them.

Her fingers brushed mud, and she knew the bottles had been crushed. She continued to feel around between two boulders, her fingers going numb as they came in contact with sharp rock.

Crunch. A water bottle rolled beneath her fingers, lodged in an air pocket. She twisted it, careful to pull it through the hole intact. Her own mouth watered at the sight. Another crunch, and she pulled another bottle free. Miracles in her chaos.

They would have to conserve them. She prayed Sophia would be back soon.

"Sarah Beth, water. Thank the Lord you are so unorganized."

Sarah Beth coughed. Her chest rattled beneath the slab pinning her. "Bet you never thought you would say that."

Kaylan poured sips into Sarah Beth's mouth. She coughed and gurgled the tepid liquid. Kaylan took a small sip and placed the bottles nearby. She lay back down and curled her body as close to the rock pinning Sarah Beth as she could. The earth continued to tremble. Kaylan grasped her friend's limp, cold hand, recited stories of their childhood and graduation, and mentioned ideas for decorating Sarah Beth's classroom. All delayed the inevitable story she would one day remember.

Sarah Beth was hours away from meeting the Maker for whom she had sacrificed everything, and every reassurance to the contrary would be a lie, something Kaylan and Sarah Beth had sworn to never allow in their relationship. Kaylan's faith mirrored Sarah Beth's broken body.

God, don't take her. She just wanted to follow You. She's the one who wanted to be here, not me. Take me. Kaylan's heart fought against the words, but every fiber of her being had reached the breaking point.

"Stay awake, Bubbles. Don't leave me." Kaylan felt as if she were back in kindergarten, but Sarah Beth would not be able to help her laugh her way through this.

Darkness became their constant companion as the wailing and screams for help pierced the night.

Chapter Seventeen

ISN'T THERE A way to get there faster?" Micah's agitation wore on Nick's nerves. He had already come close to knocking Nick out over his seeming calmness toward the situation. Inside, Nick boiled. His strength in battle came from maintaining an outward calm. It allowed him to walk into deadly situations focused and prepared. The attitude had only intensified since he'd become a believer, but a blow this personal was about to break his discipline.

Their team had gathered in the living room during the course of the night. Senior Chief was assessing the resources being sent to Haiti and the possibility of temporarily allowing Nick and Micah to head down with the Marines to search for Kaylan. So far, the process was slow, hence Micah's impatience.

"Working on it, Bulldog. Calm down."

"It's my sister, Hawk. Do you get that? My sister. And I can't protect her."

"I understand, but being angry with me won't solve anything."

"Do you understand? You don't even have a family, and when you did, you didn't appreciate them till they were gone."

Nick resisted the urge to hit Micah. As quickly as his anger rose, Micah's shoulders hunched in defeat. "I'm sorry. I didn't mean it. It isn't your fault, and I know you loved your parents."

"Don't worry about it, man." Nick popped more chewing gum into his mouth and held the package out to Micah.

"Does chewing that actually help?"

"Menial task, minor motion, something familiar." Nick shrugged. It was his vice.

Micah popped a piece in his mouth and resumed his pacing, his eyes on the news. Nick crossed his arms and allowed the wall to take his weight. If Kaylan was alive, she wouldn't be sleeping tonight. Neither would he. Coffee brewed in the kitchen, and the aroma stirred his senses, reminding him of the muddy coffee and long night watches in the Middle East. His senses were gearing up for battle, but it was a war he didn't understand, with no enemy except the earth itself.

Where was she?

For the thousandth time, he tried her cell and heard the annoying tones of a busy signal. A few calls were coming into the news from Port-au-Prince. It didn't look good. His team knew how to fight terrorists. How did one fight this? It was a mark of their closeness that the team had come to keep a silent vigil. Some of the guys kept Micah occupied by shooting darts. Micah's aim was good, even in his panic. Dart after dart hit the bull's-eye, and the other guys finally gave up.

In a few hours dawn would break over the West Coast, and for the first time since leaving Kaylan, Nick dreaded the new day. He had no idea if he was facing a sunrise that would find Kaylan dead an ocean away. His hand dove into his pocket as the phone rang. Every eye focused on him. Micah stood in front, making sure he heard as Senior Chief's voice blared through the phone.

"I made some calls. Just don't ask to who. You leave tomorrow. You will rendezvous with the 22nd Marine Expeditionary Unit and arrive in Haiti on Friday the fifteenth. That's as fast as I can get you there. The Marines will be in charge of getting critical supplies to the locals. As soon as you find that girl of yours, I need you back on the plane and here, you got that?"

Nick's heart galloped, ready to board the plane. "Is there no way to get there today?"

"The government over there is in shambles and unresponsive. We are doing as much as we can to get men and supplies on the ground, but that takes coordination we weren't planning on. The 621st Air Force Contingency Response Wing is taking over the airport in Port-au-Prince to direct traffic. You can transport supplies into the city. You're on your own once in the city, though."

"Yes, sir, I understand."

"Carmichael, have you thought about what you and Richards will find over there?"

He gripped the phone tighter. "Yes, sir."

"And you're sure you want to go? If she's alive, she'll call when the lines are open. The embassy is identifying and locating all American citizens. If she's not on a list yet, she soon will be. She won't be one of the nameless."

Micah shook his head hard, and Nick silently agreed.

"If you were in our place, what would you do?"

"I probably wouldn't have asked for permission."

"We won't leave her there, sir. We have to know. No matter what." Tears stung Nick's eyes, but he rejected them.

"Then God be with ya. I hope you find her alive, son. Good luck."

The line went dead. Nick closed his eyes and prayed for a miracle.

Chapter Eighteen

THE CRACK OF rocks falling jarred Kaylan awake. Her bruised body resettled on the floor, aching in protest. She'd fallen asleep. She couldn't do that. She shook Sarah Beth.

"Sarah Beth? Bubbles, you've got to wake up."

Nothing. The shifting of rocks continued. Another aftershock?

"Hello?"

"Kaylan?" It was Abraham. Sweet, strong Abraham. The teen's voice shot hope through Kaylan.

"Help! We're in here."

She shook Sarah Beth again. The room was dim and stuffy. Kaylan wondered if it was close to sunrise. She imagined the brilliant colors peeking over the Caribbean Sea. The sky remained indiscernible through the cracks in the rubble above her head—only dust and more dust. The earthquake obscured everything. The typical calming effect of the early morning hours fell flat on Kaylan's nerves.

"Hurry, Abe! Sarah Beth's in trouble."

"We are hurrying, Kaylan. People are coming to help, but everyone needs help out here. So many..." He stopped, and she didn't dare ask for more. "It may take a while. The roof collapsed, and there is much debris. Hang on. We are going as fast as we can."

Kaylan couldn't reply. Sarah Beth didn't have days. She didn't have hours. She might only have minutes. Tears pooled in her eyes, and she grabbed one of the water bottles, tipping the precious liquid into her cracked mouth. Only a little. They could still be trapped for a while.

She looked at the bottle in the dim light. Life in a bottle that hadn't been crushed. She poured some on her shirt and smoothed it over Sarah Beth's face and lips.

"Sarah Beth, you can't sleep. You have to wake up."

She stirred at the gentle touch, and Kaylan risked a little more of the precious liquid.

"Kayles?" Her thin, airy voice brought tears to Kaylan's eyes, and she blinked them back. Sarah Beth's usual bubbly, vivacious voice filled with life and joy and excitement was fading.

"Hey, Bubbles, thanks for joining me. I was getting bored." She sniffed back tears and wrestled her body to a hunched position, resting Sarah Beth's head on her arm and dribbling water onto her cracked lips. Sarah Beth coughed, flecks of blood issuing from her mouth to decorate the gray stone on her ribs. Kaylan wiped her mouth with the T-shirt.

Kaylan leaned closer to hear Sarah Beth. "What time is it?"

"I think it's almost sunrise. I'm guessing, but it isn't quite as dark."

Sarah Beth nodded. "I'm so cold. The sun would feel so warm. First thing I'm going to do is lay out on the beach and find an American-sized hamburger and fries."

"With diet pink lemonade?"

"You know me." She drew a rattled breath. "What about you, Kayles?"

"Call my family, get you fixed up. Find some chicken fingers and gravy like Mom makes. Go for a long ride in the woods across from the house."

"Mmm, I'll do that too."

Rock continued to shift, and Kaylan prayed they would hurry. She didn't know the extent of the damage, but judging from the roof hanging a precarious few inches from her head, she guessed it could be awhile. She surveyed Sarah Beth, planning how to get her out.

"Sarah Beth, if we try to lift the rock from your chest, do you think you could roll out?" Kaylan eyed her legs lying at odd angles and wondered if Sarah Beth's spine was broken. The blood from her mouth when she coughed warned Kaylan of broken ribs and possibly a collapsed or punctured lung. She needed help faster than it was coming. Kaylan refused to think otherwise, but her medical training wrestled with her heart.

"I can't feel my body, Kayles. Can't move."

Her voice cracked. "Try, Bubbles, please try."

"Just be with me. Hold my hand?"

Kaylan felt blindly beneath the slab until she found her friend's fingers. Icy. Tears trickled down her cheeks.

"I can't breathe, Kayles. Don't waste...your strength. They'll get you...out."

Sarah Beth's eyes fought to stay open, and her voice receded to the faintest whisper. Kaylan rested her forehead on her friend's. Tears flowed freely. This was good-bye. She could feel it in her soul, and yet she rejected it. How did she say good-bye to a lifetime of memories, to the most beautiful person she'd ever known?

She remembered meeting Sarah Beth again, remembered the dance recitals and the football games with her brothers. She remembered the slumber parties spying on Micah and his friends and watching old Doris Day musicals. She remembered Pap teaching Sarah Beth to ride a horse and painting their faces for football games in college. She remembered the late-night study dates, the coloring sessions for Sarah Beth's education classes, the flash cards where Sarah Beth made up silly acronyms for the medical terms Kaylan couldn't pronounce. She remembered graduation day. Sarah Beth had bounced in her seat, her hat tipped to the side on her curls. She had cheered and hollered as Kaylan walked across stage and then skipped to receive her own diploma. She never cared what the world thought. Living life was what she did best, and she changed people wherever she went. She made it her personal mission to spread joy and color and the abundance of life with Jesus with whomever she met.

Kaylan's tears drenched Sarah Beth's forehead, and sobs racked her tired body. Sarah Beth stirred again, her free hand limply brushing Kaylan's hair.

"Remember when we first met. You're my best friend. You always will be. Don't cry. Don't be mad, Kayles. I'm going to see Jesus. He'll dance and laugh with me." Her chest shook, and Kaylan strained to hear. "He's life, Kayles. Even in this. Don't be mad." Her hand dropped with a thud on the rocks, and Kaylan knew her nerves were numb to the pain.

Rocks continued to shift, but it no longer mattered. They wouldn't make it in time. They waited in silence as the scratch of rocks and shouts shook the air. A hole grew in the middle of the rubble, but it wouldn't be wide enough in time. Sarah Beth drew a rattled breath, and Kaylan froze, her heart stopping.

"Kayles…" And Kaylan knew. It was time. She'd never imagined this day would come. Not like this. Never like this. Life would go on without her best friend, and the thought was unbearable, unthinkable.

"Bubbles, no. You can't leave me." Sobs racked her body, and she shouted the words as she ran her hands through Sarah Beth's hair and onto her cheeks. "You can't leave. You wanted to be here. We aren't done yet. We have to go home. You have to get your burger and go riding with me. We have to dance again. You can't leave!" She whimpered, shaking her friend ever so gently. "They're almost here. Hang on."

With the little strength she had left, Sarah Beth tipped her head, her blue eyes meeting Kaylan's. Her lips brushed Kaylan's cheek, her blood leaving a cold trace. "I love you, Kayles. Tell my family we did good. I love them. I'm going to see Jesus. I'll…save you a spot."

She coughed. More blood spattered the rock. "Don't be mad. Jesus...plan even...in this."

Her chest heaved and her voice was softer than wind. "Look. The sun's...beautiful this morning. Do...do you see it?"

Her eyes closed, and her body went limp, a smile tipping her lips as she basked in the sunshine of her last moments on earth. Kaylan wept, her tears mingling with Sarah Beth's blood. Her back ached from bending over, and her hands cramped from holding her friend, but she didn't care. She cradled Sarah Beth's head, rocking back and forth.

Shouting came from outside, and a loud crack rose over Kaylan's sobs. A beam of light appeared on Sarah Beth's face from a hole in the debris. Her tears blinded her, and she didn't care if she ever left the room. Sarah Beth was gone. Nothing mattered.

Abraham's head appeared in the hole, and Kaylan wanted to rage at him for being late. She couldn't pray, couldn't think, couldn't speak. Sarah Beth was gone, taking laughter, beauty, and color with her. Kaylan's sobs joined the multitudes mourning in the streets. The color had left Haiti. Dust made ghosts of both the living and the dead.

Chapter Nineteen

L EAVE ME ALONE, Abraham." Kaylan's feeble shoves did little to deter the teen. He shimmied over a beam and shoved rock aside to clear a path for them, but she didn't care.

"I will not leave you."

A mild aftershock shook the neighborhood, and Kaylan threw her arms over Sarah Beth's head, shielding them both. Abraham covered her with his body.

"You're going to get hurt. Just leave me." She played with Sarah Beth's hair, her fingers stiff and caked with dried blood and dust.

"We have to go. Your leg looks bad. Let me take you to Ms. Rhonda."

"I won't leave her, Abe. I won't leave her. Sarah Beth, please come back." Tears blurred her vision and fell on her friend's forehead, pink skin peeking through the caked powder of settling debris. She desperately wished life were like a fairy tale and the magic of tears and love held the ability to bring others back to life. But only one Man had ever held that power. And He had chosen to take her best friend.

"Kaylan, we must go now."

"I won't leave her," Kaylan yelled, the sound tearing through her body. She couldn't see Abe through her tears.

He shook her. "Will you join Sarah Beth? You are not the only one hurt. Sarah Beth is not the only one who died." Anger colored his voice.

She shoved against him. "It doesn't matter."

"Please forgive me, Kaylan." Without waiting for an answer, his palm connected with her face just enough to get her attention.

More tears colored her vision. Abe's voice sought to soothe this time. "Get control. Fight this, Kaylan." He shook her shoulders again. "Fight so others do not end up like Sarah Beth. Honor her. Let's go."

Kaylan didn't have energy. Couldn't process. Couldn't leave. But Abe's words hit the hole in her heart left by Sarah Beth. She bent over Sarah Beth again, cradling her head, sobs racking her body.

"Stevenson." Abe's voice drifted through her foggy mind. Another black head appeared in the small hole carved by a few Haitians. He squeezed his lanky, underfed frame through the hole and joined Abraham in front of her. Their long bodies hugged the floor to avoid scraping the precarious ceiling. Their whispered Creole did little to soothe her. The earthquake destroyed more than buildings. Her body, her heart, her soul were irrevocably shattered beyond repair.

Hands grasped her arms and gripped tightly, dragging her backward. Sarah Beth's head slipped from her lap to the floor. Kaylan kicked and fought with her remaining energy as Stevenson and Abe hauled her to the opening and handed her to the waiting hands of the gathering crowd. Glass and rock cut her bare legs. The hot morning brought welcome light to the relief efforts but illuminated an ugly new reality. Dust choked the air.

"Take me back. I won't leave her. Take me back."

Abe took over as the faceless hands set her against Rhonda's dilapidated home and moved silently to the next house, hoping to hear voices beneath the rubble. She remembered what Rhonda had told her about Haiti: it would be saved one life at a time. She had felt hope at the realization. Now, she only felt despair and despondency. Haiti wouldn't, couldn't be saved. This was too big, too devastating.

She blinked in the light and fought the urge to throw up the little water in her stomach. Bodies littered the streets from flying debris. The earthquake had caused buildings to explode and crumble. Hotels and other multistory buildings lay pancaked, each floor indistinguishable from the next. Arms and legs hung at odd angles where doorways had collapsed, trapping those inside. A mother lay on the ground in front of a building down the street, wailing and crying to children trapped, possibly dead inside.

She shook her head. Abe grabbed her face and checked her scrapes and bruises, then finally her leg. Nothing hurt. She couldn't feel. Maybe that was a good thing. Sophia ran to her, wrapping her arms around Kaylan's neck. No laughter, no dancing. Just pain, blood, chaos. The bump on Sophia's head spoke of her own battle. It roused Kaylan as she remembered Abe's admonition. She gently moved the girl away and checked her for any other cuts or bumps.

"Are you okay?"

Sophia nodded and leaned against her again, arousing Kaylan's senses to the war zone around her. In Sophia's young eyes, she saw Sarah Beth as she had once been, blowing bubbles, happy to dance. In the mother lying on the street, she saw her own desperation to save her friend. She cradled the girl close, helpless to protect or shield her.

"Abe, help me up, please."

His look made her question her appearance. Did she look as she felt inside: one more aftershock and she would fall to pieces? Haiti had beaten her.

"Please, Abe. Take me to Rhonda. People need help." *And I need to get Sarah Beth out of that house.* She would find someone to help her later.

Stevenson grasped her other arm, and she hobbled between the two boys, murmuring a thank-you. The trek to the clinic a few blocks away seemed to take hours. There were no visual landmarks: no restaurant with a green sign to let her know she should turn left, no rainbow-painted tap-tap to let her know she had arrived on a new street, no impromptu art gallery to let her know she should turn right. Bodies, shambles, and weeping swirled with the dust, blocking visibility.

Kaylan's leg bled in earnest, and the boys formed a gurney with their hands, lifting her through the debris and potholes. A block before the clinic Kaylan knew she was close. Sheets hung from poles hastily stuck in the ground. People stretched out or sat on the dusty ground, solemn, emotionless, staring into space. Others cried and wailed. The clinic had withstood the quake, a small miracle in Kaylan's mind, a tower of refuge in the midst of a battle-torn city. Rhonda's red bandana-covered head traveled from person to person, helping where she could, calming. Her eyes found Kaylan's through the heavy dust, and she rushed to meet them.

"Oh, thank God. Are you okay?"

"I'm alive."

"Better than many, then." Rhonda looked behind them, scanning the crowd. "Where's Sarah Beth?"

"She's…" Kaylan couldn't tell her. "At home."

Rhonda's eyes traveled between Stevenson and Abe, and Kaylan knew the moment it registered. Rhonda's eyes shot to Kaylan's. There were no tears left. Kaylan gritted her teeth, and Rhonda squeezed her hand.

"I'm so sorry."

Kaylan remained silent.

"I need to get you fixed up. Can you walk?"

"I sliced my leg open on a wire or pipe in the debris."

Kaylan understood the reason for the sheets outside. A few doctors and Haitians ran between patients. The clinic room overflowed with humanity and blood. Kaylan smelled the brine and iron of the red liquid. Only a day before the sight had marked a new life. Now, it signified death.

Rhonda shouted instructions to another doctor and motioned to her office. Several men and women stood cramped in the small room, bruised and cut. A child lay unconscious at their feet. Rhonda motioned for a man to stand up. The teens lowered Kaylan into the chair then left to dig more bodies out of buildings.

Rhonda removed the blood-soaked T-shirt from Kaylan's leg. She didn't wince. Pieces of glass and rock caked the wound.

Rhonda's eyes met hers. "This wound is getting infected. I have to clean and stitch it up. You'll be hobbling for a while, but I need you. We're short on medicine until someone gets here with supplies, so you're going to have to deal with this unmedicated. Can you handle it, Kaylan?"

"Do I have a choice?"

Kaylan jumped as Rhonda knelt before her and took her hands. "I'm so sorry for what you've faced." Her fingers soothed the cuts on Kaylan's hands and almost drew tears to her eyes at the first gentle touch outside Sarah Beth's she had experienced since the earthquake. She longed for her mother, for Alabama, for Nick's comforting arms, for Micah to carry her away.

Instead, she remained in Haiti, shaken and bruised. Home was an illusion, a wonderful dream to which she hoped to return. Reality was death and devastation. How did Nick fight against this daily? Where did he find the strength?

"I'll help. Stitch me up." Rhonda hesitated for a moment, but Kaylan allowed no chance for further pity. Work would dull the pain. Every face would bear Sarah Beth's smile or eyes. Every child would remind her of her bubbly best friend. Every cry for help would motivate her never to allow someone else she loved to die, if it was within her ability to stop it.

It was no longer her body that felt the keen sting of pain, but her soul, as if it too had been shaken. Forced tears poured as Rhonda removed debris from her leg in a hurry to help those outside. Within moments of the needle tugging her skin, Kaylan slipped into pain-driven oblivion, the cries for help smothered by blackness.

Chapter Twenty

FOURTEEN HOURS HAD passed since the earthquake, but Kaylan couldn't remember the day of the week. More people arrived at the clinic. More bodies lay in the streets. Kaylan hobbled from patient to patient, stitching, cleaning, and applying salve and bandages until supplies ran out.

Aftershocks rattled remaining bodies, sending precariously perched rubble tumbling down. With every rumble, people sprinted to the middle of streets, covering their heads and wailing. Sometime during the day a voodoo candle was lit and placed in the middle of the street. The thick dust stamped its glow, but people instinctively ran to it during each aftershock—anything to get away from the crumbling buildings. As the shaking died away, hymns replaced the wailing, and the soothing sounds of Creole chants filled the streets, a true picture of the combination of Christianity and voodoo in Haiti.

"Help! We need help over here." Rhonda and Kaylan rushed to a stretcher Abraham and Stevenson placed on the floor. A young girl, no older than sixteen, lay unconscious, her arm broken and protruding below the elbow. Kaylan gagged and averted her eyes, scanning the girl for more injuries.

"Where was she, Abe?"

"In a house up the hill. A boulder was on her arm. She passed out when we moved it."

Rhonda pulled Kaylan aside. "We have to amputate, but the only medicine I have left to give her is Tylenol. Put these in her mouth and make sure she swallows them. I'll need you to hold her down."

Kaylan's mouth fell open in horror. She had to be joking. "Can't we just set her arm? Maybe it's a bad break."

"Believe me, if that was the case, I would do it in a heartbeat. I need your help, Kaylan."

"Rhonda…"

"She'll die if we don't."

Kaylan looked at the girl and saw Sarah Beth's twisted legs, blood slipping from her mouth, and unfocused blue eyes. Kaylan blinked away the images. "Just tell me what to do."

Rhonda instructed Stevenson and Abraham as Kaylan gave the girl pills and water. The grind of a chainsaw drew Kaylan's gaze. Abraham braced the girl on the table.

"No, Rhonda. You can't use that."

"We don't have anything else. Lay across her, and hold her still."

"Rhonda."

"You think I want to do this? It's her only option. Now, do as I say or leave and let Stevenson help." A tear slid down Rhonda's cheek.

Stretching her body over the girl's torso, Kaylan angled her head away from the grinding noise. The girl's body jerked as she screamed. Kaylan fought the urge to move off the girl as something warm splattered the back of her neck. She squeezed her eyes shut and then quickly opened them as the image of Sarah Beth flashed before her with a vengeance. Kaylan tightened her hold.

"Kaylan." Kaylan glanced up from changing a woman's bandage to find Abraham and Stevenson towering over her. She stood slowly, grabbing the stick that helped her hobble from patient to patient. She hadn't said anything to Rhonda, but she was worried about infection.

"Can you come outside?" Kaylan nodded and followed them out

of the clinic, past the line of tents that stretched from the doorway around the block. A body lay on a stretcher, a dirty hot pink towel obscuring the identifying features. The hand brushed the dirt, and Kaylan saw Sarah Beth's neon nail polish and pale skin.

She reached to pull the towel back. Just a glimpse. Abe grabbed her waist and held her fast. "No, Kaylan. She is not there. She is with Jesus."

"Sarah Beth."

"We don't sorrow as those that have no hope," he whispered in her ear, slowly releasing her.

"Where's the hope in this, Abe, where? My best friend is dead. She loved Haiti. She wanted to be here." She covered her face. "Why?" The word was barely audible.

Abe hugged her, remaining silent. Stevenson observed them, his face etched in stone. They had found young Reuben that morning in the doorway of a building near Rhonda's house. He had been huddled around his soccer ball when he was buried. Stevenson hadn't shed a tear, but he wouldn't leave Abe's side. Abraham's classmates had been buried in the seminary. Few remained alive to bring their people the gospel. Kaylan's heart broke for the teens who only wanted better for their people.

Why, God? Why here? Why Sarah Beth? Why sweet, precious Reuben, who only wanted to play soccer?

Abraham released her and, with Stevenson's help, lifted the stretcher. Kaylan balked at the shovel tucked under Sarah Beth.

"I need to take her home. She can't stay here. I need to take her back to Alabama to her family."

"If we do not bury her now, she will be thrown in a mass grave or burned in the street. I am sorry, Kaylan. This is the best way for you and for Sarah Beth."

The boys hastily dug a grave outside the city and lowered Sarah Beth inside. Abraham read Scripture and prayed while Stevenson fashioned a cross out of two sticks. Kaylan couldn't speak, couldn't process the events surrounding her. This couldn't be happening. She would never hug Sarah Beth again, never hear her tinkling laugh or smell her flowery perfume. Sarah Beth wouldn't have a class in the fall. What would Kaylan tell the students she had tutored and taught last semester? Would they understand that the woman who'd loved them, who'd brought them snacks from home because some hadn't eaten all weekend, was gone forever? The grave was permanent.

"All things work together for the good, Kaylan."

"Where's the good in this, Abe?" Leaning on her cane, Kaylan felt the cool poison of bitterness seep through her veins and wrap around her heart. Then, so only Abe could hear, she met his brown eyes and whispered, "God left Haiti, just like He left Sarah Beth." A tear coursed down her face and landed near the cross. The wind dried its track as she hobbled back to town to help.

Kaylan's mouth felt like cotton. She licked her lips and winced when her split lip stung in protest. The man stretched out on the cot before her was dying. She'd failed again. His wife and adult children hovered around his pallet on the ground. Kaylan ran a cool rag over his forehead and checked his pulse, again. There was nothing she could do. Another part of her heart chipped away. Helpless and useless, she made herself keep moving.

Lord? Are You there?

She stood, slowly, and her leg wobbled beneath her, threatening to collapse. She gritted her teeth and counted silently, focusing on the process instead of the pain. Kaylan moved to the next patient, one who could be saved. A flurry of activity behind her made her spin back around to the dying patient. The man drew a rattled breath, and as his chest fell, his head drifted down his pillow and became limp. His wife and daughter threw themselves over his chest, crying and wailing, his son attempting to console both women.

Kaylan couldn't bear it. All around her, under the makeshift tents of the medical clinic, people wailed or sat in utter silence, too numb, too shocked to react. She needed to get away, but death had become a constant companion. She couldn't stop it. She tried, but the grave respected no person. She fought a losing battle.

"I'm so sorry." She hurried toward the clinic door, limping and dragging her leg. She needed refuge, respite for just a moment.

The sound began as a wail and morphed into a melody, quiet at first and then gathering in intensity. The air around the clinic charged with energy as the wailing fell silent.

The Creole words soothed her as they had in her few weeks in the country. As the song gathered, she recognized the melody and stopped cold. She sank to the ground facing the woman who lost her husband. "Great Is Thy Faithfulness" intermingled with the dust. For the first time since the quake, the earth was still. The woman's hair and arms were coated white. Dark eyes reflected her sorrow, but they weren't fixed on her late husband. They were tilted to heaven, pouring their sorrow out to the Lord. For a moment, Kaylan wondered if she were an angel in disguise, come to lift the souls of the downtrodden.

One by one, other voices joined the woman's until a chorus of Creole enveloped the clinic. Abe and Rhonda appeared from the clinic, mouths hanging open. Tears coursed down Abe's dust-covered cheeks, and his lip quivered. As the chorus began again, he added his voice to the throng, louder and louder still. He threw his arms open wide, his face tilted toward heaven.

"All I have needed Thy hand hath provided; great is Thy faithfulness, Lord, unto me!"

Chills coursed down Kaylan's spine as the refrain ebbed into silence. The woman hummed and swayed, tears weaving down her dust-stained cheeks, a small smile on her lips—like the one Kaylan had seen on Sarah Beth's face as she slipped into eternity. The woman had just lost her husband, and yet peace radiated from her chalky face. Kaylan had never seen anything like it. Just as the earthquake united their plights, the song bonded their hearts.

Abe helped her to her feet and moved with her to another cot. The atmosphere had a different feel, as if the song had morphed the area from one of gloom and despair, to hope.

Abe whispered in her ear, "That is the first time I have seen something beautiful come out of this chaos." A small smile graced his lips. "Now I know, I remember that we will be all right." The fervency of his words made her pull away and study his eyes. They were no longer filled with fear, uncertainty, or the ghosts of the many he had pulled from debris. Peace rested in their depths.

Uncertainty settled in her heart. She had lost one she loved dearly. These people had lost everything. Where was her peace that life would be all right? What was she missing?

Chapter Twenty-One

THURSDAY MORNING DAWNED bright through the dust still coating the air. Another day without Sarah Beth, another day of bodies and chaos. Kaylan had slept for two hours on a pallet beneath one of the sheets next to the girl who'd lost her arm.

Two nights and a day had passed since the earthquake, and she still hadn't called home. Rhonda needed her, and phone lines were still down. A member of the American embassy had found her and Rhonda and registered their names on a list with Sarah Beth's. Families were to be contacted, but she had no way of knowing if her family had been called. They would be frantic by now.

"Rhonda, Kaylan." Abe's voice carried before he reached them. "A truck is here. Doctors, supplies. Water and food. Hurry."

"Kaylan, you go with Abraham and Stevenson. Bring back what you can." She hobbled after the boys as they raced ahead.

Home was a lifetime away, and she wondered if she would ever see the sun shining on the lake again. Moisture was absent from her mouth and lips, and her stomach had ceased to speak. Hunger pains had become familiar sensations, a new normal. Food was scarce. Kaylan passed her rations to Sophia and her friends, her water to Yanick and her baby. Kaylan wondered where Tasha and Kenny were. Would she see them again? Were they alive?

She grew weaker by the hour but powered through, determined to save one more life. Each nameless face bore the soul of Sarah Beth, of little Reuben, of the girl who had lost her arm. One more. Save one more.

More died by the hour.

Maneuvering around rubble, she finally arrived at the trucks. People shouted and shoved. A man hollered indiscernible noises, and she realized he was deaf. As she pushed to his side to help, the crowd shoved him to the ground. She lost sight of him in the throng. Anyone with a disability in Haiti was considered of less importance than the local animals. But she could do nothing to help as the crowd pushed her back and megaphones blared in an attempt to bring order.

Her leg ached, and she struggled to keep her weight off the wound. Blood seeped through the bandage. The stitches had busted. She gritted her teeth and welcomed the pain. It motivated her race to help the people around her—one more who wouldn't experience the same fate as Sarah Beth. Their pain was hers. They were survivors of this tragedy. She would model their resiliency. Her pain would become her strength. The weak would not leave Haiti alive.

Water bottles were passed, and crackers flew into waiting hands. Kaylan was once again jostled, but Abraham and Stevenson appeared at her side and gripped her arms. They waded into the crowd and arrived at the truck carrying men and women in American camouflage. She scanned the faces, wishing Nick and Micah were among them, but their SEAL team would never let them come to Haiti. "I need food."

"Help us, please."

"Money, shelter."

"Clothes."

"Medicine."

"Water, please, God, water."

Creole and broken English swirled around her head like a whirlpool, and the stench of sweat and blood assaulted her nose.

"I work for the Hope Clinic. We need supplies. Medicine, food, water. We have a hundred under our care and haven't anything to eat or drink."

"A lot haven't, ma'am."

The soldier's russet hair reminded her of Seth, and she offered the ghost of a smile. "Please, anything."

"If we give you a crate, this mob will have our heads. Where's the clinic? Maybe we can bring the next truck load by there."

"A box, anything, please." She was prepared to beg. The people needed something. Many had waited in a line for hours the day before, only to be turned away, water buckets empty. An eight-month-old baby had died the day before from lack of nutrients. Kaylan didn't want that for Yanick's child. Sarah Beth had helped bring that little life into the world.

The soldier looked at his partner and handed Abraham and Stevenson each a box of water and crackers. "I'm sorry I can't do more."

"We'll manage. Thank you."

A group of men crowded around her, and she lost Abe. Hands reached upward toward the back of the truck and jumped and pushed on Kaylan's head to support their weight. She crumpled to the ground, feet trampling her.

She shielded her face, blood now pouring down her leg. "Abe. Stevenson." Her words went unheard beneath the cries of a hunger-ravaged crowd. A box nicked her head as a man grabbed it and ran into the streets. She lay dazed, feet stepping on and over her.

A hand grabbed her arm and pulled her to the edge of the crowd. Abraham's loud words gained the attention of a few of the men and they parted briefly as she was pulled to her feet.

"Kaylan, you okay?"

She sagged against him, her head pounding. Survival had driven the people to primal behavior. Only those strong enough, determined enough to fight for food and water would avoid starvation.

"When will this nightmare end, Abe?"

His smile was sad. "It is always a nightmare for the people of Haiti. But we know how to survive."

"How do you survive this? No water, no food. No place to sleep. How do you live like this?"

"It is Haiti, Kaylan. We live like this because we must." He threw her arm around his shoulder and supported her weight. Her eyes threatened to close. He squared his shoulders, his head erect. "Someday, things will change for us. I have hope for my people, hope for a better Haiti."

"What hope?" She nearly shouted.

"You are alive, are you not? So am I." His sharp, steady gaze challenged her to argue.

Abraham led them through the markets and back to the clinic. Blood had become more common than water, and crying ceased to have meaning. The smell of human flesh permeated the air from piles of bodies on fire in the street. Troops and reporters arrived, bearing cameras instead of supplies. Food, water, and medicine sat at airports in Haiti and the Dominican Republic, unable to travel the rutted, pothole-riddled roads to people in need.

Broken people, bruised bodies, shattered lives, shaken faiths, missing loved ones. No soccer games led by a group of rowdy children, no worship bells. Kaylan's heart broke.

A group of people gathered at the end of the street around a pole leaning on the side of a dilapidated restaurant. Cheers and cries seemed foreign to her ears. She stopped, and her breath caught as the red and blue of the Haitian flag pulled into a sky clearing of dust. Blue shone through for the first time since the quake. A child sat on his father's shoulders, hoisting the cloth higher and higher until it billowed in the air.

Abraham stood tall. "You see, Kaylan? There will be a better Haiti. One day. God is still in control."

In the ashes and rubble the flag spoke of *lespwa*, hope despite the harshness. Kaylan didn't understand it, couldn't believe it. Too many lay dead, too much destroyed. Still, the image of the flag nagged her.

"How are you so strong? You pulled bodies and people from buildings. You braved the quake to save others when you could have died. Why?"

"You would have too."

"I wanted to hide. I wanted to die when Sarah . . . when my friend died."

"You kept going. You will rise above this."

Kaylan didn't think so. Something inside her had died when Sarah Beth breathed her last.

A cold, delirious voice halted Kaylan. His shouts filled the street.

"You, you brought this to Haiti. Where is your God?"

Eliezer rocked on the sidewalk like a drunken man in tattered and torn clothes. A gash stretched from his eye to his jaw. Kaylan instinctively stepped toward him, driven to inspect the wound.

"Eliezer, you're hurt. Let me see."

"Everyone is hurt. Why do you care?'

"I care. Let me see if I can help." She released Abraham and stumbled toward Eliezer.

"Where is your God now, white woman? Haiti has crumbled, and my people are joining the spirits of their ancestors. Our graves overflow. Does your God care? No! If He is real, He let this happen." He spat at her feet. "You serve Him, so this is your fault. They are buried in mass graves. They are forgotten and disrespected. Your fault. You and your government. You and your God."

He pointed a bony finger in her face, his breath warmer than the afternoon air. "You should never have come to Haiti. My people die because of your God. Where is He?" A manic laugh burst from his lips, and Kaylan shrank back in fear. "Where is your pretty friend, white girl? She dead? Your God abandoned her too. And yet you live. Her death is on your hands. Curse you, and curse your God."

Tears burned in her eyes. Abraham stepped in front of her, shouting at Eliezer in Creole.

"You should never have come to Haiti." Heads, shaken from despondency, turned toward them in the street.

"Eliezer, your face could be infected. Let me help you." She remembered Sarah Beth's cuts and stepped forward again, unwilling to let him suffer when she could ease his pain.

He spit again. "Don't touch me. I do not want your help. Leave Haiti. This is your fault. Your God is to blame."

A crowd began to gather, and Kaylan glanced at Abe, his eyes filled with anger and fear. Tucking her under his arm, he hurried them down the street.

My fault Sarah Beth is dead. All my fault. I shouldn't have come to Haiti. All my fault. Where are You, God?

Her leg buckled, and her head pounded. Abe shouted in the distance. Spots danced before her eyes, and the ground welcomed her fall. Her last thought was of the food she had failed to procure. She would have to try again tomorrow.

Chapter Twenty-Two

PORT-AU-PRINCE RESEMBLED THE site of an explosion. Bodies littered the streets amidst ruptured and scattered structures. People, catatonic or frantic, wandered the streets in desperate attempts to locate food, shelter, clean water, or loved ones.

Micah resembled a ticking time bomb. Nick wasn't sure how he would get him through the hours to come if they couldn't find Kaylan—or, worse, if they found her dead.

Their plane had landed before dawn Friday morning. Supplies sat at the airport, unattended and incapable of being moved. Nick and Micah hopped on the first convoy into the city.

"You boys ready for this?"

"Ready for what, exactly?" Nick eyed the camouflaged soldier riding with him and Micah in the back of the truck.

"Haven't you been watching the news? We're driving into a war zone. The people are going crazy, looting. One of the prisons collapsed, and some of the worst criminals from the slums are on the loose. The air reeks of dead bodies and desperation."

Nick smelled smoke and leaned out the back of the truck. A flash of white sent him jerking back into the truck before he realized the headlights had reflected off the frightened eyes of people camping along the road leading to Port-au-Prince.

"They're getting out of the city. There's no food or water, and they don't expect to be able to distribute much for the next few days. It's Katrina all over again. Haiti's government officials are scattered and hiding, and we're left to defend the people and pick up the pieces. Kinda messed up."

"What's burning?"

The man hesitated, and Nick no longer wanted to know.

"Bodies. Mass graves. Some are worried about disease, and there are too many to bury individually. I heard tell some are breaking into their family crypts and stacking as many bodies inside as possible."

"How many are dead?" Micah spoke up, his voice shaky.

The soldier shook his head. "I heard best case is one in ten. Could be more, could be less. What are you frogmen doing here, anyhow?"

"My sister. She's working at a clinic here."

"I'm sorry. Most of the hospitals and clinics are rubble, or so I've been told. People are panicking for medical care, and more are dying because they can't find it."

Nick could feel Micah's temper begin to boil. "Is there anything you can tell us that you haven't heard through the grapevine?" His own fear was morphing to anger, and this soldier sat in the direct line of fire. He popped another piece of Juicy Fruit in his mouth, but it tasted like ash.

"I don't think there is much anyone knows for sure, unless they've been in the eye of it."

"Are many Americans dead?" Micah's voice was sharp.

"Not as many as there are Haitians."

"How long?" The truck jerked and bumped over potholes and cracks. Dust funneled under the canvas, choking Nick.

"Who knows? The road is in even worse shape since the quake."

Dawn bloomed, and Nick fought to remain calm. Bodies of the living and the dead lined the road. How would they find Kaylan? Was she even alive, or had she died quickly, painlessly?

Nick closed his eyes and bent over his knees, not wanting to worry Micah. His stomach churned. *Lord, I need to find her. I need to hold her again. Micah and her family need her home. I can't fight nature, and I can't fight desperation. I can't protect her. Help, please. We need a miracle.*

Nick's eyes flew open as dust assaulted his nose and tickled his throat. Somehow the bumps and jolts of the road had lulled him to sleep. Or it could have been that he hadn't slept more than a couple hours since he'd found out about the earthquake three days earlier.

"We'll hand out the few supplies we have here and then find someone from the UN and try to coordinate. You're on your own. Good luck. I hope you find her."

The soldier shook their hands, and Nick and Micah jumped from the back of the truck, sending a cloud of dust skyward.

"Did we come to Afghanistan or Haiti?"

"Hard to tell the difference right now." Nick smacked his gum. A crowd of men swarmed the truck. Clothes and shoes lay scattered beneath the debris of what used to be buildings. A pile of bodies marked the edge of the market. The Haitian flag draped one body. Nick fought the urge to look for Kaylan there.

"I don't even know where to begin, man. Mom told me the street name where the clinic is located, but there aren't any streets or signs or..."

"Buildings."

Nick scanned the people. Many stood in line, their faces expressionless. Many shoulders drooped and a couple swayed, Nick assumed from lack of food and water. Or pure exhaustion. Several men at the front of the line by the supply truck yelled and began to shove, stirring some out of their catatonic states. Angry men. Desperate men needing water, food, and medicine. Several grabbed crates or handfuls of supplies off the truck and began to run, sending the people into a frenzy as they fought for food and water. The docile crowd morphed into an angry mob with no other goal but survival.

They needed to get out of here fast. Nick and Micah elbowed their way through the crowd. A flash of auburn caught Nick's attention in the middle of the black bodies near the first truck. He took a step closer, straining.

"What? What'd you see?" Micah followed his gaze.

"I thought...no, it's only Haitians. Never mind. Let's get out of here before this riot gets worse."

Before he finished the sentence, the crowd scattered. Their traveling companion jumped from the truck, yelling. The Haitians who began the riot knocked others down as they ran into the remains of buildings, determined to carry away anything and everything that would help them survive. It was survival of the fittest.

Haitian troops joined the scene, haggard and haunted as the mob continued to shout. They struggled to restore order, but it was too late. Panicked and hungry people dominated the street. A Haitian soldier, not much older than Kaylan, closed his eyes and fired his gun into the air. With that, Nick and Micah jumped into the fray, not sure how to help or where to start but knowing they had to do something.

A woman screamed nearby, and Nick swerved toward the sound.

Blood seeped through a bandage tied around her leg barely visible beneath her dirty skirt. Her hair was dusty, the color dull, and her face bruised beyond recognition, but she was white and an American. He could tell that much from her clothes. He started toward her, fighting the crowd to reach her side. A man bowled over her, knocking her down in his attempt to scramble on the dilapidated building at her back. Nick doubled his efforts.

"Kaylan." Two black teens yelled and ran toward the woman from across the square, dropping boxes in their wake. Nick's heart skipped a beat. He'd found her.

Nick reached a clearing in the crowd just as a Haitian soldier leveled his gun at the man hovering over her as the man tried to squeeze through a hole in the building she leaned against.

"No!" Nick sprinted across the square but wouldn't get there in time. He could hear Micah pounding behind him, their morning workouts pushing them in perfect rhythm. It wasn't enough.

The soldier fired, and the man dropped like a rock on top of Kaylan. His body jerked with her terror, and Nick wanted to pummel the guard who'd shot him. Hadn't there been enough death, enough terror? Where did it stop?

Nick reached her first and jerked the man off her. His blood soaked her shirt, and her eyes were wild.

"Kaylan, it's Nick. Baby, look at me. Kaylan?"

She looked at him, eyes drooping and unfocused. She didn't respond.

Chapter Twenty-Three

W HAT'S WRONG WITH her?" Micah bumped Nick out of
the way and picked Kaylan up, cradling her.
"She's probably just dazed. Possibly in shock."
"Kaylan, Kaylan." The two teens who had yelled Kaylan's name
across the street skidded to a stop in front of them. Nick instinctively stepped between them and Micah.

"She is our friend."

Another barrage of bullets tore through the air, and Nick and
Micah instinctively ducked and ran. While Micah cradled Kaylan,
Nick scanned the area for rogue shooters. Too many were already
dead from the quake. Did their fellow countrymen not care?

They rounded a corner, and the two teens sprinted in front of
them, nimbly dancing through debris.

"Clinic this way," the one in charge shouted and looked back
to make sure they were following. Nick didn't want a clinic. He
wanted an American hospital, knowledgeable doctors, pain medi-
cation, and clean quarters. But nothing was clean or pristine in
Haiti. The streets reeked of death and dust.

Kaylan's eyes were squeezed shut, her arm draped loosely
around Micah's neck. She looked frail, sick, broken. Nick's heart
ached at her bruises and the blood on her leg. What had she lived
through? He knew from experience that the memories hit at the
worst times. What would she remember?

Lord, help her forget.

They reached a series of sheets hung haphazardly over metal
rods and sticks. People huddled under the tents, statues cracked

and disfigured after the events of the past hours and days. At the end of the row, sheets covered several still forms.

"They wait for the truck to take them for mass burial. There are too many to save. Too many to bury. I am Abraham. Kaylan calls me Abe. This is Stevenson." Stevenson nodded but remained silent. The cuts and bruises on his arms and legs spoke of desperate struggle.

"Come. We will take you to Rhonda."

A row of draped sheets faced Nick and Micah as they approached the clinic. Abe sprinted ahead, returning with a woman with blonde frizzy hair and dust streaking her face. Nick knew immediately it was Rhonda.

"What happened to her?" Rhonda rushed to Kaylan and felt her head, noting the blood seeping through the bandage in her leg. "This way."

Nick and Micah followed her back to a matchbox office. "Set her in the chair." Rhonda reminded Nick of his Senior Chief—quick and efficient, removing emotion and niceties to complete the task at hand. No wonder she was still on her feet. She hurried from the room to collect supplies.

"My fault." Kaylan mumbled as Micah knelt in front of her.

"Kayles? Look at me."

"Micah? What…" Her head dropped and Nick wanted to snatch her from the chair and put her on the first plane back to Alabama.

"We're here to take you home. I need you to talk to me. Where's Sarah Beth? Kayles? Stay with me." Micah's frustration grew. "What's wrong with her?"

"Let me see." Nick took Micah's place in front of Kaylan and felt her head, searching beneath her hair for a bump or cut. A gash ran from her forehead into her hairline and was patched. Her face was blue and yellow with multiple smaller cuts.

"What's wrong with her, Hawk?" Micah looked like a caged bulldog, and if there was someone to blame for this, Nick knew Micah would hunt them down. "She's alive, and she's banged up, so why isn't she talking to us?"

"She has seen things, done things. You do not know. No one is all right in Haiti. Kaylan has lived through much, as have we all." Abraham materialized in the doorway, but Nick kept his hands on Kaylan, refusing to acknowledge Abe's statements. She was his priority until Rhonda came back.

Micah turned on Abraham. "What do you mean? Where's Sarah Beth? What all has she seen and done? Where was she when the quake hit?"

"I will show you when Ms. Rhonda returns. Best not to relive the details in front of her."

Micah ran his hands through his hair, his frustration wearing Nick thin. Maybe this was too personal. There was no way to remove the attachment to this situation.

"Chill, Bulldog. We'll get answers, and then we'll take her home."

"Nick?" Her voice was faint.

His head snapped to meet Kaylan's eyes. "Yeah, Kayles. It's me."

"What? How?"

"We came to take you home."

She gripped the front of his shirt and fell against him. "I can't leave her. My fault. All my fault."

He cradled the back of her head, wondering at her lack of tears. "What's your fault?"

"Sarah Beth. All my fault. I won't leave her. Please. I won't leave her."

"We came to take you both home, Kayles. We wouldn't leave her here."

"I won't leave her. She's all alone. She needs to be with people who love her."

Nick glanced at Micah, his face a sick shade of green, his eyes wary. Their gaze darted to Abraham, pinning him to the wall.

"What's she talking about?"

Abraham's brown eyes lowered to the floor, and Nick's stomach dropped like a rock. No. It couldn't be.

Rhonda bustled into the room. A dirty rag hung from one hand and a needle and thread were poised in the other. Nick stood to give her room and get answers from Abe, but Kaylan wouldn't release his shirt.

"Please don't leave me. It's my fault. I have to help. I won't leave her."

He cradled her face and rested his forehead on hers. "I promise I won't leave you." He kissed her forehead and carefully untangled her hands from his shirt. Her body drooped in the chair, her eyes closing as Rhonda began to stitch her wound again.

By the set of her mouth and compassionate but brash interaction, Nick could tell Rhonda had long ago ceased to confront the Haitian culture. She had adapted to it, a fact that allowed her to roll with the catastrophes that seemed to strike every couple of years. There was always something wrong with Haiti.

Nick didn't blame her. From the little he had seen of the country, it felt as if they fought a losing battle. He doubted that her attitude had gone over well with Kaylan, though. Kaylan had come to change culture, to stop the cycle. She was green, but Rhonda had roots here. Haiti had changed Rhonda. Had her short time there changed Kaylan as well?

Nick held her hand. Micah's eyes met his. They would get to the bottom of this. And they would get her home. Fast. Something was wrong. Everything was wrong.

Rhonda pulled them aside minutes later while Kaylan rested in the chair. "I'm worried her leg is becoming infected. She sliced it open in the quake and has refused medicine and proper supplies so we could use them for other patients. But she needs attention and quickly."

"I'm her brother, and this is her, well..." Micah offered a small smile. "This is a friend. We're taking her home as soon as we can arrange a ride." Micah's tone left no room for argument, and Rhonda nodded.

"I think she's also dehydrated and undernourished. I've noticed she's given the little she had to some of the children and young mothers. We ran out of food yesterday, and I'm not sure when we will have more. She hasn't slept more than a few hours since before the quake. Her mind and body have reached their limit."

Nick's desire to leave Haiti and never come back doubled. "What about Sarah Beth? We need to take her home too."

Rhonda shook her head and looked down at the floor. "Abraham and Stevenson buried her outside the city while Kaylan watched. She won't talk about it, so I don't know what happened. Abraham knows more. I would talk to him. My house is rubble, but if you can salvage anything of Kaylan's or Sarah Beth's, do so. It may help her once she gets home."

Nick nodded and studied Kaylan. What had she seen? What had she been through? He had nightmares of his own, and to help her through hers, he needed to know the extent of her injuries. Every painful detail. Flanked closely by Micah, he crossed the room and stopped in front of Abe.

"I'm sorry if we were rude. But after that scene in the market you can understand why."

"I understand."

"I'm Nick. This is Micah."

Abe nodded. "Boyfriend and brother."

"You're right on one account. Not sure Nick has earned that title yet." The first smile in days tugged at Nick's lips.

"You braved much to come here. You want to see where I found her?"

"Please. We need to know what happened. Everything."

"You ask much. I can only tell you what I saw. Kaylan will not speak of the rest."

"Show us."

Minutes later they stood outside two outer walls, all that remained of Rhonda's home. As the walls had collapsed, they had created pockets, enabling Kaylan's survival. Nick wanted to shoot something. The earthquake was an act of God, one he didn't understand. Why?

"How did she live through that?" Micah sounded close to tears.

"Barely." Nick noticed the hole through which they had pulled Kaylan. He wanted to go in. He needed to see. If he was going to walk her through this, he needed to understand.

"Abe, is it safe to go in?"

"It is difficult to say. Rubble no longer shifts, but you never know."

"What happened?" Every house on the block was dust and crumbled stone. They reminded Nick of the brevity of life. From dust he was made, and to dust he would return. Many had died. How many had stepped into eternity with the Lord?

"It took us a couple of hours to dig her out. I found her holding Sarah Beth. Lots of blood. Covered in dust. She would not leave her. Stevenson and I pulled her from the room, kicking and screaming."

"How did she escape and Sarah Beth die?"

"Part of the ceiling fell and pinned Sarah Beth. Stevenson and I came back and did our best to dig her out. She didn't have a chance."

"Can you show me where you found her?"

"The hole goes to the bedroom they were in. You have to crawl. But you cannot miss it. There is still blood."

Without hesitation, Micah dove in to the small opening in the rubble. Nick followed close behind, feeling as if he were crawling through the trenches. Glass and gravel sliced his palms. He wound around pipes and jagged cement. There was no question, he was in a war zone—a war zone of a different kind.

"Blood." Nick pointed to a large rock. Near the chunk was more dried blood on the debris-covered floor.

"Looks like she crawled too." Micah slithered over rocks, barely squeezing under the low ceiling. Nick pulled himself over to the pocket where Sarah Beth must have died.

"Is this it?" he called to Abe who crouched at the hole.

"Yes. Stevenson and I shifted the ceiling. You can see where Sarah Beth probably coughed up blood. The blood on the floor is from Kaylan's leg."

"She cut it in here?"

"Looks like she cut it on this rebar," Micah shouted. "There's blood on the tip. That's where the blood trail begins."

"Where was she coming from?"

"Her bed, it looks like. I can see more blood under the bed at the foot. Man, Hawk, the bed took the weight of the ceiling, and rocks are stacked around it. How did she make it out of that?"

Nick heard Micah shifting rubble. He studied the area where Kaylan had held Sarah Beth. Something silver caught his eye in the meager light from the hole. He shifted aside shards of rock. The necklace he had sent Kaylan lay in the rubble, the chain snapped but the lily still intact. He stuffed it in his pocket to give to Kaylan later.

"Look what I pulled from under the bed where she was hiding." Micah scooted over to Micah, his back scraping the fragile ceiling.

Nick reached for the box he had given Kaylan weeks before in the dance studio. He opened the lid and ran his fingers over the envelopes. "Wow. These letters have officially survived a war in Afghanistan and an earthquake in Haiti."

"When did you write these?"

"On our deployment. I gave them to Kaylan before she left for Haiti."

Silence descended as they both gazed around the shattered room. Normally Micah would have given him grief for writing letters to his sister, but under the circumstances...

"Find anything else under her bed?"

Micah shook his head. "She was pinned pretty tight. I don't know how she managed to wiggle out. The only reason the box survived was because it was under the bed. Apparently she made it under there before the house crashed around her."

Nick surveyed the room and crawled toward the gap. "I'm not sure I want to know the details."

"I wish there was a bad guy to chase."

"Yeah, no joke." They would help Kaylan through this, but Nick had a feeling that what lay ahead would be his most difficult mission yet.

They reached the opening and pulled themselves through, landing on the street. Abe helped them up.

Nick dusted himself off then looked at Micah. "We're outta here. Today. She needs a doctor, and she can't stay here."

Micah nodded. Nick skirted around rubble, his feet kicking up dust. Each step took him closer to Kaylan and to getting her home. But would she ever recover from what she had seen?

PART THREE

Chapter Twenty-Four

THE GROUND RUMBLED, and Kaylan gripped something soft. Her eyes flew open as she bolted upright. Light assaulted her eyes. Something sharp tugged and stung her hand.

She wrestled with the sheets and clawed at the gown on her chest. Trapped. The walls closed in, and she couldn't breathe.

Get under the bed. Get under the bed.

Rough hands grabbed her, and she fought. Everything shook. She had to hide.

"Kaylan, Kaylan, it's okay. It's just a cart. It's okay."

She stilled. She knew that voice—warm, familiar like the waves brushing the shore. Nick. She gripped his shirt and glanced around the bright, white room. An IV drip hung by the bed. In her frenzy she'd pulled the needle free.

"Where are we?"

"At the hospital in Tuscaloosa."

"How long have we been here?"

"Just a day. You slept through most of it." He rubbed her arms, and her muscles loosened.

"How? I didn't get to say good-bye. What about Rhonda and Abe and Stevenson and Yanick and the baby? Where's Sarah...? No. It was a bad dream. It has to be a bad dream."

Her hands shook, and she thrust trembling fingers into her hair. The room spun. Her eyes took in bouquets of flowers and the chair Nick had just vacated with a blanket in it. How to get out? How to get back? Sarah Beth was still in Haiti.

"Where is everyone?"

173

"Coffee run. We've taken turns staying with you."

"I...I don't remember leaving."

"You lost a lot of blood in your leg. You were dehydrated and hungry. A little dazed."

He brushed her cheek, and she moved closer to his hand, enjoying the warmth. She felt cold through her bones to her heart. Shivering, she pulled the blanket around her. She wasn't sure she would ever be warm again.

She strained, trying to remember. She remembered a man falling on her and the tugging sensation on her leg as Rhonda worked to piece her back together. She remembered the droning sound of a plane and seeing the faintest flash of Haitian countryside fade below her. But it was a blur, the images just dim snapshots in an emotional fog. Through it all, though, she remembered feeling safe again in spite of the heavy sleep that held her captive. Nick. It had been Nick and Micah who took her away.

A nurse entered the room, and Kaylan found Nick's hand and held on tight—her lifeline. The room blurred, and she was once again back in the black bedroom of Rhonda's house. Sarah Beth's hand was cold in hers, too cold.

> You remember that summer we found that mutt puppy in the woods behind the house?"
>
> Kaylan laughed softly. Sarah Beth had a thing for rescuing what no one else wanted. It had drawn her to Haiti. "We took him home and gave him a bath. He was the ugliest thing I'd ever seen. My parents said we couldn't keep him. We spent a week hanging signs, but you claimed him."
>
> "Good ole Tiger. He had red, black, and brown fur. Beautiful." Sarah Beth's grip grew weaker, and Kaylan struggled not to panic. She strengthened her hold. If she could hold on, Sarah Beth would be fine. People were coming. They had to be, because life without Sarah Beth was too awful to contemplate.

"Kaylan?" The white room snapped back into focus. She bent over, holding her stomach, her nails digging into Nick's hand.

"The lights, please. It's too bright."

Nick turned off the lights, and Kaylan released a breath. Shadows greeted her like old friends.

"Miss Richards, I need to put your IV back in." Kaylan averted her gaze from the needle and met Nick's eyes. She wasn't ready to answer his questions. She didn't want to relive the memories. But what had happened to her friends? To Rhonda and Abe and Stevenson? To the moms? To Yanick's baby?

"Miss Richards, are you ready to eat something? We need to get you back to normal."

"What's normal?" Kaylan whispered, licking her cracked lips. Nothing could be normal again. Sarah Beth should be in the bed next to her. They would talk late into the night, cry over their friends, thank God to be back with their families, and then work through the aftermath together.

"You need to eat, Kayles."

"Nothing sounds good."

"Well, how 'bout I bring you a little bit of soup and maybe some ice cream? Does that sound good, honey?" Kaylan nodded, and the woman left the room. The sun descended outside the hospital window, the sky murky and dark. When had the colors left?

Kaylan felt Nick's eyes—piercing, even from a distance. His arm around her shoulders and his hand stroking her arm reassured her, but the warmth faded as soon as his fingers left the spot. She searched the room for something, anything to focus on, but his gaze held steady. Her Hawk—always too perceptive.

"Sarah Beth's family was here."

Kaylan braced herself for bad news. They had to hate her.

"They're praying you gain your strength back soon and are waiting for a service until you're out of the hospital. I think they want you to speak."

She almost jerked the IV out of her hand again.

"Babe, it's okay. Calm down. You don't have to." His arms held her tightly, and muscle by muscle she stilled.

"I can't."

They would want to know what had happened, and she couldn't tell them. She couldn't speak of the final hours. She couldn't describe the twisted position of Sarah Beth's body. The image seared into her mind, but no words came close to describing the horror. They would hate her for surviving instead of their daughter. Sarah Beth should be here instead of Kaylan. Sarah Beth had believed in going to Haiti from the beginning. Sarah Beth should have been the one to live and come home. She'd had so much to give.

Nick squeezed her gently, and her bruises cried in protest. "What's going on in that beautiful head of yours?" He tipped her chin up, his fingers caressing her skin. "Can you talk to me?"

How could she tell him? How could she explain? How could she say that it was her fault her best friend was dead? Eliezer had said so. If she discussed it, it would happen all over again. She would smell the dust, and feel rock and glass slice into the tender flesh of her palms. She would feel the limp grip of her dying friend, taste the grit in the air and the bitter brine of tears and blood on her cracked lips. It would no longer be a dream but a reality. She couldn't.

"Nick, I don't think there are words to describe what happened. I can't."

"Give it time, Kayles. It's still pretty new."

"Time won't heal this. There's a gaping hole where...where my friend used to be. People are gone, a whole country reduced to dust and rubble. How does that heal?"

A knock sounded on the door before it opened, causing Kaylan to jerk at the sudden noise. Nick squeezed her hand and moved toward the window as her family filed in the room.

"Kaylan? Oh, honey, I'm so glad you're awake and talking." Her mother rushed into the room, enfolding Kaylan in her arms. She rested her head on her mom's shoulder, feeling like a lost child.

"How ya doing, sis?" Seth carried lilies and studied her over their mother's shoulder.

How could she answer? She offered the ghost of a smile. Exhaustion once again fought for prominence. As she leaned back against her pillow, she watched her family talk and pamper her as sleep once again crowded in. Maybe, just maybe, she would wake up again and it would all be a bad dream. Maybe.

The sun dipped below the cityscape, and the world faded to black outside the hospital window. The nurse had come and gone with the dinner that Kaylan had barely tasted before mercifully falling asleep again. The room was quiet, barred to the hospital noise just outside the door. Nick wished he could shield Kaylan from the world that easily.

Nick watched Kaylan from the window. Bruises colored her jaw line, a bandage covered the cut at her temple, and discoloration rimmed her eyes. Her grip had been strong and frantic as she fell asleep, her eyes wild and fearful, like someone fighting for her life. She had spent the last week doing just that.

What could he say to soothe the fear? To take away the pain? No medicine existed for this; no machine yet invented could rewind time or bring back thousands of innocent lives lost in a few earth-shattering seconds. Easy answers ceased to exist...only questions. Questions he too had asked God more than once.

He approached the bed and brushed a wayward curl from her forehead before bestowing a gentle kiss. As he settled back into the chair, he reached for her hand and gazed through the hospital window. Only city lights winked and sliced through the overpowering darkness.

Chapter Twenty-Five

FLANKED BY HER family and Nick, Kaylan entered the church for Sarah Beth's memorial service. It had been ten days since the earthquake. Crutches helped with the limp, but truth be told, she welcomed the pain. It kept her focused on placing one foot in front of the other.

Even now, tears refused to come. Only a gaping hole remained. Something had broken inside her when Sarah Beth had breathed her last, and that part lay buried beside her friend in the deforested land of Haiti.

Faces turned and studied her as she progressed down the aisle. Silence cloaked the sanctuary.

Sarah Beth was never quiet.

A slideshow played on the big screens on either side of the choir loft in the large room. Kaylan froze as Sarah Beth's face appeared larger than life. She was two and making mud pies, then five with her arm around Kaylan and holding a hot pink Barbie lunch box. They were seven and dancing in *The Nutcracker*, wearing pink tutus, and then ten and riding horses with Pap. They had always been a team. Inseparable. Their lives intertwined from the earliest days, like a rope that had now frayed.

"You okay, babe?" Nick murmured.

She shook her head. How could she be okay? "I can't do this." She began to turn around, knocking into Micah, who grabbed her and held her still, hugging her as best he could with her crutches. David and Seth moved forward to shield her from curious eyes. The rest of the family cocooned them as well, Kaylan at their center. Her body shook. She couldn't speak. She couldn't even walk up the aisle. Not with Sarah Beth buried next to the road in a shattered country that had sucked the life out of her.

"Kaylan?"

Kaylan's family parted to reveal Mrs. Tucker, Sarah Beth's mom. "We'd like you and your family to sit with us. Y'all were a second family to Sarah Beth, and it seems only appropriate."

Kaylan hobbled forward, Nick and Micah at each arm, to slide into the row behind Sarah Beth's parents and brother. Mrs. Tucker reached over the pew and clasped Kaylan's hand, dabbing at her eyes with a handkerchief.

"I'm so glad you are safe, hon. Sarah Beth...she would have hated if something had happened to you."

Kaylan tried to swallow the lump in her throat, but it refused to leave, much like the numbness in her heart.

Music continued to play in the background, and the occasional sniff broke the rhythm. Sarah Beth had loved loud music. No matter the song, she cranked it up on her radio or music player and sang off-key at the top of her lungs. When people stopped to stare, she sang louder. This music didn't fit her. Nothing about this proper, somber event suited her. Sarah Beth had been like sunshine and neon-colored popsicles on an Alabama summer day. Seth had worn his purple button-down and hot pink tie in honor of her, and Kaylan appreciated it more than she could say. He reminded her of Sarah Beth, of laughter and sunshine.

Scuffling and whispering voices added a different cadence. Kaylan welcomed the distraction as the class Sarah Beth had taught slipped in the back, each child with a wrapped item in hand. The teacher led them down the aisle to place their presents on the steps leading to the stage: clothes, toys, candy, bottled water, canned goods.

Mrs. Tucker whispered to her, "The kids want to help with Haiti relief in honor of Sarah Beth."

The students reminded Kaylan of her little Sophia, quiet yet happy. What would become of her now? Sarah Beth had loved playing with her, braiding her hair, teaching her. And Reuben? He was all legs and smiles, the boy who would bring joy to his country by representing his people as a professional soccer player. Sarah Beth had cheered him on. And now? Now he was buried in a mass grave, his dream snuffed out in the quake that shook more than the earth.

She looked to Nick again, her insides twisting like knotted thread. She desperately needed to deliver a speech that would honor her best friend, but everything appeared dull, lifeless without her. Above all, she couldn't talk about Sarah Beth's last moments. She couldn't talk about Haiti. The one person who would have understood remained there, her grave a bed for the spring grass.

"I can't do this." She searched his eyes.

His lips skimmed her cheek. "You're gonna do great."

She shook her head, panic returning with a vengeance. "I can't do this."

He pulled her close and she rested there, absorbing the touch but feeling nothing. Had her nerves been damaged in the quake, or was everything in the world dull now? Would it be this way forever?

Sarah Beth's brother, Tom, stood and spoke about his sister. Tears flowed, and his voice caught. His parents came to stand at his side, the Tuckers united in the loss of one of their members. Kaylan's jaw ached and eyes stung where tears should be. More music played, and more people spoke. Sarah Beth had known no stranger, found favor with everyone. Each person who spoke honored her memory as a woman who loved God and loved people. A violinist played "I Surrender All," Sarah Beth's favorite hymn. She had surrendered all, and Kaylan knew she would gladly do so again.

"Don't be mad, Kayles." Sarah Beth's voice lingered in her mind, but Kaylan couldn't accept it, wouldn't accept it. She didn't have to surrender everything, but she had. And she'd died broken.

Why, God? Why?

Nick released her. "You're up."

The walk to the podium felt like a walk to the hangman's noose. Ominous music built, and her hands grew slick on the cold crutches. Her heart beat a doleful cadence, building in intensity the closer she drew to the podium. *I can't do this. I can't do this.*

She stopped at the steps. Closing her eyes, she imagined the heat of Haiti, the rainbow-colored tap-taps hauling sweaty, boisterous people from one end of the city to the next. She imagined the paintings of brilliant color, the smell of the ocean, the welcome feel of Rhonda's home, and the laughter of twenty young mothers. In the midst of it all stood Sarah Beth, alive, whole, thriving, because she never felt more in her element than when she helped people.

Opening her eyes, Kaylan took a step and then froze. On the big screen was a picture of the two of them in Haiti, heads thrown back in laughter. She'd uploaded it on Facebook the day before the quake. Spinning around, she searched for a door, an escape. "I'm so sorry, but I can't do this. I just can't," she whispered to the Tuckers.

Ramming into the side exit, she escaped into the rain. One or all of her brothers wouldn't be far behind. And Nick. But she needed to be alone. Rounding the corner of the church, she sank down, her dress soaking in a puddle and rain drenching her face, replacing the tears she desperately wished would come. Her crutches clattered to either side. Behind her the voices of Nick and her brothers called her name, but she couldn't bring herself to respond. For the first time in her life the people she loved most felt distant, unreachable.

The only voice she could hear in the downpour was Eliezer's. "You should never have come to Haiti. Your fault. This is your fault. Her death is on your hands. Curse you, and curse your God." She covered her ears, but his voice shouted from within her. It wouldn't stop. She couldn't forget.

Kaylan tilted her face to the sky, welcoming the deluge. Maybe it would wash her away. It was her fault. She couldn't save her best friend in Haiti, and she had just failed to honor and love her in death.

She had failed again. Her fault. All her fault.

Worry consumed Nick. He didn't recognize this Kaylan: despondent, unable to give to those closest to her, running away from difficult circumstances. He followed her from the church while the pastor stepped up to smooth over her absence.

"Kaylan!" The howling wind and rain diminished his shout and the calls of her brothers, who followed behind. He rounded a corner and found her sitting in a ball, huddled against the side of the church. The picture of a broken woman.

"Kaylan?" She stirred but wouldn't look at him. He took off his soaked coat and placed it around her shoulders. The icy rain instantly soaked through his button-down. He slipped his arm around her, and she fell limply against his shoulder. A spasm of fear shot through his gut. She hadn't regained her weight yet, and her willowy body was frail, as if the earthquake had shaken her very being.

Micah stuck his head around the corner and met Nick's eyes. Seth and David bumped into him, and Micah hustled them back around the corner. Her family was including him, allowing him to operate within their inner workings. He prayed he didn't let them down.

"Remember the dance studio over Christmas break?"

He nodded against her hair, relieved that she was finally talking. *Lord, help me know how to respond.*

"I didn't realize that would be the last time we danced together. If I'd known, I would've appreciated it more, made it less about getting over Pap's stroke and more about being with her. She was strong, you know? I needed her, but I think in a lot of ways, she didn't need me."

"What do you mean? You were her best friend. You two were like peanut butter and jelly. She loved you."

Kaylan went on as if he hadn't spoken. "We were supposed to be in each other's weddings. We had it all planned, although I fought her on wearing a hot-pink maid-of-honor dress." He couldn't hide his chuckle. "We were going to have kids at the same time, a boy and a girl, so they could grow up, get married, and we could be mothers-in-law together. We were going to be those old women on the Southern porch watching the sunrise, gossiping into the evening hours, and sipping sweet tea with lemon. We were going to save the world. We were superheroes when we were young."

"Let me guess: Sarah Beth always wore pink."

"Always."

It occurred to him that she hadn't cried at all, not since he'd found her in Haiti or brought her home. Nothing.

"And what color did you wear?" The rain had let up a bit.

She turned her head and met his eyes, her own radiating pain. "I've always had a thing for blue."

"Have you?" He smiled and ran a finger down her face, resisting the urge to kiss her. It wasn't the time. Right now it would be an overflow of his heartache, his attempt to heal her.

"Kayles?" He needed to get her out of the rain, but he needed her to talk to him more.

"Hmm?"

"What happened in the earthquake?"

Her body went stiff as a wooden board, and she pulled away from him, allowing the wall to take her weight. "I don't want to talk about it."

"I think you need to." He kept his voice gentle, low, hoping she would trust him enough to let him into her pain.

"I can't, and I won't."

"I understand losing someone, Kaylan."

"Not this you don't. You couldn't. You weren't there, Nick. Only Sarah Beth would understand. And she's...she's not here anymore." Her green eyes darkened a shade.

"Kaylan, let me help you." He reached for her hand, but she jerked away.

"You can't help me."

"Kaylan."

"You don't get it. It's my fault! She would be here if it wasn't for me."

Her fault? She had mumbled that as they'd worked on her leg right after they'd found her, but he had figured she was tired and hallucinating. None of this could possibly be her fault. How could she think that?

He cupped her face, waiting for her to relax and meet his eyes. Hers reflected the storm, building and blowing, angry, confused.

"Listen to me. None of this is your fault."

She closed her eyes and shook her head, giving up her fight against him and resting her head on his chest. "You don't understand. Sarah Beth." Her voice held a hopeless cry. "It's my fault."

The thunder rolled, and Nick knew the storm was far from over. The quake had ended, but the aftershocks lingered, shaking the foundations of everything Kaylan knew or thought familiar. He wondered when she would move past it, if she ever would.

Where are You, Lord? I don't know how to help her. Help me be the man she can lean on. Help her to talk to me. Heal this.

The rain came again with a fury, sheets soaking them to the bone. He held her, shielding her with his body, powerless to stop the deluge.

Chapter Twenty-Six

NICK CHOMPED DOWN on gum and grit. The flavor had long since faded. He couldn't move. Micah was stationed on a rooftop across the street. The Marine platoon they were teamed with would come through any minute. So far, the night had been quiet.

A pebble danced in front of Nick as the ground rumbled and the convoy rolled into view. The long night of waiting and watching was over. Only one other vehicle had slipped through during the night, slowly, but that was to be expected in this bumpy pass.

Nick held his post. His legs and back twitched from lying on his stomach beneath the hide.

"Move, Hawk?"

"Hold until they roll through, and then we'll jump the convoy and head back into base with them."

"Copy." The radio fell silent. Nick peered through the scope. Dawn was right around the corner, and Nick strained to hear unnatural sounds in the early-morning stillness. This wasn't the way he liked to attack. SEALs worked at night, made the first move, and then slipped out while the bad guys tried to figure out what hit them.

A flash blinded him, and he jerked his head from the sniper scope as the lead vehicle in the convoy exploded. Men jumped and flew from the interior.

A disarray of cussing, yelling, and disbelief burst from his radio. He slammed his head into the scope scanning the area, sure he had left a bruise. How had they planted an IED? They had scanned the area all night, all during the operation.

"Bulldog?"

"Nothing. Man, there's no way. There's no way."

There was a way, and Nick's stomach lurched. He radioed to base as the area around them rattled with gunfire. Militants in tattered tan clothing emerged from the desert surroundings. An ambush. The truck in the night—it had to have dropped an IED. He smacked his gum, praying the flyboys would be here soon. They needed a fly over, stat.

He popped his gum and took aim, leveling three men in seconds. He felt nothing. His buddies were dying, and it was his fault. He should've paid more attention to the truck. Another explosion rocked his view with yellow and orange and smoke.

Nick woke in a cold sweat. He licked his lips and tasted salt. Sliding into a shirt, he stretched, careful not to wake Micah on the air mattress. Sleep would elude him the rest of the night, and sunrise wasn't far away. Maybe spending the morning with Kaylan would ease the dreams. His time with her was limited. His commanding officer had granted him and Micah personal leave for family reasons with the admonition that they could be called back at any time if their Support Activities team required immediate deployment. Either way, he would have to leave in a few days.

He tiptoed down the stairs and started the coffee, inhaling the scent of snickerdoodle. His dreams triggered a new awareness. He understood Kaylan, not just because he had lost both of his parents, but because she must see Sarah Beth the way he saw his dead buddies. He still wasn't sure what Kaylan meant when she said Sarah Beth's death was her fault, but if she felt the responsibility he had over those explosions, then he understood.

Nick understood the way of the warrior, how to face combat and loss and devastation. But Kaylan? She'd never had to face anything like this in her life. She hadn't signed up for war but had found one anyway. She'd never expected to lose her best friend, but it had happened. She'd held her as she died. He imagined holding Micah in his arms, bloody and bullet-ridden. Would he be able to recover? No. Kaylan was internalizing it, bottling it up, and he understood, at least in part—enough to help. She had become an unwilling soldier in a battle against nature, and she was losing.

The floor creaked, and Nick angled his body to the door. Micah leaned against the door frame, his hair sticking out at odd angles.

"Why didn't you tell me?"

"They'll pass."

"What do you see?"

"Those we lost. My screwups."

"You gotta let it go."

"It's not so much that I haven't let it go. I just relive it when I dream. One of these days they won't seep into my subconscious, but some of the images are still too real. Stuff like Haiti or a deployment makes 'em worse." He rubbed his eyes then met those of his sleepy best friend. "What're you thinking, Bulldog?"

"I'm thinking it's time we call a family powwow. Without Kaylan. It kills me. She's my baby sister, Hawk, but she won't talk to me." Micah blinked back tears. "If the family's okay with it, I want you to do whatever is necessary to help her. I don't relive things like you do. You may be able to help her better than any of us can."

"Of course. I'm not running this time. She won't get rid of me easily. We're just going to have to work it around training for this upcoming deployment."

The sunrise peeked through the window in the breakfast nook. Nick poured two cups of coffee and turned toward the sunroom. Kaylan would be up by now. It was odd she hadn't come for a cup of coffee.

"She's not in there, man."

Nick waved him off. "She doesn't miss a sunrise."

"She does since Haiti. She told me the colors don't look the same."

Nick walked to the sunroom, hoping to prove Micah wrong. The empty loveseat and end table devoid of Kaylan's Bible and journal stopped him short. Color broke over the tree line, and Nick knew the road ahead was long. The girl who had gone to Haiti over a month before hadn't returned whole.

He set down one of the mugs and looked around. The sunroom was Kaylan's favorite room in the house, and he felt close to who she had been here. It was where their relationship began to blossom again. He remembered their banter and quiet conversation in the early morning hours the week before she left for Haiti and he returned to work. They had discussed theology, Haiti, Sarah Beth, and Kaylan's family. They had talked about her internship and his military career. They had sat in stillness, watching the early reds and oranges spill over the dark lake. The scent of her lavender body spray and vanilla shampoo lingered. He ached to hold her, to return to the playfulness that characterized her in the few days before she'd left for Haiti.

A muscle jerked in his jaw as he took a sip of coffee. *Lord, I need Your help right now. This family just trusted me to help Kaylan get through this, and I can't let them down. I can't fail Kaylan.*

He would help her get back to normal, or at least find a new normal. Any other possibility was unthinkable.

Kaylan rubbed the sleep from her eyes at the top of the staircase. The morning light filtered through the blinds, and she turned away from its glare. Too bright. Voices drifted from below, and Kaylan moved toward the hushed tones.

Nick's voice traveled in the quiet house. "I think we may need to consider that Kaylan will never be back to normal..."

His voice faded and then her dad chimed in. "I know someone she can speak to at the hospital if necessary."

Kaylan froze. They were pawning her off to a shrink? She would never be normal again? Kaylan felt pain like she hadn't since Haiti, but this time it wasn't the pain of loss; it was the pain of betrayal. She needed their support, their help, their love, but they didn't understand.

Her feet carried her down the stairs without conscious thought, and she stood behind the couches until Nick noticed her. He paled, and the family grew silent, all eyes shifting to her. Anger boiled inside, ripping through her.

"Have you given up on me? Am I not worth helping?"

"Kaylan…"

"Save it, Nick. I don't want to hear it. I'm sorry that I'm messed up right now. I'm sorry that I'm not the happy, carefree daughter and sister who used to live here. I'm sorry that rubs off on you. But to pawn me off to a shrink, to say I'm 'abnormal,' it's not fair. How could you? You can't…" She swallowed back tears and her hands balled into fists. "You can't understand," she whispered, and her voice cracked.

"Sweetheart…"

"No, Mom."

She turned, intent on making a retreat to the stairs and back to the safety of her room.

"Kaylan." Nick caught her arm and whirled her around on the staircase landing. She wilted. No anger, no pain. Just numb. "Hear me out."

"Not now." She pushed against his chest as he tried to pull her close. Emotion fled. "I need you to be there for me, not collaborate with my family. I'm not crazy. I don't need a shrink. I just need my friend." She turned and dashed up the stairs. Slamming the door to her room, she slid down against it and hugged her knees. Alone in the dark, again. How would she ever move past this?

Chapter Twenty-Seven

THE LAP OF water against the dock soothed Kaylan's anger. She'd avoided her family for the last few hours, something she'd never felt the need to do before. The very fabric she had depended on her whole life was unraveling. Her family thought she needed to be fixed, Sarah Beth was gone, and Nick... Nick was collaborating with her family. The home she had returned to no longer felt like home. The ones who could help the most remained in Haiti.

She wrapped her arms around herself and rocked back and forth on the edge of the dock. What she wouldn't give to take the boat or Jet Ski out onto the lake, but everything was still winterized.

"Kaylan, can I speak with you?"

She whirled at Nick's slow steps and deep voice. Her foot slipped and she swung her arms, attempting to regain her balance.

"Kaylan." He dove for her and missed. Water enveloped her head, and the cold ripped through her body. Her leg twinged. Water wrapped around her, constricting her lungs, and she grew still. For a moment she wondered if this was how Sarah Beth felt as the ceiling rested on her chest and death encroached.

Another splash and bubbles surrounded her, the white foam lapping her hair. Strong arms locked around her waist, propelling her to the surface. Her head broke through, and she inhaled hard, recognizing an unfamiliar stinging in her lungs. Coughing consumed her. As air filled her lungs, the weight vanished.

"Why didn't you swim?" Nick's anger pushed hers to the surface.

"I was about to."

"No, you weren't. I had to jump in and get you. I thought you hit your head or something. But you were just content to stay down there. Why, Kaylan?" He yelled, and the sound brought her family from the house and onto the back porch.

"I don't know, okay? You wouldn't get it. Leave me alone, Nick." Her teeth chattered. She shoved away from him and swam to the ladder, pulling herself out of the water. The cold air seeped through her wet clothes, and chills racked her body.

Micah ran onto the dock with two towels. What she really wanted was a hot shower and her sweats. The chill set into her bones, into her soul.

"What happened, sis?"

"Nick startled me, and I fell in."

"Still doesn't explain why you didn't come up." Nick's voice remained checked, but his eyes roared with fire.

"What?" Micah looked from Kaylan to Nick and back again. "What's he talking about? Did you hit something? Why didn't you just swim?"

She grew tired of their questions. She didn't need to be pampered, her every action or emotional nuance questioned. "Look here, you two, back off. You"—she pointed at Micah—"why would you go behind my back? Does the whole family think I'm crazy or beyond repair? I don't want to talk to a shrink. Don't you get it? I lost someone I loved like family. I need my family to love me, to support me, even when I push you away or you don't get it. You can't put a Band-Aid on this, Micah." Her voice rose, but she no longer cared.

"And you." She pointed at Nick. "You talk a big game, but when it comes down to it, you jump in with my family to ship me off to someone else. I need to trust you, Nick. I need you to hold me, walk me through this, and realize that you can't even begin to understand the things in my head that I can't unsee. You couldn't possibly..."

"Kaylan," Nick cut her off. "You missed the majority of that conversation. Going to see a counselor was only an idea thrown out there if you wanted it. I get that you don't want to talk to anyone right now. But eventually, you might. And there are great trauma counselors who know how to walk you through healing from this."

Micah joined in. "Sis, we care too much about you to force you to do anything. We are here 100 percent, but you have to let us in. You're right. We don't understand it all."

"But we want to," Nick finished for Micah. "Please. Talk to us." He stepped forward to hug her, but she sidestepped him.

"You don't get it. You couldn't. God doesn't care about me, Nick. He doesn't listen when I pray."

"Kaylan, He never left you. He saved your life. Don't forget that. He allowed you to live."

"He left when Sarah Beth left. Why did He save me and not my friends, these sweet, innocent people I worked with? He saved me, and He saved Eliezer, but Sarah Beth died? I prayed all night. I begged. He doesn't care."

"Who's Eliezer?"

Her heart raced. They couldn't know about him. No, not now. She backed away from them. "It doesn't matter. If the Lord's in control, He chose to let my best friend die. A good, kind, innocent person who followed Him wholeheartedly."

"Kayles...."

Her teeth chattered, and her body convulsed with shivers. "I can't talk about it. I just can't. Not yet. I don't..." Stabbing pain replaced the anger. "Please, I'm sorry."

She slipped past them and ran to the house. They were trying, but to let them in completely would mean to relive it. She already relived it in her dreams. She knew she was putting them in a hard place, but she couldn't stop it. She wasn't herself. She could see that, understood it, but she couldn't regress back to her old self no matter how hard she tried to forget. Images from Haiti flashed in her head, devoid of color, dusty. Some things could not be explained in words. Some things should never have to be.

Chapter Twenty-Eight

KAYLAN JOINED THE family for lunch, thankful no one brought up the events of that morning. Instead, conversation stayed on a safe topic: the upcoming Super Bowl between the New Orleans Saints and the Indianapolis Colts. In a house full of boys, football debates could carry on all afternoon.

When the conversation finally hit a lull, Seth turned to her. "Ready to get in a light workout? You need to rebuild those muscles."

She nodded reluctantly. The doctor had recommended that she try to return to some level of normalcy. Since she couldn't do a full workout because of her leg, Seth recommended working on her core and arms with his weight set.

Half an hour later she sat in the garage-turned-weight-room, sweat dripping from her forehead. She was thankful for the brisk air, or this task would be impossible. She didn't know how Seth had worked out in here all through high school.

"One more rep, sis. We have to make sure you can throw and catch that football so we can whip David and Micah in those family games." Trying to cheer her up as she worked out, Seth kept up a steady stream of blonde jokes, but she had yet to crack a smile.

Kaylan gritted her teeth and focused her energy on getting stronger instead of hitting her baby brother. Inch by inch she came closer to her goal. Truthfully, she welcomed the pain. Her body still hurt from the quake. Every step kept her focused on her physical recovery. The battle raging inside seemed impossible to cure, but maybe she could at least regain her physical strength and stamina.

"Uh, sis, you may be pushing too hard now."

"I can do this."

"I don't doubt that you can, but I don't think you should."

"Are you going to help me or not?" she snapped, and it caught her by surprise. His wounded face mirrored her own.

"Seth…" She wiped her face and then threw down the towel. "I'm done for the day. Thanks." She pushed off Seth's workout bench and grabbed her crutches.

"Kayles?"

Seth's shoulders sagged as he met her eyes. She wished she could comfort, but there were no words.

"What can I do? How can I help you? I want to make it better." His voice cracked, and he cleared his throat.

"Nothing, Seth. I don't think anything can fix this. It's too big and too awful. I'm sorry. I just…need time and a break, a way to forget it all." She left the garage and quietly pulled the door closed behind her. *But how do you forget something like this?* She squeezed her eyes shut, but tears still refused to fall.

Nick hurt for Seth. He'd heard the last bit of Kaylan's and Seth's conversation and slipped from view as she hobbled from the garage. It was time to treat her to a relaxing night—no rehab, no recovery, no questions. Just light and fun.

Nick hurried to intercept Kaylan. On her, sweat looked good, but he didn't figure she would appreciate the comment at the moment.

"Hey, beautiful, feel good to work out?"

She turned, not quite meeting his eyes. He missed the way her eyes lit up like she had a secret she wanted to share with the whole world. Now they were shadowed, a shade darker, like winter had crept in to overshadow the summer green.

"Seth's trying. I'm trying. It hurts."

"It's a slow process. Keep going. You'll be healthy and walking normally in no time." But no matter how quick the recovery, her leg would always bear a scar, a painful reminder. Nick bore a few of his own. Not all were external.

"That's what everyone keeps telling me." Her attempt at a smile broke his heart.

He closed the distance between them and slipped his hands around her waist, taking her weight. The crutches hit the walls as she gripped his arms. He leaned his forehead against hers and waited until she relaxed.

"Want to go on a date with me tonight?"

"Nick."

"You and me, and maybe your brothers if they decide to crash."

"Nick."

"C'mon. You need a night to relax and be with people who love you and want to spend time with you. Laughter cures the pain of any heartache. Or so I'm told."

He didn't bother to tell her that he would need to leave in the next couple of days. He tugged her closer, intentionally working to pull down the walls she had built. Walls never healed the pain; they gave it a place to fester and grow unchecked.

"We won't have to leave your house. Dinner and a movie. I'll even ask David to cook, so you have something decent to eat."

She shook against him.

"Was that a laugh?"

"Don't tell Seth. He'll be jealous."

"I think he already is."

"Why?"

"I'm stealing the sister he adores, and he's not sure I'm worthy."

The silence lingered. She looked...haunted. He had to work harder. Every day she gave in to her memories. They shaped her reality, one that would always be half empty, absent a friend who thrived in daily memory.

"In your defense, you're still here."

He kissed her forehead and swallowed back his growing frustration. Once again his job would pull him away from her when she needed him. Where was the balance?

"Dinner, movie. Tonight. On me."

The flat screen over the fireplace in the Richards's cozy living room came alive with fish and crabs. Kaylan enjoyed the story of *Finding Nemo*. The ocean reminded her of Nick, and it seemed appropriate that she sat wrapped in his arms on the couch. Unable to escape the chill, she bundled up in sweat pants, her Alabama sweatshirt, and a blanket.

She envied Dory. The lighthearted blue fish had the ability to forget. Kaylan wished she could forget…forget the earthquake, forget Sarah Beth's broken body, forget the endless dark hours and the cold that had crept into her life since Sarah Beth had left. She snuggled closer to Nick.

She also related to Marlin, the clown fish whose son is lost. Fleeing from sharks, jelly fish, and swimming across a vast ocean, he was a small fish in a big pond, desperate to reunite with the one thing he loved most, his son, Nemo. If she could cross the ocean and find the best friend she loved and lost, she would jump the first plane, swim if she had to. If only it were that simple. If only Sarah Beth were lost, kidnapped, or just in a hospital somewhere. But she had left the planet. Kaylan could fly to Haiti a thousand times, but nothing would change. Only a dusty grave awaited her.

The fire roared and popped. Sharks appeared on screen, larger than life, and despite their best intentions, the biggest shark was determined to devour Marlin and Dory. Music blared and speakers rattled. Kaylan bolted upright and jumped from the couch as Nick's cell phone vibrated on the end table. The room shook and pulsated. Kaylan grabbed her head. It was happening again. She had to leave.

"Kaylan?"

Not even the sound of Nick's voice could hold her in place. The room could collapse any second, and she would not be trapped again. Never again.

"Run!"

She tore through the room, ripped open the front door, and ran onto the open driveway. As soon as she was clear of the house, she crouched and covered her head, no longer able to discern anything but the shaking of her own body and the pounding of her heart and head. Without her bidding, Haiti flooded her mind, consuming the driveway, the house, and Nick's strong voice calling her name. Alabama once again grew distant.

"Kaylan. Kaylan!" Nick shook her. She moaned but didn't open her eyes. "Kaylan, look at me. What happened?"

"Not again, please, not another one."

He sat down on the driveway and pulled her into his lap. She came willingly, curling into a ball. He wished he could wrap her in a bubble and shield her.

"Everything started shaking. I can't do it again, Nick, I can't."

He groaned and held her head against his chest. "I'm so sorry. I didn't think." He kissed her forehead and continued to hold her. He should have turned the surround sound off. The room had rattled, and even the slightest vibrations set her on edge. The phone vibrating on the table hadn't helped either. Flashbacks came at the oddest times, and he would need to warn the family of what to expect.

Chapter Twenty-Nine

ISS RICHARDS, THIS is Mary Ann Adams from the San Diego Dietetics Program. I understand you are going through a bit of a rough patch, but I am calling to encourage you to turn in the rest of your application by the due date in a few weeks. My recommendation letter for you is through, and you have unofficially been accepted to the program because of your college project and grades. Miss Richards, I need to stress to you the importance of this program for your future. If you fail to submit the material, I will be powerless to help you succeed in this field. Think about it, and let me know what you decide."

The message ended. Kaylan clicked off her cell phone and rolled over in her bed, the room still in shadows. The sun hung in the sky, a new workweek had begun, but she had been unable to rouse for a sunrise. She didn't want to do much of anything lately. Unable to face the Tuckers because of what happened at the memorial service on Friday, she had begged off from attending church yesterday, and instead she had stayed home with Nick for company, watching reruns of *I Love Lucy.*

She curled around her pillow and thought of the message. How distant college and graduation felt. Only a month before, she had left for Haiti, and that decision had ended one life and radically altered another. She had returned to a different life, one lacking. The internship seemed unimportant now. Everything seemed less important. She didn't care to make a decision. At the moment, she never wanted to leave her room, let alone go to California.

A loud tap sounded on the door, and Kaylan jumped. Would she ever grow accustomed to loud, sudden noises again?

"Come in."

Pap stuck his silver head through the door. "Sugar, it's dark in here. Time to rise and shine, my morning glory."

"I'm not ready to get up yet, Pap."

"Well, I'm not asking. Get up, get dressed. We're going for a ride."

"A ride?"

"Let's go see that horse of yours. She's starting to feel neglected."

Kaylan sat up on the bed. Her mind zipped back to the dark rubble of Rhonda's house. She was supposed to take this ride with Sarah Beth. They had promised each other, before... She shook her head hard, her hair stinging as it slapped her cheeks. "I'm not going, Pap. Not today."

"Now, Sugar, I want to spend the morning with you, and you need to get out of this house. You have two options: get up on your own, or I'll call Nick or your brothers to haul you out of this room and put you in the car in your pajamas. Now, what's it gonna be?" He threw open the blinds on the window, causing Kaylan to wince—too much light. Pap had morphed back into the famous Alabama state judge. He had just banged the gavel, giving her an ultimatum. He meant business.

"Yes, sir."

"Lover boy's coming with us, just so you know. I need some help getting around these days, and I don't figure an old man on a cane and a gimpy young lady, however pretty, should be hobbling around together alone without a strapping young man to help out."

"Pap..."

"No complaints. Get dressed, and be down at the truck in twenty minutes." The door closed with finality behind him.

Shivering, she crawled out of bed and walked to the window, squinting in the light. Her room had become a cave, her hiding place. She closed the blinds, returning the room to its dim state. Peering into the mirror, she started. She didn't recognize the woman before her—skinny, her eyes dark and dull, her hair limp and unkept. The woman before her was a skeleton of the girl who had gone to Haiti. She wondered if she would ever see that woman again.

Her breath hovered in the crisp, chilly air. Kaylan pulled the sleeves of her sweatshirt down over her arms. Nick leaned against Pap's truck, studying her, much as he had the day he'd arrived. Leaning into his hug, she felt safe, if only for a moment.

"Morning, beautiful. How'd you sleep?"

"Okay." The dreams had flirted around the corners of her subconscious, her twisted sheets evidence of a fitful night. "Pap made me get up."

"It's almost time for lunch. I hear you never sleep this late."

"I didn't used to."

"You'll find your sea legs again. You ready to see Black-Eyed Pea?"

The silence stretched. Did she tell him that Sarah Beth was supposed to be here for this? That they had planned it under the ceiling of Rhonda's house in Sarah Beth's last moments? The ride would be absent one bubbly blonde.

"We were…" She cleared her throat and tried again. His patience amazed her. "We were supposed to ride together when we got back. Sarah Beth and I. She wanted to lie out in the sun, eat a greasy hamburger, and go riding with me through the woods."

His arm tightened around her waist, and she rubbed her face against the wool lining of his jacket, finding comfort in the contact. He handed her his cup of coffee, and she took a sip. The liquid warmed her from the inside out.

"She would want you to enjoy the ride this morning and remember her as she always was—smiling."

"She liked you, you know. Called you my knight in shining

armor. I was the damsel in distress. She couldn't have known how true her words were."

He tipped her chin up, and she once again met eyes that reminded her of the ocean in a fog. A storm brewed there, churning and ready to break.

"You were rescuing others long before I arrived to rescue you." The intensity in his eyes made her catch her breath. "You are the real hero, Kayles. Beautiful and brilliant and brave."

"I'm not any of those things. I'm a royal mess, Nick. Broken beyond repair."

His voice was low and husky, warming the frigid, aching places of her heart. "Never beyond repair, Kayles. We serve a God who heals what is broken and mends our sorrows."

His gaze brushed over her lips, and she pulled back, heart racing and dread crowding out the breathless feeling of moments before. She couldn't deal with this right now. What right did she have to be happy when Sarah Beth was gone? She tore her gaze from the hurt buried in his eyes and climbed into the truck.

Nick left to fetch Pap. After all three of them were crowded into the pickup cab, Nick started up the truck, then filled the tense silence by humming along to the country songs on the radio.

After parking outside the barn, Nick helped Pap out of the car. Watching Pap's slow movements, Kaylan felt another twinge of bitterness. God had already taken Sarah Beth, and her strong Pap was weaker because of a stroke God had allowed. What next?

Pap leaned on his cane, and Kaylan trudged beside him into the barn, where she inhaled the familiar smell of hay, earth, and warm bodies. Horses snorted and shifted in the stables. The clack of hoofs on the wooden floor welcomed Kaylan, and a sharp pain of longing for days gone by shot through her. Black-Eyed Pea nodded her head in the stable, standing strong, quiet, confident, steady. The sight of her favorite horse was a taste of normal, but the taste was bittersweet without Sarah Beth.

Nick paused at the door, and Kaylan wouldn't meet his eyes. The moments stretched, the awkward silence creating a barrier between them. Always the gentleman, Nick bowed out of the silent standoff. "I'm going to take a walk."

Pap wrapped his good arm around Kaylan's shoulders. "All right, son. Come back when you're ready. I don't think we'll be doing much riding today."

Nick nodded and left. Pap's eyes found Kaylan's. "Now, what did you do to that boy before I got out to the truck?"

"Nothing, Pap."

She felt a lecture building in Pap's gut and braced for it.

"Sugar, I won't pretend to understand what happened in Haiti. I won't pretend I understand what it feels like to lose a friend as close as Sarah Beth. But, Sugar, depression and bitterness don't solve anything."

Some part of Kaylan fluttered to life at the mention of Sarah Beth's name.

"She was supposed to be here today, Pap." She grabbed a brush, slipped into the stall, and began to brush her horse.

"Lots of memories of the two of you in here. Do you remember when Sarah Beth almost slipped off her mount because she wanted to hold her hands in the air like she was on a roller coaster?" He chuckled. "I don't think she ever let go of the saddle horn again after that."

"I don't want to talk about her, Pap. It hurts too much."

"Well, then you can just listen, because I want to talk about her. You aren't the only one here who needs to heal. I loved that little girl like another granddaughter. I remember the first time she spent the night with you. Gran and I were out at the lake house. The boys were playing basketball in the driveway. She walked right in the house and said, 'Hi, my name is Sarah Beth Tucker Richards, because Kaylan and I are best friends. I figure that makes me part of the family now.'

"We were all so shocked that we just laughed. Spunky and beautiful, that was Sarah Beth. She was your sister, you know, in every way." He hobbled into the stable and grabbed another brush.

"Pap, can you please stop?" She remembered every detail of that night. They had stayed up late, watching Disney movies, and the next morning her mom had made them her famous Mickey Mouse pancakes.

"Remember when I taught the two of you to ride?"

"I said I don't want to talk about it," she snapped, then immediately recoiled. She never snapped at Pap. It was as though a snake had risen, untwisting from her gut, and struck, spitting poison at anyone in the vicinity. She felt it curl back, preparing to strike again.

"Now, look here, young lady. We love you. That young man loves you, or he wouldn't stick around. We miss Sarah Beth too." He leveled his finger at her nose, and she drew back, the cobra within hissing an angry warning. "But if you don't let us in, if you don't talk about it or let the Lord heal this hurt, it's going to fester like the ugliest sore. You deal with it now, before it eats you alive." He patted her cheek. "I'm here when you're ready to talk."

Never had she been so angry. He didn't understand. This couldn't be fixed, and God didn't care. How could He? Poison bubbled in her stomach. She leaned her head on Black-Eyed Pea and felt a single tear trickle down her cheek for the first time since Sarah Beth's death, leaving a scorching trail in its wake.

Chapter Thirty

NICK WAS JEALOUS of a horse. It could share in her tears while she held Nick at arm's length, fearful to let him close, hesitant to feel happy. He had watched Kaylan from the barn doorway as the tears finally fell, silent and steady. He'd watched her in the rearview mirror all the way back to the house, her face fallen and eyes red. And he'd followed her into the house and watched as she climbed the stairs and quietly shut her door. Yet he could do nothing.

He was a SEAL, trained to recognize the faintest nuance. He had patience to wait out an assailant, to act when necessary and at the opportune time, never to leave a man behind, but this woman had him completely stumped. A horse, really?

He wandered into the kitchen and fixed himself a sandwich for lunch. It was time for answers, time to understand what had happened. How could he help her cope with this? In a mission, if one of his brothers were injured or killed, or if he took someone's life to defend one of his own, there was no other option except to push forward. Misplaced emotion meant dead frogmen, and he couldn't live with that. It was kill or be killed—kill them, or allow them to kill Americans, and that was purely unacceptable. Adrenaline pulsed through him at the very thought.

But Kaylan wasn't accustomed to pushing through. Her sister had fallen, and the Lord had allowed it. Nick had long ago ceased to ask God why things happened. He still wondered, still grew angry, but he had learned that the Lord was good in spite of his circumstances. Kaylan needed to see the Lord as her stronghold. But how could he help her see that?

The phone vibrated in his pocket. He picked up and recognized Senior Chief's voice on the line. "Carmichael, you and Richards get your butts back here and help your team get ready to go. We are outward bound and need all hands on deck."

It was time to deploy. To where and for what were unknowns, but Nick and Micah had to help plan portions of the mission. That meant leaving Kaylan now, when everything was uncertain, when she needed him, and when he had promised her family he would stick around as long as he could.

"Yes, sir. We'll make the arrangements." Nick ended the call and sighed.

Now what, Lord?

Kaylan had crept into his heart. He no longer wondered if he was supposed to be in her life but how they could merge their lives into one. He wanted to protect her, fix everything for her. She leaned on him, counted on him to be there. It was only a matter of time before she actually talked to him about what had happened, but his departure would cut that progress short. It looked as though Seth would have to take over, after all.

Nick found Micah using Seth's weight set in the garage. Seth stood nearby, spotting him.

"Hey, Seth, can I have a minute with Micah?"

"Sure." He made sure Micah settled the bar and then left the room.

"Recall?"

"Tomorrow morning. Our flight leaves at nine."

"Where to?"

"No idea. We'll find out when we report."

"All right, I'll tell the fam and pack up."

Nick paced the room. He was picking up Micah's bad habits. He searched his pockets for a piece of gum and came up empty. "What am I going to tell Kaylan?"

Micah stilled on the bench.

"How do I leave when she needs me? She's going to think it's like last time."

"You don't have much choice, man. She'll just have to understand."

"Do you really think she will, right now? I mean, c'mon. Sarah Beth is gone. She comes home counting on us, even if she holds us at arm's length, and now you and I are bailing on her when she needs us."

Micah's jaw clenched, and Nick could tell his temper was rising—whether at Nick or at himself, Nick wasn't sure. He stood his ground.

"What do you want us to do, huh? We're doing our job."

"Look, Bulldog, chill out. I need your advice. How do I explain?"

"Figure it out. But I'll tell you this…" Micah stood toe to toe with Nick, and Nick recognized Micah's anger as fear. He didn't want to leave his sister and was worried about how it would affect her. "If you hurt her or make her for a second think that you're leaving and aren't coming back, I swear, we will have big problems."

Nick took a step back, his own temper rising at Micah's irrational mood swing. "I'm coming back. She'll know that. I'm just not sure that's how she'll see it right now."

"Well, you'd better make it clear that you aren't abandoning her, Hawk."

"I got it, Bulldog. Loud and clear."

"Who are you abandoning?" Both turned to find Kaylan at the door, Seth right behind her. "What's going on?"

"We can talk about it later, Kayles."

"No, I want to talk now."

Nick nodded. "Let's go out to the lake, then."

"Micah?"

"It's okay, Kayles. Just go talk to him." She looked between them for a minute before turning on her crutches.

Nick led her from the room. "What's going on, Nick? What's wrong? Micah looked mad."

He remained silent and prayed the whole way out to the water and as they settled in deck chairs. He fought the urge to pace. Sunshine warmed his face despite the wind chill. The water moved in the gentle breeze and reflected the sunlight. It should have refreshed him; being by the water usually did. Yet this time was different. He already felt the separation, and this wasn't how he wanted to tell her.

"Nick, please, I can't handle any more bad news."

"Kaylan, when you went to Haiti, I told you I would wait for you," he began. The fear in her eyes made it difficult to continue. He grasped her hand, intertwining their fingers. "I came to get you. I stayed with you. But my boss called this afternoon, and he needs my help. I have to go. Micah and I leave tomorrow morning."

Kaylan's eyes went wild. "You're leaving me? You can't. You promised you wouldn't. I need you. I can't do this alone."

In that moment Nick wondered if he had missed the mark completely. He wanted to rescue her, to wrap her in his arms and never let go, never let the world touch her. He had wanted to be her savior. He had attempted to fill shoes that were impossible to fill. It was time for him to go, to pray for her from afar, to do the job the Lord had called him to do, and allow the Lord to be her healer.

"Kayles, listen to me." He gripped her hands and leaned forward, meeting her eyes. "Don't for one second think I'm leaving you permanently. I'm going to do my job, and then I'll be back as soon as I can."

"You can't leave me. You can't!"

He stood and pulled her into his arms as she fought with all her strength. How would he get them through this?

"You're doing it again. I need you. Don't you get that? How can you?"

"It's my job, Kaylan. I thought you understood. I thought we'd moved past this."

"Why now?" She continued to push against him until he released her and grabbed her arms. "Let go."

"No, I won't let go. I want to be with you. Without a doubt. I won't let go, Kaylan. You are too important. Do you hear me?" He shook her, and she stilled. "You are what I want, Kayles. More than the SEALs, more than my search for my parents. You, Kayles." His eyes misted.

He rested his forehead on hers and wished he could kiss her. All that was in his heart poured out, his voice a husky whisper, and she unwillingly leaned into him like a magnet that couldn't ignore the pull to its counterpart. "But I need to go. I have a duty, and more than anything, you need to turn back to the God who can heal. I can't be your savior, Kayles. But I would give anything in my life to fix this."

She froze and shoved hard, stumbling as he released her in shock. The tears that had pooled in her eyes solidified. She gritted her teeth.

"You can't fix it, and clearly God doesn't want to. I lived. Eliezer lived. Sarah Beth died. It's not fair. Go, Nick. I don't want you here. Go!" She turned and ran back into the house.

Nick turned to study the water. He was out of his element. There was something else going on, something deeper. He couldn't leave things like this. Who was Eliezer? What else had happened in Haiti to turn Kaylan from depressed to bitter? He dug out his phone. He would find out now, today, before he left. Then he would talk to Kaylan again.

Scrolling through his list of contacts, he located the number for Rhonda's clinic. He tapped the number on the screen, praying the phone line had been restored. To his astonishment, he was rewarded with the sound of a distant phone ringing.

Rhonda picked up. "Hope Clinic." She sounded tired, harassed. Nick could only imagine what she had lived through—continued to live through—since the earthquake a few weeks before.

"Rhonda, I know you're busy. Is Abe there? It's urgent." After a minute Abraham's tenor voice greeted Nick, and Nick quickly explained the reason for his call.

Abraham's thick accent rang in his ear. "Nick, I am sorry, but I cannot tell you what is wrong. You must talk to Kaylan about what happened."

Nick groaned in frustration at Abraham's suggestion. With his imminent departure, he had to speed up collecting information. The only way he knew how was to talk to those who had survived the earthquake with Kaylan.

"Abe, she won't talk. She doesn't laugh. She doesn't cry. And who's Eliezer? What happened with him? When she says his name she looks…"

"Frightened?"

"Yeah. What reason would she have to be frightened?" Kaylan was probably in her room. He turned to look up at her window from where he stood in the driveway. Wind gently whistled through the trees and sent a shiver down his spine.

"Eliezer is the local voodoo priest, very rooted in the old ways. He detests believers and Americans and did not like Kaylan and Sarah Beth sharing Jesus. He got angry. Blamed her and our God for the earthquake and for Sarah Beth dying." He tapered off, and Nick gripped the phone, straining to hear over the static. "I never thought she would believe him, but she has, has she not? That is why you are calling."

Nick closed his eyes. "Yes, Abe. I think she believed him."

"Nick, my people have experienced much heartache. This is bad, but we will overcome. All is not lost. People are broken and beaten, but people are coming to church, asking to know more of God. Stories pour in daily of those saved under the rubble. We are knocked down and shaken, but not defeated. We have hope. Please, tell Kaylan."

"I'll tell her. Pray it breaks through. I'm not sure she'll believe me unless she sees it for herself."

"Then let her see it. Let her help. Let her heal. She worked after the earthquake to save people. Maybe she should again. She has the heart of a warrior, the desire to deny herself and help others. You removed her from the only place she could fight how she felt. Tell her, Nick. Help her see she still has purpose. She lives. She is strong. There is still hope."

"Thank you, Abe. I'm praying for you. Maybe I can talk Kaylan into going back to help in a few months."

"All in good time, my friend."

Nick hung up the phone, feeling the strangest mixture of hope and despair, like water and oil attempting to mix. They churned in his heart. He understood...but he didn't. How could he encourage Kaylan to go back to the place where her world was shattered? Even if he could talk her into it, should he?

I know You never left her, Lord, but this seems pretty hopeless. You'll have to make this very clear, because I won't encourage her to go unless You tell me to.

Chapter Thirty-One

YOUNG MAN, YOU look like you are carrying the weight of the world." Nick whirled, frustrated he hadn't heard Pap enter. After a subdued family dinner, Kaylan had gone on a walk with Micah, and Nick had retreated to the sunroom to think and pray. The sun had set, and the room rested in murky, black shadows.

"Just a lot to think about, sir."

"I imagine. Micah told me you are leaving tomorrow." Pap lowered himself to the couch and patted the seat next to him. Nick sank into the cushions on the wicker furniture, feeling more exhausted than he had in a long time.

"You know, David whittled this for me." Pap extended his cane for Nick to see. "Look at the intricate knife-work, the detail and precision. It was a labor of love. But you know, each detail took time and effort." Pap rubbed his hands over the smooth wood. "This used to be an ugly, disproportionate piece of wood. It was uprooted and knocked off its parent tree. David took it, invested in it, and made it something beautiful. A treasure. One-of-a-kind."

"I don't have time. I've run out."

"Takes time to fashion something beautiful out of what has been broken. And it's not ultimately your job. The only One who can heal and refashion something this beautiful is the Creator."

"I just want to fix it and make it better. I want to be here for her. I made a promise." He raked his hair in frustration. "I'm letting her down. I can't fight this." Pap rapped Nick's shin with the cane, causing it to sting. "What was that for?"

"Come on, son. Have you told her yet?"

"Told her what?"

"Told her you love her? That you want to be with her?"

"I can't tell her that yet. Not when she's like this."

"Talk to her again. Reassure her, and then go do your job. She isn't thinking straight. Let her run to the only One who can fix what is broken. He knows her better than you, and He understands. You see, He was with her in the earthquake, even though she thinks He has forgotten her." Pap's eyes bore into Nick's, a silent challenge lurking in their depths. "And right now, she doesn't need you to play God."

The words stung. He could be her knight in shining armor, but only when she knew the King had her best interest at heart. The best thing he could do for her was leave. There was a distinct possibility that it would break his heart, and...

"What if she doesn't forgive me?"

"Well, that's not in your control, either. Son, do you believe that the God who created you, got you through SEAL training and a deployment, and brought Kaylan into your life is capable of getting you two together at the right time? He's a big God. Why did He allow the earthquake? Why did He allow Sarah Beth to die? Why is Haiti in shambles, without the means to recover fully? I don't know, but I do know the reports I've heard of people coming to the Lord, of others coming together and giving. Big things are happening in the wake of a big disaster. I won't pretend to understand why God allowed it to happen. But this God who is big enough to move the earth and unite cultures is big enough to heal Kaylan and heal you."

Nick squirmed like a fish caught on a hook. Had he limited God to his own capabilities? He hadn't trusted the Lord in this situation. He had prayed for wisdom, for the Lord to work through him, for Kaylan to heal, but he hadn't prayed that the Lord would have His way.

"I see you have more to think about. Gran and I are leaving. Be careful, son. We'll be praying. Pray for Kaylan, and leave her in the capable hands of the God who has her wrapped in His arms, even though she can't feel Him right now."

Nick stood and shook Pap's hand, loving the man. "Thank you, sir. Thank you for the family you invest in."

"You're as good as family." He hobbled to the door and paused. "Son, have you looked into your birth parents anymore?"

The question caught Nick off guard. "No, sir. We've been training, and then everything happened with Kaylan. It's on the back burner until all this is resolved."

"I have a lot of connections. People in powerful places with access to records. I may be able to help when you're ready."

Red flags waved in Nick's mind at the way Pap studied him. He knew something he wasn't saying. "I'll take you up on that. Thank you."

Nick turned back to the windows and the blackness permeating outside. He opened the door and walked down onto the dock. The late January night chilled him. Outside the city lights, a few stars blinked. Nick loved the night. It was his time to thrive as a frogman. Nights in the desert on a mission had left him gazing at the stars.

"Lord, Your Word says You know each star by name, which means You see Kaylan and me and the people of Haiti. Please, Father, do big things here. Give me the courage to let go and trust that if this is right, You'll bring us back together at the right time."

In his weariness, he felt a measure of peace. The knots in his heart released, and he walked back to the house to pack and get ready for bed. He needed to sleep, or he would be worthless on the upcoming mission. Hopefully he would have one last chance to talk to Kaylan before he left. Meanwhile, he released the happenings in Alabama into the hands of a good God.

Screaming pierced the dark, and Nick slapped the night stand for his gun before he realized where he was. Micah crouched low on the floor as another cry sounded and a door slammed.

"Kaylan," they said together. She had come back from her walk with Micah in a relatively peaceful mood but quickly retreated to her room for the night, exhaustion and depression still constant enemies. Apparently her body's need to sleep was no match for the nightmares.

Nick hit the floor at a dead sprint with Micah on his heels and slid in front of Kaylan's door. The sound of crying and glass breaking continued for seconds before all fell still.

"Go slow, Bulldog. We don't need to startle her anymore."

Micah pushed the door open and hit the lights. The lamp lay on the floor along with a broken picture frame.

"Kayles? Where are you?"

"Sis?"

"Hide! You have to hide. It's happening again."

Nick crept to the closet in his bare feet, careful to avoid the glass. The sight broke his heart. Kaylan sat curled in a fetal position in the corner of her closet, clothes hanging around her head. She rocked back and forth, tears streaming down her face.

"Bulldog, go get your mom."

David and Seth tore into the room and stopped to survey the damage. Nick studied the flickering emotions playing on their faces in rapid fire succession. Shock. Pain. Grim acceptance. Helplessness. They needed to feel useful.

"David, can you get something to clean up the glass? Seth, we may be up for a bit. Can you start some coffee?"

They both nodded and ran from the room.

Nick crept into the closet slowly and folded himself into the corner with Kaylan.

"Sarah Beth?"

"Kaylan, honey, you gotta wake up. Sarah Beth's not here."

"Hold my hand. She wanted me to hold her hand."

Nick linked their fingers. They were cold and trembling.

"She was so cold. I'm cold now. She...she was twisted. It kept shaking. Wouldn't stop shaking. Why won't it stop? Everyone screamed and wailed. People, so many people. Blood, dust. I couldn't breathe. No fresh air. We told stories. She coughed up blood. I couldn't move the rock. No matter what I tried. I couldn't stand, only crawl. I didn't want to leave her. Why does everything keep shaking? Sarah Beth?"

"Kaylan, she's not here. Are you awake? Let's get you out of this closet."

She panicked and clutched at his bare chest. "No, everything will fall out there. We can't leave. We're safe in here. We can't leave." Her voice rose, and Nick feared she would start screaming, her mind trapped in the earthquake.

Her parents came into view, along with Micah. Nick tried to stand, but Kaylan clung to him, her strength flowing from a place of panic.

"Don't leave me. You have to hold my hand. I don't want to die. You have to hold my hand. It's not safe."

Her words pierced him like machine gun fire. She wasn't just frightened of the shaking or reliving the deaths of her friends and countless others. She saw herself dead. His stomach churned. Her knuckles were white in his. With his new understanding, his priority shifted. He needed her to wake up and snap out of this flashback. There was only one way to do that.

"Mrs. Richards, can you go turn on the shower? Make it as hot as you can get it without burning her. Micah and Mr. Richards, can you move anything that might break or be in the way? I'm going to have to carry her out of here, and she may fight me the whole way."

Kaylan whimpered now: "All my fault, all my fault."

He pulled her close and felt a tear slip down his chest. "Baby, we're gonna get you past this. But I need you to come back to me. Wake up." He avoided shaking her and instead kissed the top of her head.

"They didn't get to us in time. Rock kept shifting. The ceiling was too close. They tried. I tried. Sarah Beth was white. Her body. Oh, God, she was so hurt. I didn't have any medicine. I couldn't stop it. I couldn't save her. Why didn't God save her? She was so good. She braided Sophia's hair and played soccer with Reuben. She loved the women." Her voice cracked, and a tear splashed onto his hand. She was crying. Finally, she was crying. "Why? Sarah Beth...why not me?"

"Nick, the water's ready."

"Mrs. Richards, I'm going to need your help. Is everything moved?"

"Yeah, Hawk, you're good to go," Micah answered for his mom.

Nick gritted his teeth. He wasn't sure how she would handle this, but he had to do it. In one quick movement, he was up. Flinging her arm over his shoulder, he lifted her from the ground. As soon as he exited the closet, she began to kick and shout. She closed her eyes against the light.

"Put me down. It's not safe. It's not safe. I won't leave her. Sarah Beth! Take me back."

Nick walked into the bathroom and stepped into the large, open shower with Kaylan as Mrs. Richards held the glass door. Kaylan's eyes flew open as water hit her face. She shivered, and tears intermixed with the water. Steam rose around them.

"Kayles, are you awake?" He cupped her face with his hands, studying her eyes as they struggled to process her surroundings.

"Nick." She covered his hands with her own and glanced around the shower and then at her mom through the open door. "Mom."

"Honey, it was just a bad dream. I'm so sorry."

Kaylan's eyes flew back to Nick's. "It was so awful, Nick. I was there, and I could hear you, but I couldn't leave. It was like I was stuck in that building with Sarah Beth." Her eyes pooled. He thanked the Lord that she was awake and coherent. "I'm so sorry. I hate that you're seeing me like this. I'm so sorry." He hugged her, accepted the towel from Mrs. Richards, and slipped through the glass doors.

"Ma'am, I'm sorry I had to do that. She may need your help. She's still a little hysterical and confused. The flashback is still close to the surface. Tell her to work out the tension in her shoulders with the hot water. The guys have coffee ready downstairs when she's ready."

"Thank you, Nick. I don't know what she would do without you." She kissed his wet cheek, and for a moment he missed his own mother.

"I'm sorry this is happening," he told her.

"She's tough. She's going to get through this. Now go get cleaned up and let me take care of my daughter."

"Yes, ma'am." Nick slipped into dry clothes and prayed Kaylan would be ready to talk when he got downstairs. There would be no sleep tonight. He wasn't sure how to heal this precious woman he loved, but if she could find the strength to get through this, then so could he.

Chapter Thirty-Two

KAYLAN SAT ALONE in the sunroom. She felt warmer—a subtle chill still remained, but it was an improvement from the cold that had permeated her bones like frost since coming home from Haiti. The family had gone back to bed after she reassured them that she was better and just wanted to stay up and watch the sunrise alone. Nick was somewhere in the house, probably showering and preparing to leave. She knew he was going to do his job, but she felt abandoned. She craved stability, and she wanted Nick as part of that, but his job didn't allow it.

This was the first sunrise she had seen since her return home. She felt no joy, no new beginning, just loss. Dim light appeared over the tree line, but no color. She wished the darkness would remain a while longer. She wasn't ready for the morning. She had cried and cried and cried. The release felt wonderful and awful, like a dam had finally burst but now wouldn't stop gushing water. She didn't want the physical reminder of her pain.

"Hey, beautiful, can I watch the sunrise with you?" Nick joined her on the wicker loveseat.

His warm, low voice infiltrated her nightmares. She had wanted to reach for it, but to leave the Haiti of her nightmares meant to leave Sarah Beth again. But, just like Stevenson and Abe, Nick had pulled her from the darkness kicking and screaming. She couldn't escape the pain. Water could wash away blood, chase away nightmares, but it could never erase scars. Hers festered, still raw.

"Feel better?" He ran his hands through her wavy, wet hair, and she leaned into his open arm.

"I'm tired."

"Go back to sleep."

She let the silence settle. "I fell asleep. After the quake. I woke up and panicked. I had to wake Sarah Beth. I was scared she was already gone. Her hands felt like ice. I kept giving her water, wiping away the blood, but it kept coming. It was a sick, horrible nightmare. When she was gone, I couldn't believe it."

"Kaylan, I know you don't think I understand, but I do. More than you realize."

"No one gets this, Nick. You took me away from all the people who would understand." She wished there was a way to help. Anything would be better than the daily pain. In Haiti she'd grown numb, unable to feel because there were still people trapped, other Sarah Beths still needing help, water, healing, hope. Here, she was helpless, with too much time to think, too much time to remember, in places and with people who made the memories vividly alive.

She'd given her heart to Haiti and been betrayed. She'd given her heart to Sarah Beth and been abandoned. She'd given her heart to Nick...she didn't realize it until now, and he was breaking it, betraying it, and abandoning her. This was almost worse than Sarah Beth dying, almost worse than the earthquake. The one she pinned her hopes on was leaving...again.

"Kaylan, look at me. I understand your nightmares and flash-backs. I know what you live with. I have nightmares and flashbacks, as well. I wrestle with men I lost, with those I couldn't help, with two buddies who died right in front of me. I see them. I relive the moments in too much detail."

She studied him. How had she missed this? What else did she not know?

"I know what it's like to lose a loved one, a friend. I lost both of my parents, although not to something as shattering as an earthquake."

She shuddered. That word had the ability to shake her all over again. It should be excommunicated from the English language.

Silence engulfed them. He understood in part, but she wasn't sure she could tell him the rest. She couldn't discuss Eliezer. To say his name, to talk about him, would be to invite him into her home, put substance to her fear, her guilt. It was still her fault Sarah Beth had died. Maybe if she had chosen to stay home, Sarah Beth would have stayed too. Maybe if they hadn't come home from work early to take a nap, she would have lived. The sky above the distant tree line tinged a light pink.

"Sarah Beth's favorite color was pink."

"You've told me."

"She was like a little kid in a woman's body. She loved life, Nick." The snake reared its ugly head again. "It's not fair that she's gone. Why her and not me? She wanted to be there."

"Kaylan, don't ever say that again. Sarah Beth wouldn't have wanted that for you either. You wanted to be there too. God wasn't playing favorites. It was just her turn."

Tears flowed again, and she swiped them away. She needed to get a grip.

"It's okay to cry, Kayles."

"No, it's not. I don't want to cry in front of you anymore."

Nick pulled her into his arms, rubbing her back.

"I know you have an assignment. But what happens if I never see you again?"

Nick wished he could promise her everything would be all right. He wished he could reassure her of the safety of the mission, just routine training. No reason to worry. But the world was crazy, as she had discovered. He couldn't control whether or not he came back alive or draped in a flag-covered box any more than he could control the weather.

"You'll get through. Your family will be here. Time will pass. Life will keep going." He talked almost mechanically while his mind raced. Should he tell her she should go back to Haiti? He shuddered at the thought. *Not now, Lord. Please, not me, and not now.*

Her soft voice sliced through his prayer. "Life is unbearable enough without Sarah Beth. What would it be like if you didn't come home?"

Her words sank in, stopping the roar of his thoughts. He smiled. "So, I rank now, huh? Does that mean you're officially my girl?"

He'd caught her off guard, and his smile deepened, but she needed to know he was sticking around in a permanent way.

"You promised you would be here."

"I have a job, Kaylan. A job that is more than a nine-to-five workday. It's a calling to me. I'm asking you now to believe in my calling as I believed in yours to go to Haiti. This isn't a permanent leave. I'm not running away. How can I hold my head up if I ignore my commitments?"

"Any other time, I would accept that answer, but I need you. Can't you ask for more time? They can take someone else."

"Kaylan, my team needs me. And you don't right now."

"Yes, I do. I can't do this without you."

"That's what you think. Babe, I think I've moved from the place of heroic knight to savior king, and I can't be that. The Lord has to be your everything before I can help you anymore."

"He doesn't care."

He couldn't argue with her. Wouldn't. He lifted the cedar box full of letters onto his lap. He would save the necklace for later.

Her eyes grew wide and her tone softened again. Her hand flew to her mouth. "Where? How?"

"I went to Rhonda's house. I saw what happened."

"But this was under my bed. Why would you go in there? Why would you do that? The rubble was unstable. It could have shifted and killed you."

"Kaylan, to help you, I needed to see what you lived through. I wasn't in the earthquake, but I saw its aftermath."

"You saw, didn't you? You saw where she died."

"I saw it all."

Silent tears poured down her face again, and she ran her hands over the top of the box. "I thought I lost this."

"I loved getting your letters. Maybe if you write to me while I'm gone and keep them for me here, it will feel like I never left. It's good to get your thoughts on paper. Since I can't tell you where I'm going anyway, you can just send them to me when I get back."

She wrapped her arms around his neck, and he pulled her close. Her tears soaked his shirt. "I wish you didn't have to go."

It broke his heart to break contact. He had to leave. He kissed her neck, her cheek, her forehead, seeking to comfort, though who he was comforting was unclear. He knew if the circumstances were different, she wouldn't be this desperate for him to stay. "I'll come see you when I get back."

"Nick, please."

He leaned forward to whisper in her ear. "The Lord never left you, Kaylan. He loves you more than I ever could. He is good, even in this."

She stiffened, and he pulled her arms from his neck, rising to leave before he changed his mind. "Bye, babe."

"Where's God's goodness in this?" Her whisper, dripping with bitterness, reached him outside the door, and he stopped as if his feet were cemented to the floor. He almost turned around, but he couldn't. Clenching his fists, he put one foot in front of the other, forcefully removing himself from the equation. Only God could help her now. He'd been the only One who could accomplish it all along.

Chapter Thirty-Three

THE STEADY HUM of men preparing for battle greeted Nick and Micah as they reached the team building in Coronado after a long day of travel. It was a familiar sound to Nick. As much as he and Micah loved the brotherhood of SEAL Team 5, serving with Support Activity 1 allowed him to lead and gave them autonomy. They received a mission, executed, and returned home to their place on SEAL Team 5. Fewer guys served with Support Activity, but he respected the relationship they had to build in a short amount of time. Ten guys checked weapons, boats, communication equipment, and radios throughout the room in a calm, controlled manner. Jokes and insults flew in the quiet rhythm of a team who fought and played in sync.

A white board waited against one wall. Frag-O filled the top of the board in messy handwriting. It looked like this mission came straight from the top dogs. A timeline stretched across the board, and Nick's and Micah's names each had assignments. As a sniper, Nick was responsible for the first two stages of the mission, route planning on insert, the final foot patrol into the target, and then getting everyone out. It would demand all of his focus.

Senior Chief Collin "X" Williams bent over a table of maps, writing, erasing, and writing again. He was so named for Professor X from his favorite comic, *X-Men*. His ability to control a situation, not with angry words but with sheer will, immediately commanded the respect of those who followed him. He had the innate ability to read his men, assess their strengths and weaknesses, and send them into combat prepared. He knew the enemy like the back of his hand. It was almost as if he could read their minds. It kept his team alive. He was a veteran and Nick's mentor.

Nick knew this would be big, and he knew his input would be required. This mission would test him to his limit, and he wasn't sure he was up to the task. His heart remained in Alabama, and his head felt muddled from lack of sleep.

"Carmichael, Richards. Thanks for showing up, ladies. Now we can get down to business." The men stilled and gathered around the maps. "Our friends up in Washington have passed on intel that a target by the name 'Janus' has resurfaced after a four-year hiatus and is officially making arms deals again. Based on info, the time has come to catch this guy before he sells to our dear friends in the Middle East and they get hold of something that kills a couple hundred of America's youth. Our job is to gather the last bit of intel—a picture, types of arms, contacts, et cetera. We take him if we can, but we give the bigwigs enough to form a more concrete profile of this guy. Janus is the right-hand man of a much bigger fish. We want to catch both.

"The destination is Nicaragua, and I don't need to tell you men that this mission is important. If we don't catch him in the jungle, we'll have to catch him in the desert, with tangos much more adept at warfare than these druggie goons down south. Make your plans. Hawk, Bulldog, you'll coordinate and give me a workable plan with multiple options in twelve hours. We leave in thirty-six."

Nick studied the maps as men moved with a quiet urgency. The target position and extraction point meant humping through the jungle and leaving by sea. The target was meeting a little too far from the water for his comfort. That meant they would need to get in, get the intel, capture Janus, and get out before the sun ascended.

"What do you think, Hawk?"

"I think we have a lot of work ahead of us. And I desperately need some coffee."

Micah slapped him on the shoulder. "Head still back in Alabama?"

"I hate the way we left things. Too bad I can't be in two places at once." He slapped the table, drawing the warning looks of several in the room.

"Get your head in the game. We need you. I'll get you some coffee."

"Carmichael." Nick tensed at the demanding tone. He sauntered across the room to X's locker and immediately faced the full brunt of his senior chief's passion for the job. He fought the urge to react and clenched his jaw. Alabama was no longer in his vision. He saw red.

"Now look here, son. This team needs you, and I need you. Lives are on the line. This is much bigger than that pretty lady of yours. I need to know you can pull it together and take the lead on this target. Lover boys have no place as frogmen. She doesn't exist on missions. When you enter this room, the only people who exist are your brothers and the guys we live to fight. Got it?"

"Yes, Senior." Nick gritted his teeth, now angrier with himself than X.

X studied him, and Nick met his eyes, refusing to show weakness. The man could read Nick like one of the comic strips he loved so much. X's look softened. Regardless of his tough exterior, he cared about each man.

"How is she?"

"Messed up, sir. But she's tough. It's just going to take time."

"She'll have to be tough to date a SEAL. This isn't for the faint of heart." X would know. Wife number three waited for him at home.

Nick nodded and met Micah with his coffee. There was yet another thing he and Kaylan needed to discuss if they wanted this relationship to last. At the moment, he would have to learn the balance. It had been easier on his deployment with Seal Team 5.

Kaylan had been a dream, a regret, but nothing concrete. Now, he could still feel her, hear her cries, smell the lavender on her skin when he hugged her. She was real, and she needed him. Yet he had a mission, a pursuit he believed in with his whole heart.

Sorry, Kaylan. You can't exist in this room.

Nick raised his coffee toward Micah. "All right, Bulldog, let's get this show on the road."

The lighthearted smile that had been absent since before Haiti lit Micah's features, and he raised his mug in reply. "Let's go get us some bad guys. Save the world. Get you the girl."

Nick chuckled. "Just another day in the office. And, man, seriously, we've got to find you a girl."

Chapter Thirty-Four

DECISIONS. THE ONCE overwhelming word now also carried emptiness. Sarah Beth wasn't here to bounce ideas off of, to cheer her on, to eat ice cream, or to call when the circumstances were too hard to bear alone.

"She isn't here," Kaylan said into the empty room, startling herself with the sound. Nick and Micah had left a week ago and were somewhere halfway around the world. Pap wasn't feeling well and Gran was taking care of him. Kaylan feared he would have another stroke. Seth was working an off-season high-school football camp at the college and didn't get home until late. Now into February, David was swamped with tax season and exhausted, absent. Her parents were attending conferences for work. The house was empty, lonely, and far too big.

Life had continued, and everyone's schedules with it. Kaylan felt the gaping hole in her heart, as if shrapnel had sliced away uneven chunks, embedding and releasing a bitter poison. She didn't know who to call and didn't really want company. Had she truly been alone without someone close by since her return from Haiti? She didn't think so, but the quiet granted too much time to think, too much time to feel. She could pray about these decisions and knew she should, but if God wouldn't talk to her, she wouldn't talk to Him either.

Crying, aching, longing—nothing changed the reality that her best friend was gone. Anger consumed, but with nowhere to channel it, she had come to a conclusion since Nick had left: she had to do something. She was tired of dwelling on it, of the nightmares, of the questions from family and friends. Maybe if she worked herself to exhaustion, the dreams wouldn't come, and the sharp pain would recede to a dull ache.

She spread the paperwork in front of her on the table. Her laptop hummed, and the cursor blinked like an annoying pest on the empty page. She perused the internship applications. It was the first week of February, and they were due in a few days. She was basically guaranteed the spot in California if she applied. Mississippi, Texas, Alabama, and Virginia were also options on her list. She'd completed the essays before leaving for Haiti, but she needed to tailor them for the different programs.

Kaylan tossed her pen on the table. "What's the point?"

She knew the point: if she didn't complete her internship, her degree essentially meant nothing. But Haiti had changed everything. She had chosen the less traveled of two roads and had wound up the loser. The course of her life had shifted. If only she could go back and change her mind, convince Sarah Beth to stay.

"But then I wouldn't have met Abe and Stevenson, and Rhonda, Yanick, and the baby, Kenny and…" She couldn't finish. Not even those friends were present or could help.

"Enough!" She shouted into the room. She was tired of thinking about Haiti. Her pen attacked the pages with a fury, and within an hour, the applications were filled out to every school. She could decide which one when and if acceptances came back. For now, she simply needed the distraction.

Clouds played on the lake outside the breakfast nook. Nick and Micah were somewhere on a mission, and she wasn't allowed to know their location. She was angry they had left, fearful they wouldn't come back. Would their fate be the same as Sarah Beth's? Would they too wind up dead in a country that didn't truly appreciate their sacrifice? The silence became a burden, and she flipped the radio on. The first strains of "My Girl" flooded the room.

The lyrics started drifting through the speakers of the house, and Kaylan slammed fingers on the machine, changing the station.

"My Girl" had been one of Sarah Beth's favorite songs. Was she destined to be taunted by the memory of the best friend she couldn't speak to or see anymore?

"Why do You hate me? She's dead. And it's my fault," Kaylan yelled at the ceiling. She needed to get out of the house, maybe go for a ride. She snatched her shoes from the floor, grabbed a lightweight jacket, and threw open the front door.

"Mrs. Tucker!" To her surprise, Sarah Beth's mom stood on the porch, her hand hovering over the doorbell. Every inch the Southern belle, she was poised and put together even in the midst of her grief. Mrs. Tucker's blonde hair held a few gray streaks, and her eyes resembled Sarah Beth's so much that Kaylan's stomach did a small flip-flop.

Kaylan thrust a hand through her tangled hair, feeling unkempt. Her fingers caught, and she yanked hard, pulling strands loose as she backed into the house.

"Hi, Kaylan. May I come in?"

She wanted to yell, "No!" and slam the door, but without a word she ushered Mrs. Tucker into the sprawling family room, gestured to a chair, and sat as far away as possible.

Mrs. Tucker glanced around, allowing Kaylan a moment to compose herself. "Your mother has done it again, dear. The house is beautiful."

"Thank you, Mrs. Tucker."

Her eyes were devoid of tears. She seemed rested, at peace. How was that possible? She had lost her only daughter. Kaylan was a mess in comparison.

"Your mom told me how you're doing."

"I'm fine. You didn't need to come." She stood quickly. "I have somewhere I need to go."

Mrs. Tucker crossed the room, put her arm around Kaylan, and lowered her to the couch again. "Just give me a few minutes. I heard you decided to complete your applications for the dietetics internship. Sarah Beth would be so happy for you."

Kaylan avoided her eyes. "I'll hear back sometime in April. I'm not sure where I'll end up or if I'll even go."

"Why wouldn't you, dear?"

"It seems kind of pointless now."

"The things and places the Lord sends us to are never pointless, no matter how they turn out. Sarah Beth loved you, and she would have wanted you to look for God's hand in all this."

Kaylan was on her feet again. "How can you be so calm? Your daughter is gone. My best friend! She can't come back. Where is the purpose in that?"

Mrs. Tucker reached for Kaylan's hand and gently tugged her back down onto the couch, maintaining her contact. "Sarah Beth loved those children. She loved you. She was changing lives and following the Lord. That was her purpose. It was not empty and not unfulfilled. Don't disrespect her legacy by criticizing what the Lord did. Don't forget the people of Haiti, Kaylan. They are the reason you went."

"I couldn't help her. I couldn't do anything. How do you not hate me?"

"You did something for her that we never could have done. You were present in her darkest night. And at the end of that night, her new day never shone so beautifully. She was with the God who loved you enough to use you in the lives of people who have nothing. She had you." Mrs. Tucker drew back, tears spilling down her cheeks.

Kaylan looked away. She knew what Mrs. Tucker wanted to know but didn't dare ask—about Sarah Beth's final moments. What she had said. How she had died. But how could Kaylan possibly relive that moment, that horror? Kaylan shook her head, barring the images and the awful scent of dust and blood.

Mrs. Tucker rose to leave, Kaylan trailing behind her. When

they reached the door, Mrs. Tucker placed her hand on Kaylan's arm, her eyes sad. "We're planning a trip to Haiti for the first of July. It will have been six months, and we want to help with what Sarah Beth started." Tears gathered in her blue eyes, and Kaylan again ached to see Sarah Beth in them. "Kaylan, my daughter loved you, and I know she wouldn't want you hurting yourself over her death. I know it's not that easy, but will you come with us?"

Her heart halted before taking off at a gallop. Go back? No way. There was no way.

"That country killed Sarah Beth. How could you even consider going?"

Despite her grief, Mrs. Tucker's eyes held resolution. "Because they need help. Because my daughter loved the kids. And because it will be good for me, help me feel close to her. She wouldn't have wanted you to hate what she loved."

She didn't know what she was asking. "I'll think about it."

"Pray about it."

She offered the hint of a smile. She couldn't promise that. "Thanks for coming by." As she closed the door behind Mrs. Tucker, she remembered Sarah Beth's words. She couldn't tell them what had happened, but she could give them this.

Kaylan ripped open the front door and ran after Mrs. Tucker. "Wait. Sarah Beth…she wanted me to tell you that she loved you and that we did well. You can be proud of her. People loved her. And in her last moments, she talked about the beautiful sunrise."

Mrs. Tucker's eyes brimmed with tears, and she threw her arms around Kaylan again. "You both did well. God is good, even in this. Don't forget, Kaylan."

She kept hearing that, but how was He good in this? What good had come from the earthquake? Sarah Beth had died; Kaylan was a shattered shell of what she'd been. The people were broken and needed food, water, and homes but couldn't pay for any of it. No, nothing good had come from the quake.

Chapter Thirty-Five

NICK'S GREEN FACE paint seemed to sweat on its own. Mud seeped through his uniform from his position on his stomach beneath the hide. The wetlands of Nicaragua were hot and sticky, and so far, this assignment was one huge, wild goose chase. Kaylan would kill him if she knew he was in the epicenter of earthquakes and volcanoes.

Nick didn't move. Five hours and counting, and no one had appeared at the rendezvous point. Three weeks scouting the area, pretending to be on vacation, and still nothing. In that time he'd learned the places to eat without acquiring food poisoning. He knew to sit with his back to the wall and never eat with more than two of his buddies at a time. While half the men were on surveillance duty, the other half attempted to blend into the surroundings. Nick itched to surf.

The hide packed in heat like a sauna. Their CIA friend hadn't surfaced all week, and Nick was beginning to wonder if Janus knew he'd been made. Granted, the Nicaraguan terrorist organization was pitiful in comparison to its brothers in the desert across the pond, but these guys were in America's backyard. One well-aimed nuke or missile, and the United States would experience the largest crisis since the twin towers.

"Hawk, there's nothing here, man." The whisper came over Nick's earpiece after hours of silence. Nick's trained reflexes prevented his body from responding. Micah was positioned in a tree grove on the other side of the rendezvous point.

"I'm starting to wonder if this is a setup. We stay put until we know for sure."

A click sounded over the earpiece, and silence settled again. Sweat dripped down his face, and the scent of earth and dirt tickled Nick's nose. He remained as still as a statue. A slew of disgruntled parrots catapulted into the sky, squawking in indignation. Someone approached.

Caveman materialized out of the jungle, his uniform designed to blend into the foliage. He tapped Nick's shoulder, then held two fingers to his eyes, signaling tangos. Terrorists. It was time.

A man sauntered into the clearing near the bungalow. A long, bulky pack hung over one shoulder, and a straw hat sat cocked to the side on his head. He could have been a farmer, but his eyes shifted around the clearing, and Nick knew he was no friendly. The bundle most likely contained weapons. Over the next few hours three more men arrived at the hut, all dressed like locals, no weapons visible, but all shifty and too intent on the trees and shrubs.

Come nightfall, four men resided in the small bungalow. No sound issued from inside. A single lamp remained lit in the window. Nick felt a tap on his shoulder. Caveman bent in his line of vision and held a finger up. One more on the way. This was it. This had to be Janus.

A head bobbed into view, and Nick immediately knew this was their guy. His hands glowed a pale white in the moonlight, and a scarf of some sort shrouded his head. His small frame didn't appear to carry any weapons. Nick didn't dare move. The man knocked three times and then knocked another three. Inside the bungalow, the men tensed and stood. Nick knew they had their man. Janus had arrived.

"Bulldog, you get his face?"

"Negative. Looking through the window. Why didn't we get ears for this convo?"

"Too dangerous." Nick breathed over the earpieces as he studied the landscape. Eight men hid, but not one moved. "Stick to the mission. We confirm the weapons. Get a good look-see at this dude and then shoot to kill if this thing goes south." Seven clicks sounded over Nick's earpiece. He could feel his pulse in the index finger resting on the trigger of his rifle. He slipped on his NVGs and perused the bungalow through the green hue. A commotion came from inside, and in a flutter of motion Janus's head covering slipped free.

Whispers spilled over his earpiece. "Do you see what I'm seeing?"

"No way."

"We sure this is Janus?"

"What kind of info did they feed us?"

Nick craned his neck to get a better look. What was going on? He immediately pulled back. It couldn't be. No way the Russians would be that stupid.

"Hawk, are you seeing this?"

"They sent a woman. Janus is a woman. No wonder we couldn't catch 'him.'"

"Zip it." Nick's command ceased the abnormal level of chatter.

Micah broke radio silence as they studied the activities in the hut. "Hawk, are you sure this is it?"

Nick hesitated, but their orders were clear. "Wait to see if they make the deal, then we move in."

A man exited the hut and stood outside. Nick's finger twitched. Caveman tapped his shoulder again and signaled Nick should circle the perimeter and get closer. Nick acknowledged and slowly inched from under his hide. His legs ached from lack of use. He pulled his gun with him and stood when he was farther back in the foliage.

"Friendly on your six."

Micah appeared at his side; Nick signaled Micah should circle one way and he would go the other. His body moved like a jungle cat, careful not to disturb the nesting parrots far above or the leaves on the earthen floor. He circled closer, voices carrying through the windows in the humid air.

Spanish. Nick thanked the Lord he had endured conjugating all those verbs in high school and college.

"You have what we asked?"

"Partially. You will be directed to the remainder when the money is wired." The woman's voice was thickly accented and strangely familiar.

"That was never the deal."

"Well, this is what I am allowed to give. Take it or leave it."

"We could end this now. Your boss would miss you, but we are not so easily ignored." Nick heard a sneer in the man's voice. "He must be pretty stupid to send a woman such as yourself into the company of men such as we are."

The click of a gun switching from safety alerted Nick, and he tensed, wishing he had a piece of gum.

"I would not be so stupid. You will never see your supplies if I do not return. I am part of the deal." Her voice was dead and cold as the Arctic.

A harsh laugh met her words. "Who are you, a small woman, against four armed men? You are stupid." He spat, and Nick could feel the tension build in the muggy night. This was about to get ugly.

Straining to hear, Nick shifted to see through the window. The woman's revolver was still leveled at the man who appeared to be the head of the gang.

A gun appeared in the man's hand, and a shot cracked the stillness, sending parrots into the sky. The man's body crumpled. "Anyone else, or can we get back to business?"

Silence greeted her, and she lowered the gun. Nick still couldn't see her face.

"We've got positive identification. Take it out." Nick could barely hear Micah's command to withdraw. She had just killed the head of her negotiations, and the other men in the room remained impassive. Something wasn't right. His brain clicked through a thousand possibilities like a slideshow on speed.

"Trouble incoming! Get out of there now!" The whisper sounded over the earpiece, and Nick melted into the night, Micah joining him. The ground rumbled, and the air exploded. Yellow, orange, and red flames shot into the air.

"Hawk, move!" Heat seared Nick's face as he flew against a tree trunk and crumpled to the ground.

Chapter Thirty-Six

THE STEEPLE LOOMED over Kaylan's head as she carried a box of bottled water across the church parking lot. Her heart churned. She hadn't felt the urge to pray this strongly since the earthquake, since Sarah Beth had died. Nick weighed on her mind—and had since his departure three weeks earlier. She knew she needed to pray for him, but she and God weren't on speaking terms. It wasn't so much that she was still mad. Her anger had fizzled after weeks of waking every day to life without Sarah Beth. But the pain and longing remained for their daily friendship.

The urge to pray for Nick grew. The longer she waited, the more overpowering the need. What was wrong? Surely God wouldn't take him too. Sarah Beth's death had beaten her. If Nick was hurt, it would finish her off. She fought the need to pray. It was just her frazzled emotions.

"Kaylan, are you all right?"

Kaylan started, shifting the box in her arms as she ran into Mrs. Helms at the main doors. "Yes, Mrs. Helms. Fine. Just taking these things to the storage closet."

"Okay, then I'll see you in church Sunday." Mrs. Helms waved as she headed to her car.

Kaylan trudged inside the church and headed for the storage closet. It hadn't taken long after her talk with Mrs. Tucker for Kaylan to find something to do. Rhonda had called, and her blunt manner and dedication had finally roused Kaylan to find some way to help from the States. The moment she began working on Haiti relief, life took on a clearer focus—still fuzzy around the edges, yes, but at least she had made some progress.

The Pantry Project, Kaylan's idea, was well underway at the church. So far, two truckloads of supplies had been collected for Haiti relief. Kaylan slid the box onto a shelf, then stood back to survey the pantry. Almost full. Collecting the food had been the easy part. The hardest part of the project had been the comments she had to endure.

"Kaylan, dear, I'm so sorry to hear what happened."

"Everything happens for a reason."

"Keep your chin up. It will get better."

"I'm here for you."

"Sarah Beth would want you to get on with your life."

"I was devastated when my dog died. I understand what you're going through." It took all of Kaylan's control not to reply with an ugly retort and well-placed shove at this comment. Seth had taught her how to tackle, and she strongly considered using her skills.

Kaylan took the comments in silence, thinking of ways she and Sarah Beth would have laughed and joked about the pitiful attempts at consolation.

She couldn't be in Haiti, but she could help in this small way. She hoped transportation on the ground in Haiti was better than when she had left. Reporters had arrived in the city while supplies sat on tarmacs unattended and forgotten. She touched a box of bottled water, thinking of the dusty faces after the quake, of haunted, dark eyes with no hope.

After the quake she'd coped by helping every victim. Everyone had been Sarah Beth. She'd seen her blue eyes, her pink lips, hair she'd braided, lives she'd touched. She thought if this one was saved, then Sarah Beth would be all right. It never came true.

Raising support and aiding the relief efforts was the equivalent. She felt Sarah Beth again; her hands helped Kaylan stack goods and box water bottles. She made jokes inside Kaylan's thoughts as Kaylan packed medicine and mangled the medical terms.

Kaylan ran her fingers over the smooth cardboard of one box. "I miss you, Bubbles. You should be here."

Another project came to mind from the year before. Sarah Beth had organized a food drive for low-income families in Tuscaloosa. During the summer months many students went hungry because school meals were no longer provided. Sarah Beth was determined to avoid this. Community members had donated canned goods, pasta, and fun drinks. Sarah Beth had been ecstatic.

"Can you believe this, Kayles? It's amazing! It actually worked."

"Well, you are quite persuasive, Bubbles. Who would tell those big, blue eyes, 'no'?"

"Good point. I might as well use them to my advantage."

Kaylan shoved her, laughing.

"Seriously, Kayles, this is a total God thing." They packed boxes of food while they talked. "I mean, some of these kids don't think anyone loves them or cares. This brings them hope."

Kaylan picked up a box. "They'll never forget this."

Sarah Beth slapped another Bible verse into the finished box. "It's like we're being His hands and feet, you know? I mean, we can share the gospel all we want, but when it's not accompanied by this, meeting needs, how can we be effective? How can we truly show them that Jesus loves them?"

"Hands and feet of Jesus." Her voice broke the silence, and she sank into the corner of the closet. "The people in Haiti are hopeless. This won't even make a dent in the problems."

No, but it helps one. The answer whispered across the dark recesses of her soul, and she inhaled sharply. She hadn't felt that in months. Peace. She remembered Rhonda's coaching in Haiti after they'd lost a baby. Kaylan had been devastated and angry, much like now.

"Kaylan, how do you finish a test?"

"One question at a time."

Rhonda's voice lowered to a whisper, burning with passion. "Kaylan, how do you change a country?"

Recognition dawned in Kaylan. She lifted her chin and squared her shoulders. "One life at a time."

"One life at a time, we will see Haiti changed. One mother understanding the intricacies of the life within her, one child knowing the love of two parents and a full belly, one father knowing how to provide for his family. One by one."

The urge hounded her again: to pray for Nick, to pray for Haiti, to find her way back, but she wasn't ready. She imagined Nick's blue eyes and strong presence. Her head pounded, and she closed her eyes, thankful for the cool, quiet recess. Something was wrong. She could feel it.

She forced the words out of her mouth, breaking the stillness. "Lord, I know I haven't spoken to You in a while, but I think something's wrong with Nick. Whatever it is, please keep him safe. Don't take him away from me. I can't bear any more."

She hugged her legs and rested her forehead on her knees, remembering what she had felt after the earthquake, waiting for Sarah Beth to die, praying she wouldn't. She rocked back and forth. She couldn't take anymore. Darkness crept in, but panic didn't follow. Instead, she felt a warm, unexplainable feeling course through her body and mind. Peace.

Pap lumbered down the sidewalk, leaning on the cane. Kaylan grasped his other arm and prayed he wouldn't fall. He had wanted to come outside, breathe fresh air and soak in the later winter sunshine. "Maybe we should go inside, Pap. It's kind of cold out here."

After dropping off the supplies at the pantry, Kaylan had decided to drop in on her grandparents. Gran was off grocery shopping, but Pap welcomed the visit. He had slowed down since his mild stroke, but he refused to acknowledge it.

"I'm old, but I'm not dead. I'm gonna die moving, although I don't plan on doing that today. Now, quit your yapping and let me enjoy my walk."

"I don't get it. Why do you push yourself so hard?"

"Soon as you stop trying, you stop living." Pap stared into her eyes, and she refused to look away. The snake that had reared its ugly head the last time they had visited the stables lay dormant. Kaylan wanted to try. She wanted to live. The bitterness, the anger, the pain—they were eating her alive. She wanted, no needed, to understand why her family still had hope, why Sarah Beth's family still trusted the Lord wholeheartedly.

She'd been raised to love the Lord. Until the earthquake, she would have said her faith was deep and growing. But after Sarah Beth's death, she'd discovered her faith had shallow roots. It was depressing and discouraging. She didn't know how to take her faith from where it currently existed back to the place she had perceived it to exist... or on to a deeper place.

Pap pointed to the oak tree growing in his yard. "Sugar, you see that tree? What do you think made it grow so tall?"

She studied the tree—unbending, unyielding, majestic.

"Its roots are far-reaching and shallow. They suck the nutrients from the soil and push the tree taller." Pap continued as they approached the back porch.

Kaylan helped Pap to one of the wicker chairs. Gran's lemonade waited in a crystal pitcher on the end table. "I thought all roots grew deep."

"There aren't as many nutrients down deep, Sugar, at least not for an oak tree. Roots have to spread and grow, sometimes even past the canopy of the tree. The bigger the tree, the more widespread the roots. But all those shallow roots feed back into one big tap root, which penetrates deep into the earth and stabilizes the tree. No matter what shakes it, the tree doesn't move because that tap root keeps it stable and strong. Both shallow roots and tap roots are necessary to grow and stabilize the tree."

Kaylan felt like her tap root was missing. She had been shaken and found wanting. Her roots had been too shallow to help her stand tall. Had she leaned too much on her family? On Sarah Beth?

"My roots are messed up, Pap. I can't handle any more."

Pap rose to his feet, gripping the chair until his cane was firmly in his hand. He waved off Kaylan's help when she began to stand.

"Sugar, I once heard that we turn to God for help when our foundations are shaking only to learn that it is God shaking them. So you might want to ask yourself why the Lord chose to shake your foundations. Look hard, in here." He tapped his chest, right over his heart. "You might learn something."

He turned and hobbled into the house, leaving Kaylan alone and more confused than ever.

Chapter Thirty-Seven

ALABAMA CALLED HIS name. Five weeks had passed since leaving Kaylan, and Nick missed her more than ever. He groaned as he rolled in bed. Every muscle hurt. He had taken hard hits before, but that explosion had severely bruised his back. He was back home in Coronado on medical leave until the doctor released him. It would be a week, maybe more, all while his team planned and trained harder than ever.

They'd walked into a setup. He should have seen it from the beginning. Janus had killed the head of the terrorist group, and no one had so much as blinked. It was an execution of the worst kind: kill the leader to make way for another brutal, yet easily manipulated man, and take out those tracking her at the same time. They never expected IEDs to be buried around the bungalow. That lack of awareness spelled danger for his team. He was angry, boiling even. As much as he missed Kaylan, he wanted to hop the next plane to Russia and find the shrew.

"Are you still wallowing?" Micah leaned against the doorframe, grimy from a day of training.

"Nursing my enormous ego and bad temper. I'm just a little banged up."

"So, you aren't currently pining away for a certain auburn-haired beauty in need of Prince Charming, however incapacitated he may be?"

Nick threw his pillow at Micah.

"Man, why don't you go see her? You won't be back at work for at least a week. They won't even let you come into the office. Get out of here."

The idea was appealing, but he didn't want Kaylan to see him like this. "It can wait until I'm fully back on my feet."

"What's the problem? More male ego?"

Nick met Micah's eyes. "She just watched her best friend die and patched up half a city. She doesn't need to see me and worry."

"Don't you think that Kaylan is tough enough to handle it? If y'all are going to label this as a relationship, you better learn real quick that your problems are her problems, just as you've already adopted hers. Don't handle this alone."

"I can't tell her anything, man. Keeping secrets has never been so difficult."

"You tell her the truth. You're a little banged-up but on the mend. A few days, and you'll be as good as new." Micah grinned, and Nick wondered what was coming next. "And you tell her that nothing gets a guy back on his feet more than the loving ministrations of the girl he adores. Tell her that, and you're gold. She'll forget you're hurt."

Nick's grin now matched Micah's. "It's that easy, huh?"

"Well, you know, I have a world of experience in this area."

"Right. When I get back, we've got to find you a girl."

The dance studio hummed with the laughter of little girls and the memory of two best friends. Kaylan had applied to teach dance lessons until she left for her internship, assuming she was officially accepted. She had interviewed over Skype the week before with the San Diego Dietetics Program, and the head of the department informed her that she would most likely be accepted to the program. For now, though, she was back at her old summer job, doing something that reminded her of Sarah Beth every day. Her heart was still raw, and she still wasn't sure how to heal.

Little girls in tap shoes and tutus had filled her time with endless hours of distraction, but the studio was silent now. Kaylan held the keys to lock up. She drifted toward the small auditorium. She had performed her first ballet here, played Belle in *Beauty and the Beast,* and practiced with Sarah Beth. The empty stage mirrored her loneliness, the hole created when the star of the show leaves the spotlights after a breathtaking performance.

She hadn't danced since the night of Pap's stroke. Pop music had blared through the practice room, and she and Sarah Beth had twirled in perfect rhythm, the picture of two girls now women who had lived a lifetime together. Neither one of them knew that lifetime was coming to an end.

As she hit play on the sound board, Michael Bublé burst into song on the speakers in the auditorium. She slowly walked to the stage, dragging her fingers along the seats as she went. She didn't know if she had anything left to give, anything worthy of the well-worn platform. She climbed the steps, hesitating before placing her foot on the polished wood panels. They were familiar friends.

The strains wafted across the room, and Kaylan could almost see the orchestra as she heard the rich plucking of strings and the wailing of the saxophone. Notes drifted across the room, as if floating on a gentle breeze. Kaylan stood center stage, swaying, eyes closed. She could do this. It was another step back, another way to remember Sarah Beth and never let go. She couldn't forget, wouldn't forget. One more way to heal.

> *"You jump here, and I'll spin across stage here, and on eight we'll meet back in center stage for the finale. Ready, Kayles?"*
>
> *"You sure this will work?"*
>
> *"Are you doubting our awesome skills? We are going to nail this recital. Best one yet."*
>
> *"Okay, I'm ready."*
>
> *"Five, six, seven, eight."*
>
> *Kaylan leaped, calling on all her years of dance. She imagined herself as a gazelle, gracefully leaping over the African*

*Serengeti. She landed on her feet and met Sarah Beth in center
stage as the last strains of the song faded into silence.*

"We nailed it. I told you, Kayles."

*They sprawled out on the floor, sweaty and proud. "Bubbles,
how do you do it? How do you know everything is going to turn
out okay all the time?"*

"I don't."

*"Sure you do. You are the most optimistic person I know. You
don't have that nickname just because of the bubbles incident in
kindergarten. You embrace life. How do you do it?"*

*Sarah Beth pushed up on her elbows, and Kaylan met eyes
that sparkled. "I guess because I've learned to let go. You want
to fix everything, Kayles, make it perfect. I know I can't. No
fear, no expectations. I just live life to the fullest. You bury what
happens to you. I know God is big enough to take care of it for
me. I trust Him."*

"So do I."

*"Don't get defensive, Kayles. I know you do. I'm just trying
to explain. I've learned that even shade is an indication of
sunshine, and darkness is pierced by the reflection of daylight
in the moon. God is good, Kayles. If I were to lose everything
tomorrow, that sun is still present, just dimmer. I let go and let
God be who He is. There is such freedom and joy in it."*

The memory swirled to a sickening stop as Kaylan sank to
the stage. Tears stung her eyes and spilled over her cheeks. "It's
not that easy. It's not. Letting go of you means forgetting. I can't
do it."

Cracks broke through her fragile armor. "God, I can't do this.
Why did You take her? She trusted You. Loved You. Helped
people. She was the best of us. Why not me?"

She ran her hands over the scuff marks on the floor. That's
how she felt, scuffed up, less than perfect, a mockery of who she

used to be. From a distance she looked like the stage, glowing, polished, pristine, but up close she was a marred image of what she had been.

"Do You hear me, God? Did You hear me in Haiti? Do You still care? How do I do this?"

"Remember when we first met. You're my best friend. You always will be. Don't cry. Don't be mad, Kayles. Don't be mad. I'm going to see Jesus. He'll dance and laugh with me." Her chest shook, and Kaylan strained to hear. *"He's life, Kayles. Even in this. Don't be mad."*

Sarah Beth's last moments mingled with the mellow music. God was life. He was still good, even in this. Sarah Beth now danced with Jesus, whole, healthy, and as bubbly as ever.

"Nothing makes me happier than helping people, Kayles. If I die doing this, life will end perfectly." Sarah Beth's words after a day working with the kids in Haiti rang through her mind. If her friend could be content with circumstances, not blaming God in her death, how could Kaylan do any less? But it was much easier said than done.

She wrestled with the words. They bubbled from her heart, and she fought them back. The battle raged. The snake reared its head, but this time she denied it. She was tired of its venom. It was eating her alive.

With a cry, words spilled from her mouth: "I can't be mad at You anymore, Lord. I still don't understand how You're good in this. Sarah Beth could have done much more good, more than I ever can. I don't see any hope. I'm angry, and hurt, but I can't fix it. Sarah Beth knew how to let You heal. I can help bodies, but You heal what is broken. Jesus, I need help. Show me the way back. Show me how to trust. Show me the good in this." Her voice cracked, and the plea came from the bottom of her heart. She wasn't sure God would answer, but if He heard her, she needed this most of all. "Give me new hope."

A hand touched her shoulder, and Kaylan jerked backward.

"Hey, babe."

Chapter Thirty-Eight

NICK HAD SEEN the fall. He'd seen the breakdown, the honest plea to God, and he'd sat in the back of the auditorium, praying her through. At the sight of her tears, he stood, needing to comfort her, but stopped in the middle of the aisle, riveted by the scene onstage. She was the picture of a broken woman asking for healing. The stage lights illuminated her. Absolutely breathtaking. The light highlighted the red in her wavy locks, and her tears looked like crystals pooling on the dance floor. When he could stand it no longer, he approached the stage.

"Hey, babe."

His heart broke at the pain in her eyes and the desire for something to live for—purpose, hope, release. He'd need to thank Micah later for persuading him to come.

"Nick, what are you doing here?" She swiped at her face, and he gingerly bent down and ran his thumb over her wet cheek.

"I told you I'd come back. I just got a little banged up in the process." He winced as he lowered to the floor next to her. "I'm okay, babe. Just had to take some time off and thought I would come see you." The panic in her eyes slowly faded as he pulled her into his arms, careful to make sure his back could handle it but determined to hold her.

"But...but you're here. How long have you been here?"

"Long enough to know that the Lord answers prayer in unusual ways."

Her body wilted against his. "I miss her, Nick."

"I know you do. You always will. But she would want you to

remember her with laughter, not tears and anger. She'd be proud of you, you know."

"There's not much to be proud of. I'm a mess."

"Never true." He brushed the hair out of her eyes. "Your mom told me you've been helping with Haiti relief. Do you understand how much courage that takes? How much strength? Babe, I'm so proud of you."

"I'm not strong. Not like her. She had this innate strength and peace."

He cradled her face in his hands. "You are one of the strongest people I know, Kaylan Lee Richards. You know what she told me once? Sarah Beth said you had this quiet strength and loyalty that everyone sees but you are completely unaware of." He rested his forehead on hers. "I see it in you every day I'm with you."

"Really?"

"Absolutely." He pulled her to her feet and swayed to the music, letting her tears soak his shirt. They were no longer tears of pain and bitterness. They were liquid healing.

"Thank you for braving the aftershocks and bringing back my letters. You have no idea how much they've helped."

"I have something else for you too." He let go of her and reached into his pocket. "Turn around."

A spark of playfulness returned to her eyes, and he realized how much he had missed it. He returned it. "You trust me?"

"Who wouldn't trust a SEAL? You came back, didn't you?"

"I'm touched you recognize my chivalry. Please, turn around?"

She turned, and he slipped the chain with the lily on it around her slender neck and fastened the clasp.

She gasped as her fingers brushed the trinket. "Nick, where did you find this? How? I thought I'd lost it."

"I found it in Rhonda's house. It was covered in dust and rock chips. I had it cleaned."

She faced him as she studied the petals. "Impossible. I thought for sure it was gone for good."

"The metal's strong, Kayles. It may have taken a beating and been lost, but nothing lost and bruised is ever without ability to find and repair."

"Thank you."

"My pleasure."

Pulling her into his arms, he twirled her around the stage, enjoying the closeness. It was a comfort after weeks in the jungle.

"Did you know that white lilies are the epitome of everything intricate, beautiful, and pure? They stand for virtue. When the time is right, they open for everyone to see. They are everything I admire about you."

"I think you may have given this to the wrong girl."

"No, I got the right girl this time. I couldn't have picked someone more deserving. What do you say, Kayles? Wanna make it official? Be my girl."

"Nice of you to ask."

He chuckled. "I'm not sure I'm asking anymore."

"What you see is what you get, Nick. I have a long way to go. And what about the SEALs? I'm not sure I can handle not knowing where you are. Or what happens if I lose you too?" Her eyes widened, and Nick smoothed the wrinkles furrowing her brow.

"One step at a time. You can handle it."

They rocked to the music, and slowly she relaxed in his arms.

"Remember the last time we did this?"

"How could I forget? You turned me down flat. Quite a blow to my pride."

She smiled and lowered her eyes, a blush highlighting the freckles around her nose.

"What's with the blush?"

"Well, do you think we could try it again?"

His body stilled, and he studied her eyes.

"Are you sure?"

Her palms grew slick, and her heart raced. Was she ready for this step in their relationship?

"Nick, I told you I wanted this to be the way we said hello, but life changed everything. I can't tell you I'm the girl you held months ago. She's gone. But I do know that today I took the biggest step back to myself. For the first time in weeks, I want to find my way home. My head and heart have been in Haiti with my friend. But Sarah Beth prized life." She brushed the hair from his forehead. "This is life, Nick."

He leaned close, his lips hovering over hers. "Welcome home, beautiful." His lips touched hers, and for the first time in what felt like ages, she was present, her mind engaged in what could be instead of what had been. He explored, pulling her closer, his touch tender and passionate, saying all she had longed to hear. She wrapped her arms around his neck, swaying, lost in his strength and goodness. And in his arms, she felt treasured. Safe. Loved.

She was finally home.

Somehow, in that moment, a piece of her heart buried in the dust of Haiti found its way back to its origin, easing the wound like a salve. It was a piece of hope, of healing from the only One who could answer her prayers and bring them together.

He pulled back slightly to look in her eyes, and she resisted the urge to touch her lips.

"You never answered my question."

A soft laugh slipped out, the first time she had laughed in weeks, and she relished his responsive chuckle. "I would love to be your girl."

Chapter Thirty-Nine

S HE WAS TERRIFIED. Kaylan poured a cup of coffee and trudged to the sunroom, pulling her robe tighter around her. Her body was readjusting to waking before dawn. Tugging a blanket over her legs, she covered a yawn as she studied the subtle, rosy hues pouring over the tree line.

He was taking Sarah Beth's place, and it both terrified and thrilled her. She'd realized it after the kiss. Sarah Beth had been her best friend, a shoulder to cry on, a well of wisdom, someone with whom to laugh, someone with whom to walk through life. Sarah Beth couldn't be replaced, but Nick was becoming equally if not more important in a shorter amount of time.

"Morning, beautiful."

She nearly jumped from her skin. "Nick Carmichael, stop sneaking up on me."

"Sorry." He placed a gentle kiss on her lips. "It's my job to take the enemy by surprise and then leave without a trace."

It felt good to laugh. He left more than a trace. "I'm the enemy?"

"When I can't sleep because I'm thinking about you, and then I force myself out of bed after not sleeping so I can be with you, you are definitely the enemy."

"I didn't do anything."

"I beg to differ. That kiss was far too memorable."

The kiss. She slipped her hand from his grip and hugged herself.

"Something wrong?" His brow furrowed in confusion.

"Not exactly."

"Well, why don't you tell me what exactly is bothering you?"

"I'm not sure I can."

"Try."

"I'm frightened."

"Good. If I don't frighten the enemy, I'm dead."

The blood drained from her face, and her hands began to shake. "Don't say that. Don't ever say that again."

"Kaylan, I'm sorry. I didn't think about it."

He pulled her to him, and she rested her head across his chest, watching the sunrise. She couldn't help but think about Sarah Beth's last sunrise. Kaylan had held her, denying and raging against the inevitable. All her tears, screams, and clinging couldn't keep Sarah Beth from slipping away.

"Your job deals with life or death. What happens if you don't come home? I can't handle it, Nick. I can't lose someone else I care about."

"Kaylan, neither of us can control that."

"Don't do it."

"Don't do what? My job? Kaylan, you are very important to me. I would do anything for you, but please don't ask me to give up what the Lord has called me to do."

"How do I know you'll be okay?"

"Yesterday, you prayed that the Lord would help you trust Him. Trust Him with me. Let Him be God, Kayles. Let Him be in control of my days. Besides, I have too much to live for now to be stupid."

She nodded.

"You want to tell me what the real problem is?"

"Not really."

"Why don't you humor me? Pretend I'm your ever-loving boyfriend who wants to calm your fears, if at all possible."

"You would play that card."

"Time to accept reality. You said yes yesterday. This is part of the package."

She pulled away from him and struggled to gather her scrambled thoughts into a coherent sentence. "When you kissed me, something happened that frightens me."

"Your heart stopped beating, and butterflies fluttered in your stomach? It was that good."

She shoved him and smiled. "Be serious, Nick."

"Sorry. You just make me happy." He leaned in to kiss her again, but she pulled away.

He sighed. "All right, talk to me."

"I think you're taking Sarah Beth's place, and it scares me to death because I don't want to forget her, and you are becoming all too important to lose, and I don't know how to handle this." The words burst from her mouth as she panicked.

His eyes probed her like the machines at the doctor's office, testing each place for the source of pain. "I could never fill the shoes of that relationship. They are far too big and amazing to fill. This is our own relationship, a piece unique only to the two of us. You won't lose me, Kayles. I'm not going anywhere. And you won't forget Sarah Beth either, because I won't let you."

Tears filled her eyes, and she realized she'd been holding her breath. "Really?"

"I promise, and I don't break my promises."

She settled back against his chest, feeling the weight of the Haitian rubble lift for the first time. "Know what she told me as we were lying there, waiting to be rescued?"

"What?" His voice was low and warm, and the sunrise seemed deeper, richer.

"She told me not to be mad, that God was still good."

"He is, Kayles. I won't pretend to understand. When I lost my buddies, it was like a part of me died." He kissed her head and whispered the words against her hair. "Then you danced into my life."

She met his eyes, once again feeling at home. Suddenly the pain wasn't as sharp. "Do you think we give pieces of ourselves to the people in our lives, and that's what makes it hurt so badly when they're gone?"

"I think if we are truly investing ourselves in the people around us, we inevitably give them part of who we are, and they give us part of who they are. We swap pieces. It's one reason we're always changing, always growing. We're like puzzles who share pieces and in doing so become more intricate. Better versions of ourselves."

"I like that image. Sarah Beth's piece is bright pink and huge with tons of daisies and sunshine. She would have liked that. It's the gift she gave to me."

"She gave you an even bigger gift than you realize. She gave you permission to live, guilt-free. God is still good." He tilted her chin and rested his forehead on hers. "Kayles, she gave you permission to love her and remember her without pain, without shame. She gave you hope. Don't ever forget it." He kissed her, slow and long, melting away the ice around pieces of her heart. When she pulled away, the sun rested high in the sky, welcoming a new day, a brighter beginning.

"I wish I could tell her about this." A tear trickled down her cheek; it was no longer one of sorrow but of sweet remembrance.

"She knows. She would be happy for us."

Kaylan settled against Nick and felt the once familiar urge to pray. She no longer wanted to fight it, but she still didn't understand. God still felt distant, as though she had left Him in Haiti, buried with Sarah Beth.

"I wish I could still believe God is good. I have hope for us, but hope for this larger picture, Nick? I don't get it. Where's the good? Where's the hope? Where's God in all of this mess?"

Nick had been praying for the right words to say all through his restless night. When words hadn't come, an image had. He

259

pictured Kaylan and him in Haiti, helping to rebuild, revisiting Sarah Beth's grave, saying good-bye the way he should have allowed her to do before ripping her back to Alabama.

He dreaded her response. He knew she had been contributing to Haiti relief, but that didn't entail being back in the war zone that had first plummeted her into this depression and pain. Could she handle it? Would she want to? Regardless, she needed to.

Your words, not mine, Lord.

He took a deep breath and shifted Kaylan away from him. "I want to talk to you about something, and I want you to listen and consider before you say anything."

The faintest hint of distrust colored her eyes, and he wished he'd begun with a more graceful opening.

"The way Micah and I brought you home from Haiti wasn't right or fair. We were terrified your leg was infected because of how sick you were, but that's no excuse. I've talked to Rhonda and Abraham, and I think you need to go back to Haiti."

Her face went stony. "You, of all people, should know better than to say that." She tried to stand, but he caught her arms and held her in place, willing her to look and listen.

"Kayles, I know that place ripped you apart." He ran his thumb over the small scar above her eye. "I also know how much you loved it, and how much Sarah Beth loved it. I think it would give you perspective to go back, maybe see the hope you are desperately denying. Abe said things are happening, people are changing. I think you need to go see for yourself how God can work wonders in the midst of the rubble of our lives."

"What if there's another earthquake? What if more of my friends died? I can't, Nick, I just can't. Sarah Beth's mom already asked me to go, and I've thought about, and I don't think I could bear it."

"Think about it, babe. Pray about it. I think it would be good for you."

"I haven't really prayed in months. Not like I did in the auditorium."

Nick almost asked her to repeat the whispered words. "Then maybe it's time to start. You lived for a reason, Kaylan Lee Richards. Don't waste it. Talk to that God who dug you out of the rubble. There's your first indication of good in the midst of this. You aren't finished yet." He wouldn't back down on this. She needed to hear. It was time to put things back in order, time to remember the beauty in the midst of brokenness.

"You aren't going to let this go, are you?"

"I'm nothing if not persistent. And I would never do this if I thought you couldn't handle it. I really feel like the Lord placed this on my heart before I left, but the time wasn't right to bring it up. Now it is."

She gazed at the lake, and Nick prayed, gripping her hands to bring reassurance. She didn't look at him, but he heard the soft words: "Will you go with me? As soon as you can get another leave?"

He thought of his assignment with Janus. He was headed back to his team in the morning. They would train harder than before because a killer was loose, armed, and deadly, and his team had been given the task of taking her out. He wished he knew when they could go to Haiti, but he didn't know when new intel would come and he would have to disappear again. Yet he had to figure something out, because to ask her to face her biggest fear and pain was unacceptable unless he was present to help her through it.

"I'll be there. I won't let you down." It was his promise, the promise of a SEAL who never left a teammate behind.

Her hands shook as she nodded, and he prayed she wouldn't fall apart. He watched her silent struggle and recognized the moment she found her strength. Her shoulders straightened, and her eyes met his, clearer than they'd been in months. "I guess we're going back to Haiti."

Some way, somehow, he would be there for her. He prayed that the timing would line up.

PART FOUR

Chapter Forty

NOTHING HAD MOVED. Little breathed. It was as if she'd never left. Haiti in the heat of July was a shadow of the colorful place it had once been. Street painters didn't greet her. Tents suffocated open land and streets. Little seemed to have changed in six months, and Kaylan felt defeated. The heat and humidity suffocated her, and she struggled to draw a deep breath.

Black hands encircled Kaylan, Nick, and the Tuckers. She changed her mind. One thing had changed: there were even more desperate people.

"Food."

"Money."

"Hungry."

The Creole voices threatened to break her heart. She hadn't brought money on purpose, but she reached into her bag and placed candy into groping hands. She slowly made her way up the rubble-filled street to Rhonda's clinic. Shops remained closed, buildings crumbled and uninhabited, churches devoid of bells or people. Rubble resided where people once lived. It was as Kaylan had suspected: hopeless.

"Kaylan, you came! Welcome back to Haiti, my friend. So good to see you on your feet." Abraham walked forward and wrapped her in a hug. She did her best to muster a smile.

"You look well, Abe."

"I feel well. Even better, now that you are here. Come, see what we are doing."

The sheets that had sheltered victims of the quake were gone.

The clinic resembled a lighthouse welcoming the hurt and down-trodden of Port-au-Prince. Women waited in chairs in the small room while children played on the floor. A few elderly people sat in one corner, engaged in animated conversation. The broken did not inhabit the room, but rather those receiving healing.

Kaylan shook her head, confused. She had expected something similar to what she had left. Whereas the outside showed scars of the quake, the people no longer resembled ghosts of the living. They lived.

Rhonda emerged from a back room, carrying one of the children. The child laughed as Rhonda handed him a lollipop and allowed him to run to his mother. Waiting to be noticed, Kaylan felt a pang as she remembered Reuben. Nick stood quietly at her side, her rock.

Rhonda looked up, her professional demeanor vanishing as she smiled. "Kaylan!" They met in a tight embrace that spoke of love and loss and survival.

"Hey, Rhonda. Looks like you're pretty busy today."

"All in a day's work. I have lots of help right now." She led Nick and Kaylan to the back room, and Kaylan stopped short when Yanick turned to face her from the supply cabinet, a beautiful baby tied to her back.

"Kay-lin, welcome home." Again, Kaylan was engulfed in a hug, and her confusion doubled. She felt as if she were on the receiving end of a gigantic joke. How could these people smile and welcome her home? Had they been outside lately? Did they not see that their home was still rubble, and no one seemed to care? Haiti had been forgotten in the six months after the earthquake, but work was far from over.

Rhonda cooed at the baby before smiling at Kaylan again. "I'm training Yanick to be my helper. She continues the weekly meet-ings with the moms in your absence. Now, more than ever, these mothers need help knowing how to care for their families. I've taught her to sew and cook. She teaches the other women. It's the first step in helping them make money for their families. They get off the streets and into their homes making purses, skirts, scarves, and T-shirts. We even set up a website."

Yanick held out a scarf to Kaylan. The purple, red, orange, and yellow threads intertwined, adding a splash of color to the Haiti of Kaylan's memory. "*Lespwa*, Kaylan. For Tasha. For Sarah Beth. For you."

Kaylan looked to Rhonda.

"They named their business *Lespwa*, hope, because you and Sarah Beth cared enough to teach them." Rhonda squeezed Kaylan's hand. "You changed lives, Kaylan. Sarah Beth changed lives. One at a time."

"I don't understand. Does this actually work? People can't afford anything here. How are these women making money? Rhonda, this isn't a good idea. They'll become depressed when this doesn't work."

"What happened to the girl who wanted to change Haiti?"

"What happened to the woman who said I couldn't?"

"I never, ever doubted you could. I simply told you to focus on one person at a time. You did that. You may have left, but you're still making a difference, and these people thank God for you and Sarah Beth every day."

"The slums have grown. People live in tents. Sarah Beth is gone. What is there to thank me for?"

"They live, Kaylan. They are gaining the ability to work and take care of their families. They have life." Rhonda looked from Kaylan to Nick. "Kaylan, what happened to you?"

"The earth shook more than my body. My best friend died, and this country will never be the same. How can you have this hope?"

"Hope." Yanick grabbed Kaylan and Nick's hands and dragged them to the door. "Come. See."

Kaylan looked back at Rhonda.

"Open your eyes, Kaylan. The Haitians are like ants whose mound has been crushed. They rebuild, slowly but surely. Look. See. Believe. And remember."

After visiting the clinic, they had continued the tour of the neighborhood, Kaylan pointing out old sites. Not much had changed. She headed toward the church, anxious to see if it was rebuilt. Men shouted in Creole, and Kaylan heard a loud crack. She ducked, angry for being so skittish.

"It's just shifting rock, babe. Everything's fine."

Nick held her hand, and again Kaylan was thankful for his presence. "Have I told you thanks today?"

"For what?"

"For coming. For being with me."

"I can think of a better way to tell me thank you."

"Oh, yeah?" Kaylan leaned forward and kissed him, thankful for something comfortable and familiar. "Thanks," she whispered against his lips as another crack split the air.

As the church site came into view, Yanick spotted them and pulled them forward to meet her husband, Rolin, with Abraham stepping in to translate. Kaylan studied the area for the first time. The small structure had completely collapsed in the quake, burying the pastor beneath its walls. Men crawled over the wreckage, shifting rock and clearing the area.

"What's happening?"

Rolin spoke first. His face glistened with sweat, and his smile spread. He opened his arms and gestured to the work behind him. Kaylan loved the Creole tones.

Abraham translated. "This is the project Rolin began with some of the men. He says that Haitians must have a place to worship the Lord and thank Him for life. Every day a new man joins the team."

Kaylan recognized many men from Cité Soleil. "Abe," she whispered, "aren't some of these men, well, dangerous? They were part of the gangs in the slums the last time I was there."

"Who better to reach the slums of the earth but those who live in them? They are all new believers, thanks to Rolin. The man does not give up."

Hearing his name, Rolin spoke again. Again Abraham translated. "He says to thank you. He owes you the life of his child and his wife. Someday his son will know the Jesus you and Sarah Beth spoke of. One day he will know a better Haiti. And one day he will worship here…" A smile lit Abe's face. "Where I have been elected pastor. Can you believe it, Kaylan?" The child in Abe broke through, and Kaylan truly smiled for the first time.

"That's great, Abe. I'm proud of you. And of this. I can't believe it."

"There is one more surprise." He whistled, and a teen stopped his work. He shaded his eyes, and Kaylan squinted to make out his features. White teeth cracked his face, and he shouted.

Within seconds Stevenson landed in front of Kaylan and reached for her hand. He opened her palms and placed a finger in the center, smiling at her the whole time.

"I met the palm reader Jesus. I am His palm reader now."

Kaylan looked at Nick in awe. His eyes sparkled at her joy.

"Stevenson, I can't believe it. How? When?"

The youth pointed to Abraham, who explained. "After you left, Stevenson went back to Eliezer. He tried to convince him that Rhonda was making a difference and helping. But Eliezer told Stevenson to steal food from Rhonda for the two of them. It was as if Stevenson's eyes opened for the first time. But he refused. When he came to me, I told him more about Jesus. He never looked back.

Several who followed Eliezer are now here, helping Stevenson and myself tell the people the hope that is in Jesus Christ."

"How, Abe? How do you still have that hope?"

"God never left Haiti, Kaylan. He shook me, and I grew stronger. Many died, but more now live life for Jesus as a result of what they saw and experienced. I do not know how better to explain. There is a vein of hope that runs through Haiti. One day the world will see it."

Chapter Forty-One

NICK WIPED SWEAT off his brow and took the drink offered by Kaylan.

"Sweat looks good on you, soldier."

"Funny, I was going to say the same thing about you."

Kaylan, Nick, and the Tuckers toiled over the church, making it a labor of love for Sarah Beth and the people of Haiti. Little food existed for the inhabitants of the city, but what little was present was shared with their American band. Nick was honored. He could see why Kaylan had fallen in love with these people. These men and women had weathered an earthquake and, although shaken, stood tall. Hope wasn't an elusive concept but a present reality, and they clung to it as if it were food and water.

His phone rang. Nick dropped the cement block he was carrying to fish out his cell. Seeing the number, he moved away from Kaylan before answering. "Hey, Bulldog."

"Hawk, how's she doing?"

Nick studied Kaylan as she distributed water bottles. Her smile was lighter, and the circles under her eyes continued to fade; she was active and aiding a cause she was intimately linked to. "Better. She's getting there."

"I hope you were right about this trip."

"I was right. But something tells me that isn't why you called. What's up?"

"Janus is back. Made a reappearance in Ukraine before slipping her shadow. She's good, Hawk. One of the best I've seen."

"We're better."

"We'll have to be. That's why I'm calling. X wants everyone back, stat. Time to catch ourselves a killer."

Nick could almost taste the desire. This woman didn't think twice about whom she hurt or the clients to whom she sold weapons. She was cold-blooded, a viper, and she must be stopped before another 9/11 landed on their hands. Nick needed to do his job, but he worried what Kaylan would have to say. They had a lot to talk through.

"I'll be there in the next forty-eight hours. Can you hold down the fort until I get back?"

"You got it. Take care of my sister."

"Always. Hey, man, be praying for tomorrow. We're visiting Sarah Beth's grave, and I'm not sure how she's going to hold up. Pray we don't have a relapse into the Kaylan of the past couple of months."

"You got it."

Nick closed his phone and took another swig from his water bottle. Children flocked around Kaylan, including little Sophia. Nick couldn't thank that child enough for finding someone to dig Kaylan out.

Kaylan was holding up well, even thriving. She had accepted the internship in San Diego to be closer to him. After it was over, she planned to become a dietician for a natural disaster relief organization based in California. Having been a survivor of one of the worst earthquakes of the Western world, she understood the challenges of a crisis and had a passion to help others survive the trauma.

Despite her plans and the strides they'd made in their relationship, he knew the hurdles ahead were daunting. She would need to learn how to trust God with Nick when Nick entered deadly situations. He knew the sacrifice he was asking of her. He had lived through it himself when he hadn't known whether she was dead or alive.

Nick tensed, unsure what had set him on guard. He surveyed the men around him. Each had stopped work and stood with his shovel ready. Quiet, strong, they resembled statues that had survived an onslaught and were preparing for another. Kaylan glanced up and paled, her eyes looking beyond him. Nick turned, his fists balled, braced to face whatever had upset her.

Kaylan shuddered and almost dropped the box of water bottles. A man strode at the head of a mob. Tall, bald, commanding, his eyes were those of the living dead—Eliezer. Surly teens drifted behind him, their features chiseled in stone, hardened by life in the slum, brainwashed by a man who promised power and the riddance of the white man.

Kaylan tensed and turned to the children. "Run to your mothers. We can play later." She jerked as a hand grabbed hers before recognizing Nick's touch. Her breath caught in the oppressive humidity, and she fought the panic rising in her heart.

"Eliezer?"

"I didn't want to see him, Nick. I didn't want to see him."

"It's fine, babe. Maybe he just wants to see what we're up to."

"You don't understand. Eliezer has studied the history of Haiti. He still believes white people only cause havoc in his country. The only way for the people of Haiti to have a better life is to do what the slaves did long ago, rid their country of white influence."

The men had moved from the rubble pile and now stood around Nick and Kaylan. Ex-gang members gripped shovels tightly, and Kaylan worried that more Haitian blood was about to be spilled. Fear of this man was irrational, but Kaylan was more worried about what he intended to do to the men working than what he could do to her.

Lord, help.

273

Eliezer appeared calm, almost regal, but the men behind him shifted and clenched their fists. Kaylan was thankful they hadn't brought guns onto the streets. Dusk was hardly the time to attack this far from their territory. They were unsure and angry, the remnant of one of the slum gangs. She searched their eyes for understanding or compassion. Hatred boiled in their depths, though she wasn't sure if it was part of their nature or if they despised her.

"You are not welcome here, Kaylan Richards. Why did you return?"

Nick stepped in front of Kaylan, and she gripped his arm. "Eliezer, I'm glad to see you are no longer in pain. Did Rhonda help you?"

His eye twitched, and the scar along the side of his face tightened. "I did not seek her help, nor did I want it. You should not have come back." He gestured to the devastation around him. "As I have told you, this is your fault. You and your God. You should never have come to Haiti, and your return is unwelcome. Go home, and take your God with you. He has only brought pain to us."

"Eliezer, my God isn't one who inflicts pain. *Se jezu sel ki kon geri* —it's only Jesus who can heal. And He came to heal you and me and Haiti and America because He knew we are helpless and hopeless without Him. He loves us." She pleaded with him to understand.

"Is this His idea of healing?" His voice rose, and Kaylan noticed the pulse throbbing in his throat.

"I don't know what this is, but good things are happening among your people, Eliezer. Don't you see? I came back to see if things were better, and they are."

"They are not better. There is no one here helping Haiti. Your people helped, and then left us to our filth and destruction. No homes, little food, disease. This is not better. You have angered the spirits. Leave, Kaylan Richards, or we will make you leave. You are not one of us."

The men behind Eliezer stepped forward as the men from the church surrounded Kaylan and Nick, pushing them to the back. Rolin stood at the front of the group, eye to eye with Eliezer. His Creole was quick and passionate, but firm. Abraham translated for Nick and Kaylan.

"She is one of us. She has the heart of a Haitian. She lived through what we lived through. Her God is now our God. We rebuild from the ashes to make a better Haiti. Help, or be gone."

"You would side with her over me? Who helped you when your wife ached with child? Who came to your aid to yank Yanick away from the ways of this woman and her God? You dare turn on me now?"

"Her God gave me hope to live tomorrow, and so I rebuild a place where those of our city can worship Him. You have no power here. My God is bigger than you or your spirits. He is hope and love, not manipulation and anger. In the name of Jesus Christ, leave. You will not harm this woman today. She brought a message of life to Haiti. This earthquake was not her fault."

Kaylan closed her eyes and fought tears at the outpouring of love from these people. She had given them pieces of herself, and they had given pieces of themselves to her. They formed a tapestry of color and loyalty. She had poured into them, invested all of who she was. When they were broken, she was broken. In their hope, she now found hope. Another small piece of her heart felt the warm sensation of healing.

Stevenson stepped forward, and Eliezer's eyes blazed. "You left me."

"You asked me to harm the people you claim to protect."

"You have turned your back on our heritage. You are no student of mine." As he raised his arm to strike Stevenson, Kaylan surged forward before Nick could catch her.

"Stop."

Eliezer's hand froze in midair, and his eyes focused on her, surprised, angry.

"We don't have to do this. You once told me we could both help Haiti. Help us now, Eliezer. Help us rebuild."

"I will not. Haiti will not be saved with your religion."

"No, it'll be saved because of my God. The Bible says the Lord binds up what is broken."

Eliezer seemed to lose the ability to talk. He advanced toward her again, the men behind him rooted to the ground. He bared his teeth, but Kaylan stood her ground. She remembered her place. She remembered her identity and why she'd come to Haiti. She remembered her calling to stand for the less fortunate, and her fear fled. No more would the past months destroy her hope. As Nick moved to her side, she laid a restraining hand on his arm.

"I will not fight you, Eliezer. My purpose is to help, not hurt. Will you inflict more harm on those of your own blood?"

His eyes blazed, and he studied the men surrounding Kaylan. He took a step backward, then another, before swiftly turning and fading back into the dust, leaving those around him confused, adrenaline crashing without a fight. The church members swarmed around them, talking, sharing the gospel.

Nick watched it all, but most of all he watched Kaylan. She had never looked more beautiful. Her hair knotted under a bandanna, dirt smudged her cheek, and her clothes were sweaty and crumpled. She'd done it. She'd graciously, confidently faced the man who had haunted her dreams. She'd come to the country that had nearly destroyed her, and in the process she'd emerged like the lily she wore around her neck: strong, beautiful, resilient, changed.

Chapter Forty-Two

THE MOUND HAD flattened in the past months. Kaylan laid the flowers over the grave and stepped back into Nick's embrace, tears flowing unchecked down her face. For the first time she knew she hadn't left her best friend in Haiti. She and Nick would return to this place later with Sarah Beth's family and their Haitian friends who had known her, but this was Kaylan's time to say good-bye.

Sunrise. Kaylan gazed at the horizon. The morning had never looked so beautiful, not since the earthquake. A sprinkling of grass had grown over Sarah Beth's grave. Kaylan thought it fitting. Where someone lay battered, something else took root. Sarah Beth had given their Haitian friends a taste of hope. She'd given them what she treasured the most—life, full and abundant. She'd given Kaylan that gift, as well. Kaylan could never thank her enough.

She knelt next to the mound and ran her fingers over the grass. "You made a difference, Bubbles. You changed the world, and your memory will keep changing it. They found Jesus because you loved them enough to show them how good He is. You showed me that." Kaylan bit back a cry, and Nick knelt next to her. "Look who's here with me, Bubbles. Can you believe it?" The sky came alive with brilliant displays of pinks and reds, as if the Lord were showing off this morning just for Sarah Beth, a tribute to a faithful soldier who had joined Him. "It's beautiful this morning. Your favorite colors. But you're watching them from a much better seat. Save a spot for me. We'll rock on that front porch up there for the rest of eternity." Her voice broke, and she sobbed. Telling her good-bye, letting go, was almost more difficult than the earthquake and the months of heartbreak. This was what she should have done at Sarah Beth's funeral.

"I wish you were here. I never imagined the next stages of life without you. But I'll take you with me wherever I go. And I'll remember. I still don't understand why it took an earthquake. I still don't understand why He took you, but God is doing big things here. Beautiful things that I never imagined." She laughed, tears still flowing. "He's good, just like you said. You saw it in death, and it took your death to show me that in life. I won't ever forget."

Kaylan grabbed a fistful of dirt and clenched her fist. She could do this. She could let go of her best friend. The memories would never leave her. They would push her through every day of the coming internship, of the next stage with Nick. They would make her laugh in the hard times and cry when she needed a friend. They would make her strong, because there had once existed a blonde-haired, blue-eyed beauty who'd loved a country so much she'd died to share Jesus with it, and in the process she had changed more lives than they would ever know.

"I don't know how to tell you good-bye. You were the sister I never had. How do I let that go?"

Nick's gentle voice broke into her reverie, soothing the pain. "You remember, Kayles. This isn't good-bye. You'll see her again."

"It's hard, Nick. I don't know how to do this."

He lifted her hand from her lap and held it over the mound. "She's not there."

"I don't want to forget. I don't want to say good-bye."

"Sarah Beth will always be part of you, remember?"

She nodded, tears falling on Sarah Beth's grave. Finger by finger, she loosened her grip, and dirt sifted down, coming to rest on the mound. "Bye, Bubbles. I love you."

Nick helped her to her feet, and it took every bit of resolve to turn her back on the grave.

"I'm proud of you, babe."

Kaylan wiped the tears from her face. "Can we go to the beach?"

"Absolutely. Show me the way."

The hum of Rhonda's truck occupied the otherwise silent ride. Memories of Sarah Beth flooded Kaylan's mind. She didn't know it was possible to feel pain and peace in equal measure, but it was her reality. She placed a hand over her heart. Some holes would never be filled. Sarah Beth had left a mark on her life. It was the mark of a partner in crime, a best friend, and a sister. It would not fade or blemish. It was love of the purest kind; Kaylan hoped one day to find that kind of friendship again.

Slipping her shoes off, she waded into the surf. The sun was warm and the water a deep turquoise. It showed no signs of an earthquake—no cracks, rubble, or decay. It was pristine, strong, and beautiful. She turned to face Nick, his smile as bright as the sun. It was a smile she loved, that she wanted to see more of. She rolled her eyes. "I'm a mess again. Give me a damage report."

He came toward her in the water and ran a thumb over her cheeks. "Tear trails that will fade."

"I wish scars faded that quickly."

"Battle scars are badges of honor, Kayles. They are the mark of a survivor. They're earned. A reminder of an event that changed your life. Never be ashamed to acknowledge them."

"They'll remind me of Sarah Beth, of Haiti, and of these amazing people." She nodded at the water. "It doesn't show damage."

"It masks what's under the surface, Kayles. It polishes rough edges and smooths over cracks. They exist, but they are being made better through a rough process."

"That's what the earthquake did to me."

"It shook you. But know what I've been told? When the Lord shakes us, He does it to rid us of what's unnecessary, so that we can become more of who He designed us to be. We shake off the baggage, so we can bear more of the good."

She wrapped her arms around his neck, enjoying the feel of him and the water slapping at their ankles. "Know what I shook free?"

"Bad tan lines?"

"Nick..."

He flashed a smile again, the one he reserved for her alone. "Tell me."

"Fear of letting you in. I can't promise I won't succumb to that again. I can't promise I won't cling. But I can promise that I want to try this with you. Sarah Beth always reminded me that life was meant to be lived. I want to dream big with you."

"Then California, here we come. Think you can handle being the girlfriend of a SEAL?"

"I'm going to give it my all." She turned her eyes to the water, the waves lapping at their legs. There would be days like this, when the ocean was peaceful, and days when it would rage. "We'll weather it. Together."

"That's all I can ask."

As their lips met, a wave crashed into their legs, knocking them down in the surf. Water soaked through her clothes and her hair fell in wet waves around her sandy face. Kaylan threw her head back and enjoyed Nick's laughter while the sun warmed her face, reminding her of a time at this beach when she'd laughed with Sarah Beth.

She had miles to go in the healing process, more tears to cry, and more joy than she imagined possible; she'd been given time with a friend who had utterly changed her life. Sarah Beth had shown Kaylan who she could be, and she'd shown her the goodness of the God they'd both come to Haiti to serve. They had set out to save Haiti one life at a time, and slowly it was becoming a reality, a movement spreading beyond what either of them had ever planned. In that, Kaylan recognized the goodness of a God much bigger than herself. And, in that, hope bloomed.

Coming in Winter 2015 From Kariss Lynch

SHADOWED

Book Two in Heart of a Warrior series

Chapter One

THE SKY EXPLODED in an array of fiery color, and Kaylan jerked, remembering the distant crash of buildings in Haiti only nine months before.

"It's okay, babe. It's just fireworks." Nick pulled her close on the beach, his arms reminding her of her new life in California, away from the humid, tropical landscape of Haiti, and away from her family in Alabama.

Vibrant reds, blues, and oranges danced in the sky, leaving smoky silhouettes in their wake. Nick's team of Navy SEALs and their wives and families surrounded her—her new community. A few guys lit fireworks on the beach and then darted away before they ignited, children squealing in delight as they burst. A fire crackled in front of them on the beach, and the clear night sky grew hazy under the continual pops and smoke from children's sparklers. It was the perfect way to spend the beginning of Labor Day weekend.

Kaylan wished she could freeze the memory and frame it. Laughter mixed with the lap of the waves and boom of fireworks. Children played tag, darting in and out of the waves licking the beach. Some of the guys stood near the fire, roasting hot dogs or marshmallows. The women chatted or chased down kids. It was picture perfect, and Kaylan smiled to herself. The scene seemed so normal, hiding the fact that these men could leave in an instant with just the ring of a phone. She squeezed Nick's arm a little tighter, knowing the time would come.

His strong fingers ruffled her hair, gently sweeping strands from her forehead. Despite the warm evening, goose bumps danced down her arms, and she closed her eyes.

"What's going on in that head of yours, gorgeous?"

She turned her head to meet Nick's eyes, loving the fire she found in them. "Just making a memory."

His lips brushed her forehead, and then in one quick move he stood from their sandy blanket, pulling her with him. "Let's take a walk." He settled his arm around her shoulders, and once again she treasured the contact, knowing these fresh memories would carry her through the long days to come.

A football whizzed through the air and smacked Nick on his back. "Yo, Hawk, get a room, man," Jay called, whistling at Kaylan.

Before Nick could react, Kaylan's brother Micah tackled Jay around the waist, and they both hit the sand. "I think you forgot you are talking about my sister." With one quick move Micah wrapped his arms around Jay in a headlock, his legs pinning the rest of Jay's body. Jay fought and kicked, but Micah held firm, his arm still allowing Jay to breathe. Barely.

The rest of the team gathered around, money exchanging hands as quickly as their cheers and chanting filled the air. Kids joined in the frenzy, excitement glowing in their young eyes.

"Micah totally has this."

"No way. Jay wrestled in high school. Micah is toast."

Jay squirmed. His face turned red, whether from embarrassment or lack of air, Kaylan wasn't sure.

Nick chuckled. "Looks like Micah has it under control." He turned Kaylan away from the crowd and moved up the beach as darkness settled around them.

The moon hung low in the sky, reflecting eerily on the waves capping and lapping the beach. Nick walked them toward the surf, the cool Pacific stretching to kiss their feet. Kaylan could barely see the water line, but the soft roar of each new wave soothed her.

She closed her eyes, turning her face to the gentle breeze and enjoying Nick's hand in hers, strong, tough. Her eyes flew open as her feet left the sand and Nick swung her in his arms, jogging to the water.

"Put me down, jerk!" she shrieked, awaiting the plunge in the dark, cold water. Her panic built. She saw only blackness. "Nick Carmichael, don't you dare."

His boyish laugh tugged at her heart. "It's just water, Kayles." And in they went, Kaylan's jean shorts soaking, her T-shirt hanging on her frame.

Her breath caught in her chest with the chilly water. She could barely make out Nick's grin in the darkness as she swiped wet hair from her eyes. "Nick Carmichael!" With one good swing she sent a wave of water into his face. His eyes registered surprise before his smile quirked. Trouble.

"Oh, no, you don't. You already got me wet. Nick, don't you dare." Before she could back away, he grabbed her around the waist, and they both went under an oncoming wave. The salty taste permeated her mouth.

"All right, all right." She came up, sputtering and gasping for air in the icy water. She shoved at his chest as he steadied them both. His heart pounded beneath her palm, and his warm laugh melted her heart. She joined his laughter, loving the familiarity. Just as it had been with her best friend, Sarah Beth, Kaylan was learning to read Nick's moods, his reactions. This laugh was one of pure joy. Contentment.

"Moonlight looks pretty good on you, even though you're wet."

She wrapped her arms around his neck as he pulled her close.

"You aren't too bad yourself, Mr. SEAL."

"I mean it, Kayles. Beautiful, kind, genuine, gentle. I couldn't be more blessed."

She was thankful for the darkness as her face heated. She could barely discern his eyes, but she knew that look. The one he reserved only for her. He expressed himself better than she did, and occasionally it left her feeling behind the emotional curve.

He rested his forehead on hers, the waves lapping gently around their legs. Despite the chill, she felt warm with this frogman in his natural habitat. Nothing could touch her.

The breeze ruffled her dripping hair, and on its wings came the words she longed to hear yet dreaded. "I love you, Kayles." The whispered line sent her heart pounding, and she pulled back.

"Nick..."

"Don't panic on me." He held her close, and she fought the need to pull away, the urge to run before she got hurt, before she lost another person she loved, before she fell so hard that the darkness enveloped her again. She could almost taste the Haitian dust clinging to the air, smothering the light and her ability to breathe.

"I can't. Nick, I...let's talk about something else." Sarah Beth's cry echoed faintly with the crash of buildings in her mind. Again she tried to pull away.

His calloused hand cupped her chin. "Kayles, look at me. It doesn't matter that you can't say it right now. I just need you to know. I need you to trust me." His eyes reflected the glowing moon and never wavered from their hold on her face, on her heart. "I love you." He drew each word out, making sure they reached every insecurity. "I'm not going anywhere."

She allowed the words to penetrate her fear, hoping against hope they would take root and blossom. Healing came slowly, but every day she grew stronger. Nick was key to the process. But there were some memories that could not be erased, some nightmares that bled into her daylight hours, stealing her most precious moments.

One day she would say it. One day she would feel it. But not yet, just not yet.

"Smile, gorgeous." He smoothed the lines on her forehead. His mouth tipped at the corner in the moonlight, and her body tensed.

"Don't you…" She squealed as his fingers found her rib cage. She twisted and fought, laughing so hard the nightmare from moments before receded with the tide into the darkness.

"Nick Carmichael, let go!"

"You asked for it." He released her, and she began to tip backward into the waves, his laugh echoing in her ears.

"I don't think so." She snatched his T-shirt and pulled him in the water with her, her head dipping below the cold waves once again.

Their laughter filled the air as they rose to the surface. "How can you be so nice one second and so mean the next?"

"Mean? I make you laugh because I love you. Don't be so gloomy." His chuckle warmed her to her toes, and she threw her arms around his neck.

"I like you too."

His arms slipped around her waist, and his face dipped toward hers. He could see all the way to her soul in the moonlight, and it was enough to stop her heart.

"I think it's a little more than that. But I'll wait to hear the words." His lips settled on hers, making the lingering fireworks pale in comparison.

"Ugh, break it up, you two."

Her brother's voice made her jerk, but Nick held her close, turning to face Micah on the beach.

"Bad timing, Bulldog. What's up?"

Kaylan tensed as Micah held up a phone. His silence spoke volumes. Her hands clenched in Nick's wet shirt.

"We gotta go, Hawk." His voice carried a warning over the crash of the waves.

"Is it…"

"Yeah. It's time."

Nick's hands slipped from her waist, and he waded to shore. Kaylan immediately felt cold. She followed him out of the surf.

Up the beach a couple other SEALs who were part of Support Activities kissed their wives and girlfriends good-bye before running for their cars.

"Babe, we gotta go. I'll call you later." Nick's eyes grew distant, his mind already miles away.

Kaylan refused to show her fear. "Be safe."

With a nod, they both ran to Micah's car. Moments later they peeled out behind their teammates.

Kaylan wandered back up the beach to the other SEAL families. She'd known when they left Haiti in July and when she'd moved to California the first of August that the time would come when Nick and Micah would leave. She'd come to hate every ring of his phone. But here they were, and she had the choice to panic or stand firm. She was the girlfriend and the sister of SEALs. If they could race fearlessly into danger, then she could remain their rock at home. She only hoped they wouldn't see the small cracks.

"Kaylan, Kaylan, Kaylan." Four-year-old Molly came bounding up, her blonde curls bouncing around her slim shoulders. Kaylan lifted her into her arms.

"What's up, Munchkin?"

"Where did my daddy go?"

Kaylan glanced at Molly's mom, who was busy wrestling sparklers away from her two boys. Kaylan smothered a laugh. They were as strong as their dad, Logan, the team medic and one of the older men. Molly had his curly blonde hair and pale green eyes.

"Daddy and the boys needed to work. You'll see him later."

"Are they going to take care of bad guys?"

"Yes, sweet girl." Molly was innocence in a beautiful, sweet package. The little girl wrapped her arms around Kaylan's neck as she walked them closer to the fire. Molly's blonde hair glowed, and her little hands felt sticky on Kaylan's neck. She knew the little girl was getting wet, but Molly didn't seem to care.

"Kaylan, know what?" She pulled Kaylan's head close, whispering in her ear. "My daddy's a hero just like Superman. Only he's better. He doesn't need a cape."

Kaylan's heart warmed, and she kissed Molly's sticky cheek, tasting marshmallows from the s'mores. "Your dad is definitely a hero."

"Molly?"

The little girl squirmed to the ground as her mom called. She turned back quickly to Kaylan. "Don't worry about Mr. Nick. My daddy says he is the best of the good guys." The best, the bravest, the most sacrificial. It was the latter that scared Kaylan the most. Her hero without a cape, unafraid to face the barrel of a gun— even if it meant his life.